Jolly Rogerson

RALPH McINERNY

Jolly Rogerson

1967

DOUBLEDAY & COMPANY, INC., GARDEN CITY, NEW YORK

*All of the characters in this book
are fictitious, and any resemblance
to actual persons, living or dead,
is purely coincidental.*

Library of Congress Catalog Card Number 67–19092
Copyright © 1967 by Ralph McInerny
All Rights Reserved
Printed in the United States of America
First Edition

PART ONE

Spring

1

The open newspaper entered Rogerson's study like a kite and stopped before his desk. Marge's hands gripped its sides. Behind it she emitted a long whooshing sound and Rogerson thought of cheeky winds on the corners of old maps.

"How awful." The kite collapsed. Rogerson looked at his wife's face, her eyes unseeing, still focused for type.

"What is it?"

In a vee of lowered pages, Marge shook her head impatiently and read on, her lips forming words. Rogerson looked at the book on his desk. Its lines merged like non-Euclidean parallels. He smacked his mouth several times. His daughter Barbara had made his birthday cake and after two cups of coffee he could still taste the cloying sweetness of the icing.

"Honest to God," Marge murmured.

Rogerson waited and eventually the story came. A suburban housewife had killed her children and then herself. Marge lay the paper on his desk, directed his attention to the photographs, shook her head.

"Think of her poor husband, Matt."

"Yes," Rogerson mused.

Marge left the paper with him and crossed the room. Her thighs had thickened; her household slippers were crushed in back, her walk a matter of keeping them on her feet. It gave the effect of a ruined stripper trying desperately to arouse a jaded audience. The simile ironic, Rogerson unamused. No insistent drumbeat accompanied Marge's passage to the living room couch. She sat and Tommy and Bobby cuddled to her like pajamaed brackets. Rogerson remained in the study, waiting for them all to go to bed.

Ad seipsum:

> Midway this way of life we're bound upon,
> I woke to find myself in a dark wood,
> Where the right road was wholly lost and gone.

Lost and gone. Not I, not I, but what right road? 44. Backward and forward the same but does that make it midway? Middle C on the keyboard of life and I one numb neum losing interest in reason's song. Going down from mind to street floor and imagination then lower still to the ultimate sediment, the vegetable I've always been. Fundamentals last. And pedals. Hold that simile. Confusion says, girl on bicycle peddles ass all over town. Remember to remember. Desire to desire. Not hope. Hope's for later, desire for now. St. Jerome on his deathbed shagging his equally aged sister from the room. Ah, the perils of asceticism. An octave, resolution, octet too and odd that now the sextet asserts itself, driving toward a humping heroic coupling. Wow. Sex. Forty-four-year-old father of three arrested for (by) dirty thoughts while sitting in mortgaged home at one in the morning. Crap. I hate . . .

Matthew Rogerson read it over the following morning, then let the ruled sheet drop to his desk. The night before when he had torn that page from an examination booklet he had been visited by terribly lucid thoughts which were to follow as sweetest exegesis on those lines from Dante. As it must to all men sexegesis came last night to Matthew Rogerson. . . . What had he wanted to say?

He did not destroy the scribbled effort. He saved everything. The house was heavy with his holdings: in the attic dozens of pasteboard cartons bulged with old term papers, magazines, book catalogs, examinations, scraps of notes like this. Fragments he had shored against his ruin were now a monument to it.

His coffee had cooled but he sipped it anyway. Last night he had found Marge's latest hiding place for the liquor. In the oven! Tiptoe in stocking feet like a thief and cursing the squeaking floor he had gone all too often to the Heraclitean well and now his head was a soft riot from that lonely celebration. Happy birthday, his glass raised to the unframed print pinned to the wall over his desk. A woman's face, a blown-up detail of a Rembrandt, the cover of a book catalog some years before. Thinning hair disappeared into a white cap surrounding a broad lowland face whose scrubbed shiny highlights, kind eyes and faint smile approved in advance whatever he might think or do. The woman could be observing an orgy, a birth, a death, but she smiled on, acquiescent and unbaffled.

Marge called his name, approaching, and Rogerson put his hand on last night's note. But there was no need to conceal it. Marge was not curious about what he did here and even if she were she would be unable to interpret his deteriorating hand. In the doorway she paused, glowering at a pad, then went to the leatherette easy chair and sat. With a free hand she dug in the pocket of her red housecoat for a cigarette. She hadn't looked at him and he knew what she was not remembering.

"What am I going to do about Emily Pruitt?"

The now lighted cigarette dangled from her pursed mouth and one eye squinted in anticipation of a smarting swirl of smoke. Her housecoat gaped between buttons and Rogerson considered the revealed lacy border of his wife's rounded slip. Slip of a girl, of lip, *lapsus linguae*, God, God.

"Emily Pruitt?"

"The tea. Do I have to ask her?" Her eyes drifted past him, showing her dislike for the clutter of the room, dropped to the urn on his desk, flew quickly away. He had bought the Mexican silver urn in Tijuana during the war. It was filled with cigarette ashes. Marge was horrified by it and had been since he had told her the contents were his father's mortal remains. The opening of her housecoat closed in a clutch of fingers. Rogerson felt a sudden shame at what they would not talk about.

When finally he'd gone to bed last night, slipping in be-

side her but facing away lest she smell the booze if he
wakened her, he lay breathing through his nose, aware that
he was almost drunk. Her body warm, the sough of her
breathing—it had been easy in the dark to remember a time
before her almost pathological fear of pregnancy. Her
church's stand on contraceptives had turned their bed into
a battlefield on whose coordinates he could map past
strategies of failure. A hand sent scouting returned
wounded to report the enemy was there. A frontal attack,
easily repulsed, then retreat to high ground, his side of the
bed.

But last night, rolling toward her, still breathing through
his nose, Rogerson put his hand stealthily on Marge's breast.
She stirred, slept on, did not lurch away and he felt the
familiar fatty mound respond to the gentle flexing of his
palm. In wary stages he brought himself against the plush-
ness of her bottom, continuing to caress the now exposed
breast, not caring that she slept. When he lowered his mouth
to the aroused nipple he was certain Marge was awake, her
sleep mere pretense. She suffered his attention, lying limp;
any further moves would bring the mockery of a feigned
awakening so he concentrated on that one breast as if their
marriage pact granted him only this furtive suckling. His
body tensed as if she were giving more of herself. In
imaginings lost, he borrowed a part of Marge's body to
consummate a fancied coupling. Finally, not giving a damn,
he allowed the inevitable to happen. Their thighs were
drenched with his onanistic token when she affected a slow
emersion from sleep.

"Matt? Are you awake?"

"I'm awake."

"You've been drinking."

"A birthday toast."

A sigh. She rolled away. What a union. The most she
dared offer him was her abrasive exterior on which to
jiggle his solitary pleasure and even that had to be treated
as inadvertent. Wet dreams and drydock were the prospect

for years, though God knew he wanted her pregnant less than she did.

Now Rogerson shook away the memory and looked at Marge. "Why not invite Emily?" he asked.

"She's not one of us any more, Matt. Not since Gene died. Besides, she'd have to take the afternoon off from the library and she needs the money."

"I'm sure she can afford an afternoon off."

"I wonder. What could he have left her?"

"Maybe you're right."

He refused to let his mind travel the habitual grooves of discontent. Let the goddam AAUP worry about it. They were sure they could get to Wooley on retirement benefits once the college was eased into the state system. The young bastards were already on a higher, secret pay scale. Reinhardt Schmidt had let that cat out of the bag last year and all hell broke loose. Wooley had sought to placate his unruly troops with the Faculty Club. In their helplessness they had accepted that joke as a concession.

"The other wives can't stand her, Matt."

"Do they ask her?"

Marge reluctantly nodded, tapping ash from her cigarette. Her index finger came down again and again. In moments of doubt that habit gave her an air of decisiveness. It was borrowed from her mother, along with the squinting eye after lighting up. While smoking, Mrs. Olson and Marge took on the mien of flappers. Rogerson could imagine Mrs. Olson sharing a flask with a pompadoured sheik, plucking a Lucky from a green pack. Lucky Strike green had gone to war but Marge mimicking her mother could bring it marching anachronistically home two decades later.

"Ask her. Why not? You wouldn't want to be dropped if you were her."

"You've got to be kidding, Matt. When you go this house goes and the kids and I catch the first flight to Milwaukee."

When I go. Marge looked at him with defiant bravado;

he turned from her to the friendlier face of the Rembrandt print. A small resentment rose within him then died. Marge had statistics on her side. And the insurance companies. Have you provided for your loved ones? Will their lives go on without a ripple left by your absence? What a pitch. A greedy appeal to self-effacement.

"You don't have to wait till I'm dead to go to Milwaukee."

"I might just run up this afternoon. What's six hundred miles?"

Rogerson computed it in yards and feet and inches but said, "Wait until after the tea anyway."

"Are you serious?" Marge sat forward on her chair.

"Deadly." And he was. "By train though. Flying is too expensive."

"God, I'd go by bus." She tried to disguise her joy. "I can't just leave you and the kids."

"Of course you can."

"There *is* the tea. And next week Barbara's Campfire ceremony." Marge looked at him quickly but apparently decided against bringing up his promise to write that skit.

"There'll always be something."

"Could I really leave after that Campfire thing?"

Again he said yes, embarrassed by her delight. So small a thing. A visit home. Marge was speaking of Mrs. Snow, who was dirt cheap and could come in days. Years ago Marge had gone home fairly often, taking the children with her. When Rogerson put her on the train, helping her commandeer a double seat, he had never understood her gratitude. He would have thought the prospect of the hours ahead, the transfer in Chicago, would depress her. But she had saved that for her return, treating the junket as some cruel and unusual punishment he had cunningly contrived. What was he letting himself in for now when she could go off in blissful aloneness?

Marge, wondering aloud about schedules, snatched the phone from the desk, causing a pile of books to teeter

dangerously. Rogerson steadied them and his eyes fell once
more on the words he had written the night before. He felt
distant from their tone and folded the sheet, putting it in
his paperback Dante. Marge repeated times of departure
and arrival and he jotted them down. When she hung up
she stood, her face bright.

"What are you going to do about Emily Pruitt?"

"Invite her. What the hell do I care?" Marge started from
the room, then stopped. "I better go talk to Mrs. Snow.
What time do you leave today?"

He told her, annoyed she did not know his schedule.
"I'll get dressed."

Rogerson tried to cram the paperback *Inferno* into a
bookcase but it wouldn't fit. He lay it on the desk and became aware of humming. His own. Marge was going home,
home to her parents. They had never thought of this as
home.

It's only temporary, he had told old man Olson when with
his master's he went off to teach. His father-in-law stared
at him with vacuous blue eyes and nodded his crewcut
head. Olson was a cement contractor, his hearing shot and
Rogerson never knew when the man heard and when he
didn't. That bullet head with its seamed sunburned face
echoed with the erratic syncopation of the cement mixers
he heard all day. A year, maybe two, Rogerson had told
him. "You ever want to come in with me, Matt, say the
word," Olson had told him once. He would never forgive
Rogerson his shocked disdain. Since, Rogerson had often
whimsically wished he had taken his father-in-law up on
it. He could have used the concrete experience, but mainly
of course the money.

"I'm going, Matt," Marge called. The front door squeaked
open. "It's stopped raining." The door slammed and, a few
minutes later, after prolonged whining, the old Plymouth
came to life outside the window. Rogerson went into the
kitchen to see if there was any coffee left.

Standing at the back door he looked out at a scene not unlike that which had prompted his poem "Birds Dropping."

> Downward
> as earlier
> rain caught
> now flat
> reflecting them
> wrens come
> alight upon
> a birdbath's
> knuckled edge.
> Their heads
> cock in wonder
> to surprise there
> at their feet
> the sky from which
> they've come:
> into water
> then where
> wild wings
> whip up the mirror,
> defy its blue
> immensity.

Seven years' bad luck is several seasons more than any bird can last. Rogerson looked at the wet grass wink in sunlight, lit a cigarette, created a cloud against the glass. Mortality seemed a never-never A-proposition in the April morning. All men are mortal but not this morning. Exhalation, a minor meteorology assuming vagrant shapes before his face, thunderheads, cirrus, a spinal column from which unfurls riblike the cage containing the one bird meaningful.

The phone rang and Rogerson went into the hall and picked it up. He held it to his ear, saying nothing.

"Hello," a male voice said. "Hello?"

Rogerson did not recognize the voice but what can two syllables squared reveal? He said a falsetto hello.

"This is Mr. Rogerson?"

"Hello, Mr. Rogerson," Rogerson said.

"I'm not Mr. Rogerson. I . . ."

"Then who the hell are you?"

"Who *is* that?"

"Let me speak to Rogerson," Rogerson demanded.

"But I want to speak to Rogerson."

Rogerson clucked reprovingly. "What flight is he on?"

"Is this the airport?"

"Are you calling the airport?"

"No, I am not calling the airport."

"Well, this isn't the airport. Why aren't you calling?"

There was an exasperated pause at the other end. Rogerson had still not placed his caller's voice. He said, "Do you have Prince Albert in the can?"

"Oh, no!"

The phone clicked and Rogerson hung up. Moments later it rang again. Rogerson ignored it and went back to the kitchen.

The college had been founded in the fourth quarter of the nineteenth century by a sect whose tenuous lines with the continent had soon been broken. Later in an ecumenical whorling, when most of its nominal adherents had lost their faith, it had been subsumed into a vague and creedless Midwestern synod. The school was a fitting emblem of a lost trust in the transcendent: a cold stone church in which nondenominational spring weddings were perpetrated by couples who saw no reason to let graduation interrupt an established sex life; an Administration Building whose random wings testified to a series of fires and hasty rebuilding; a library, perhaps of brick, beneath dense green growth; what was called the Arts Building, the adjective differentiating it from no other academic entity, and finally two brand-new government-subsidized residence halls, one male, one female, yearning toward one another across the city street which bisected the campus. In its post-Christian era the college had become municipal and now, under President Wooley, it aspired to inclusion in the state higher educational system and access to the suddenly overflowing coffers the legislature had provided in the terrified wake of Sputnik.

Rogerson was standing outside the dean's office where Schmidt had intercepted him, wheezing confidentially and grinning with that Continental obsequiousness sensible chauvinists instinctively distrust. The bill of his ski cap, Schmidt's winter affectation, now symbol of his doubt that spring had come, raised and lowered with the wrinkling of his forehead like a growth, like horns.

"You've heard of the fiasco?" Schmidt's eyes were following an imagined tennis match in the darkened hallway.

"Fiasco?" It could have been Schmidt's allusion to a United Nations committee.

"But how could you have heard?"

Rogerson, forgetful, smiled with what could be misinterpreted as encouragement. He was distracted from Schmidt's cap's bill by the glint of Norah Vlach's glasses. The dean's secretary was peering from the open door of the office, convulsed in silent laughter. Schmidt caught Rogerson's questioning look and wheeled but Norah disappeared in time, setting like a stage sun behind a file cabinet. Schmidt put a hand on Rogerson's elbow and sidled down the hall with him.

"What will they do to her?"

"Who?" Had they finally discovered Norah's unbridled contempt for the whole goddam school?

"Forgive me. I will start from the beginning." But first Schmidt swooped at a water fountain which delivered a wavering stream of tepid tan water. He lapped at it meditatively and, straightening, went on avoiding Rogerson's eyes.

"She had removed the book from the library." Schmidt's English was almost clear as he said this, plucking each word carefully from his polyglot lexicon. "It was in her room!"

A book? Rogerson felt pointlessly cornered.

"I had put it on reserve, Matthew, but she took it home. This is outrageous."

"Was it checked out?"

"The security man was furious."

Rogerson tried to imagine one of those relics who prowled the library furious. "Well . . ." Why was Schmidt bothering him with this?

"Since you have her in class, I thought perhaps you might know why." Schmidt's green eyes did turn on Rogerson now, bright and suspicious, alert for some telltale tic.

"Who?"

"Marie, Marion . . . Oh, what is the name?" Schmidt

pulled a slip of paper from his pocket. "Ah. Maureen Nugent."

The name meant nothing to Rogerson but clearly Schmidt had just been checking on the girl with Norah. He said, "Have you called her?"

Schmidt laughed painfully and the bill of his cap shot up. "She called *me*, dear friend."

"Perhaps you *had* better start at the beginning."

Schmidt sighed. "I am full professor, yes?"

There was no danger he would see Rogerson's angry look. Schmidt's eyes had dropped humbly at the statement of the eminence he had reached at thirty-five. A concomitant shift of shoulders made Rogerson aware of the rucksack he bore like a cross. It was angular with its burden, probably filled with library books sought in vain by students. Down the hall, Norah emerged from the dean's office but seeing them turned like the rain figure on a weather clock and went back in.

Schmidt lapsed now into the Esperanto he used when excited, running the small gamut of emotions his vanity allowed, glancing from time to time at Rogerson as if at a mirror where he might surprise his elusive essence.

"Did you tell her you wanted the book, Reinhardt?"

"Where was she? You see, that was the problem. It goes without saying . . ." Schmidt paused, then said as if it were QED, "It was Saturday."

"I see." In desperation Rogerson bent to the water fountain. Some water got into his mouth and he spat it back.

"I was reading proofs of an article. I had to have that book." Schmidt considered his life line. He wrote articles with vulgar gusto, piracies from European journals put into his inimitable English, thus diminishing the risk of plagiarism. The Old Bastards mocked him but, as Schmidt said, he was full professor, yes.

"Matthew, in Munich a student does not dare to speak to a professor unless addressed." Schmidt's eyes clouded with nostalgia and Rogerson had a vision of a youthful

Schmidt skulking along Munich streets waiting to be addressed by a professor. "*Swear* at a professor? Rogerson, it is unthinkable."

"The girl swore at you?"

"Imagine the dean's rage," Schmidt whined.

"You told Laplace?"

"I had no choice."

The stupid ass. Laplace was probably rolling on the floor of his office now. Norah's smile, more than usually manic, now made some sense.

Schmidt abruptly adopted the air of one who had accomplished his purpose. Rogerson sensed he could escape without hindrance. They shook hands, of course, and Schmidt executed his jerky little bow.

In the dean's outer office Norah took Rogerson's books, lay them on her desk and pulled him giggling into the inner office.

"Did he tell you?" she cried when the door was shut behind them.

"What's going on?"

"Mrs. Larson caught our Herr Professor in the women's residence hall," Norah managed to say. "In a room!"

"The men's room?"

"A girl's room."

"You're kidding."

"He said he was looking for a library book." Norah's voice sailed up the scale. Hands at hips, thumbs pressing her abdomen, bowing, straightening, bowing, Norah dissolved in the calisthenics of hilarity. Rogerson responded with sympathetic mirth.

"Do I have the girl in class?"

"Yes," said Norah, wet-eyed in the wake of her spasm. "Your three o'clock."

"Schmidt was in a room with a girl?"

"Oh, no. The girl was home for the weekend."

Mrs. Larson, the juiceless widow who presided over the women's residence hall, intent that their defloration

should not take place on her premises, had come upon
Schmidt in the Nugent girl's room. An elementary judo
chop had rendered him helpless and she was about to phone
the police when Schmidt managed to convince her Laplace
was the man to call.

"You mean Laplace rescued Schmidt?"

Norah nodded. Poor Schmidt. He was at the dean's mercy
now. Rogerson asked where Laplace was.

"In the Arts lounge. Telling the story."

Norah lit a cigarette and regarded her flaming Zippo like
a wise virgin, her thin lips stretched in a smile. She shared
the general contempt for Schmidt and was exhilarated by
his unaided edging to the precipice. Looking at her, Rogerson felt a slight unease. Norah had sat in on summer
courses of his and alone among his students had smoked
out his trick of attributing to fabricated contemporary poets
his own lousy verse.

"There is no Quentin Sexton," Norah said to him one
July afternoon.

Rogerson had been too surprised to deny it. "It's just as
well. His stuff is pretty awful."

"I'd like to see more of it."

"It shall be done."

Easy to say, later he could procrastinate, that was the
plan, but the next day he had wordlessly passed to her a
looseleaf notebook containing a sampling of his verse. For
forty-eight hours he had writhed in anguish. Norah returned the poems without comment and had not mentioned
them since. The episode had almost cured him of writing
poetry, one more ambition recognized too late as groundless.

Norah was an enigma. He guessed her to be thirty, more
or less. Her hair was neither blonde nor brown, exactly, and
it framed with indecisive waves an almost, not really pretty
face. Blue eyes with large irises and those damned rimless
glasses no one wore any more and her body the sexless
instrument of her keen mind. A violet by a mossy stone
and Norah among the file cabinets: it was her destiny and

a malevolent nature had given her protective coloring so that she faded unhurtfully into these surroundings. On occasion Rogerson had sensed an actor behind her role, a person peering at him through those glasses. Now, in the institutional intimacy of Laplace's office, he wondered if imagination could be inflamed enough to invest her body with minimal undulation, erase those glasses, get by the almost to a near prettiness of face. Might he emit an impossible utterance? Norah, I love you. Prithee assume a supine position there among the notices of class absence and receive a first-class semen in berth ashore at last.

Rogerson rubbed his face and stood. The great horned toad hopped to the door and cast a warty look back at Norah. A person died among the ground refractions astride her nose. Adieu, adieu. He was at his own office in the library before he realized he had forgotten his books.

When after his two o'clock class Rogerson entered the main door of the library, the place seemed occupied only by employees. Girls with a limp receptive air hovered about; men young in years or by imitation glided in a fey and hippy way over the shining floor, the code of their heels muffled and obscured by the acoustical ceiling; behind the checkout counter ladies, the old and spent, widows and maids, found in ink pads and stamps and thousands of books unread and never to be read by them a kind of nunnish meaning for their lives. Emily Pruitt drifted among the card catalogs. Rogerson was unsure what her function was but she seemed to participate in the general mystery enveloping library employees. He watched Emily free a drawer and place it on a table; her stubby fingers raced over the cards as if in search of the source of a deal so raw as hers. Rogerson made a wide circuit to a far card catalog, but minutes later Emily spoke beside him.

"Have you heard the good news, Matthew?"

Rogerson altered the position of his elbow on the table where he was jotting down the Dewey decimal number of a book. His torso turned some millimeters toward her; it was opening enough. Emily too was making little notes in a stern stenography.

"Henry Hunt," Emily said. Her mouth was turned perpetually down; her facial expressions consisted in variations on that labial declension. She adjusted her mouth to tragedy transfixed by folly.

"Henry Hunt," Rogerson repeated, glad that this was not about Schmidt's indiscretion.

"It was only fungus in his lungs."

"Really."

"The cancer report was all wrong."

"Hunt," Rogerson said again, studying the porous ceiling. "He taught chemistry for years and years."

"Oh, yes."

A vague image tried to constitute itself in Rogerson's mind but, like Emily's husband, Hunt was only an anonymous ghost that haunted the campus, a predecessor, a similitude of self, gone now into the penury of retirement or to a realer rest. For Emily the present staff was obviously inauthentic compared with the departed. Remembering Marge's reluctance to invite Emily to her tea, Rogerson understood. Emily belonged here in the library, hissing confidences about forgotten people, a chronicler of illnesses, preferably terminal. She clearly regarded mortality as the vindication of a personal hypothesis and her arthritic passage through the library was all the reminder Rogerson required of the transitoriness of life. Who in fifty years would disturb this air with the mention of his name?

"Everyone was told it was cancer," Emily complained. "I actually went down there."

"To the hospital?" Rogerson crumpled the slip he'd been filling out; it was no ticket out of this. He had written SHIT several times in the blank alloted for the title of the book.

"Oh, no. He's home now. You see, there was nothing they could do."

"Ah."

"And now Gladys is told it's only fungus." Emily frowned. "How could they make such a mistake?" She glanced over her shoulder as if sensing the approach of mortal adversaries or time's squeaking chariot. She ran a bloodless tongue over her denture and her lids closed briefly over her old eyes.

"I've never heard of fungus in the lungs before," Rogerson said. My God! He had a vision of white scaly growths at the base of trees in some childhood woods.

"Oh, it's quite common," Emily said brightly.

"How old is Hunt?" The cigarettes in Rogerson's inside pocket seemed to nudge his vulnerable chest.

"Seventy. Seventy-one."

"I think I remember him."

"Of course you do."

Rogerson left her then, heading for the stacks. When he emerged some time later and was on his way to the stairs which led to the faculty offices below, someone called his name.

Peter Dowlet with short-clipped hair, friendly if questioning eyes, a doctorate from a lesser state university, symbol of the threatening future, came across the floor, cupped the leather patch of Rogerson's elbow, and started down the stairs with him. Rogerson got his arm free and slowed his pace.

"Through for the day, Matt?" Dowlet revealed a row of white teeth in a standardized smile, his manner not quite condescending. He was Rogerson's idea of a management trainee and he marveled at Dowlet's unawareness that his choice of the academic life had removed him from the American escalator.

"I'm through."

"How about a drink at the club?"

Rogerson consulted his watch. The club bar opened at four. It was after four. He did not want a drink with Dowlet but on the other hand he wanted a drink.

"I have to stop at my office."

"I'll come by for you in five minutes."

Rogerson let himself into his office, closed the door, locked it and stood in the dark room with his finger on the light switch. When he was young his bad dreams had concerned out-of-the-way places, the corners of basements in deserted homes, a shack for ice fishing far out on a windswept lake, himself sitting wallward awaiting some terrible event. He defied the feeling now but it was there. No doubt it had a name but a name would lend it no further reality. Who needs the botanist's label when he has seen the flower? At home, a month before, alone, Rogerson had stepped into the hall closet, shut the door and stayed there half an hour. When he emerged, blinking, he had walked with heroic step to his study. Now he threw the switch and looked at his desk where a coffeepot rose from the debris. He sat behind the desk, unplugged the pot, and looked about for his Dante. It was not there. To hell with it.

"I saw Mrs. Rogerson this morning," Dowlet said when they were walking across the campus. Pustular faces of students went past them in a stream, bodiless visages.

"Oh?"

"Matt, don't take this wrong, but she is the most attractive faculty wife bar none."

Rogerson nodded as if he had been awarded a blue ribbon at a cattle show. Was she really? It was an odd thought. He supposed she could be. Hadn't it been her beauty that had prompted him to take those stealthy liberties so soon after meeting her, the liberties that had quickly cost him his?

Each tooth in Dowlet's smile seemed a trophy of conquest; he probably deserved his reputation. Coeds cooed like doves at registration time, impatient to sign up for Dowlet's English courses. The faculty wives were constantly pressing unmarried girls on him, wearing the while a look of faintest chagrin that they were out of the running. Even Marge had given her unsolicited testimonial. Peter Dowlet is tremendously sexual, she had said. What else are Peters for, Rogerson had replied, bringing Marge frowning back to her normally neuter approach to things.

"You must seduce her sometime," Rogerson said.

"First chance I get, Matt."

The Faculty Club was an old house on the edge of the campus, bequeathed to the college, once a residence for deans, now renovated. Its erstwhile kitchen, converted, contained a bar which was now the support of a raucous row of sipping instructors. The Old Bastards had withdrawn with their drinks to the living room, encircling a coffee table with chairs like a wagon train at nightfall. Harry,

the steward, came immediately to Dowlet, who consulted
Rogerson's pleasure and placed their order. Reinhardt
Schmidt stood at the far end of the bar making love to a
bottle of bock beer. When he noticed Rogerson he smiled
hopefully and began to move toward him but Rogerson
grabbed his drink and fled to the living room.

Herb Laplace sat like a fatherly wagonmaster among
the Old Bastards, his presence a promise of hope that the
menace represented by the younger men at the bar could
be cushioned if not ultimately withstood. The dean's florid
avuncular face disguised his spiritual affinity with the
young; his twenty-five years on the faculty made him,
chronologically at least, one with those who had a vested
interest in the school's historic and humane mediocrity.

"Matt!" Laplace cried, jumping to his feet. "Matt, I
think we've got the sonofabitch." Moving away from the
others, Herb nodded toward a corner and Rogerson went
with him.

"He's at the bar, Herb."

"We've got him for breaking and entering." Laplace spoke
into the glass he held to his mouth, then tipped it up and
while he drank looked at Rogerson with joyful eyes.

"What's this about some girl swearing at him over the
phone?"

"Damned if I know. Let me tell you, Matt, ole Rhi-
noceros Shit is worried." Herb's lips glistened with beer
and he licked them as if it were justice he thirsted for.

"What can you do to him?"

Laplace roared. "What can't I do? It's the goof we've
been waiting for. I'm having lunch with Wooley tomorrow
and I'm going to bring it up then."

"Come on, Herb. He just wanted a book."

Laplace dangled his glass between his knees and stared
at Rogerson. "Hey, are you defending Schmidt?"

It *was* an uncharacteristic stance. Rogerson's difficulty
was that he disliked Laplace almost as much as he did
Schmidt. Two climbers. Once long ago, before the Wooley

era, Hughes had spoken to Rogerson in a Delphic but faintly promissory way of the deanship and in the event it had gone to Laplace. Had he really wanted the job? Perhaps not, but he would have preferred refusing it to being simply passed by.

"Good God, Herb, larceny isn't what's wrong with Schmidt."

"So what? This could put the skids under him."

It was an old project, the extermination of Schmidt. Reinhardt had arrived on the campus three years before, bringing with him all the academic ambitions of his Teutonic youth. He personified everything Rogerson found distasteful in academe. He was every petty foible and vanity writ large, a caricature of the underside of all their souls. It was as if the compromising with the administration, the pompous parading before students, the dogmatic *obiter dicta*, all of it, could be heaped on Schmidt and cast out with him.

"You better find out what that girl said to him, Herb." He paused meaningfully and caught sight of Schmidt standing in the doorway looking at Laplace's back with apprehension. "You wouldn't want to build on sand."

"But I've talked with Mrs. Larson! I was there. What could go wrong? What's this crap about a girl phoning him?"

"Who knows? You better check on it."

"Goddam it, he was caught red-handed prowling around the women's residence hall."

Over Laplace's shoulder Rogerson regarded Schmidt's mournful face. Laplace talked on of his open-and-shut case and Rogerson beckoned Reinhardt to join them. Schmidt's face came alive with hope and he hurried toward them; when he arrived Rogerson arose and said he'd be back. Schmidt's obsequious babbling followed him to the stairway.

When he emerged from the upstairs bathroom Rogerson stood in the hallway and listened to the blur of voices lift from below. The steward's room was opposite the bathroom

and Rogerson went to it, opened the door and looked in.
The walls writhed with provocative nudes, disengaged from
the men's magazines that were stacked around the room.
The unmade bed looked just deserted, somehow fetid and
unclean, the room seemed to reek of masturbatory fantasies.
Harry was a parolee Felix Freeman had championed for
the steward's job last spring. Dowlet had cited statistics
on relapses of convicts and pointed out that embezzlement
was among Harry's previous offenses. Harry had got the
job anyway; it paid too little to attract the honest. Rogerson
closed the door with a grimace of distaste and had turned
when Dowlet came up the stairs.

"Harry lives here, doesn't he?" Rogerson asked. "I'd forgotten that."

"Room and wages and all he can steal. He's got it good,
Matt."

Rogerson went downstairs, looked into the living room
where Laplace was still trapped by Schmidt and turned into
the kitchen. Standing at the bar, he ordered and then
watched the steward. Harry was at least fifty, bald, the
hair on the sides of his head slicked back, his body over-
weight and weak, the perfect complement to his character.
His deferential manner was partly saved by an edge of
irony. Behind the bar, prominent among the glasses, was
the mimeographed faculty phone directory containing the
autographs of all who would give them to Harry. Rogerson's
signature was not among them.

"What were you in for?" he asked when the steward put
his drink before him.

Harry grinned; his career was a frequent topic of conversation here. "Which time?"

"The first."

"Forgery."

Chuckles along the bar. Rogerson took his drink into the
hallway and paused by the phone. It reminded him of
home and robbed him of an incipient glow of camaraderie.
The voices tuned up behind him; in the living room the

chorus of the Old Bastards went on. The two choirs were contrapuntal, the melody from the kitchen bass but lilting, that from the living room verging on tenor with melancholy overtones. Which was more senseless, the hope of the young or the despair of the aging? Rogerson picked up the phone and dialed O. A bodiless voice identified herself as an operator.

"Which, bitch?"

"What!"

"La vie est triste, trop triste, incurablement triste."

Rogerson replaced the receiver in its cradle and patted its ebony head. He put glass to mouth and drank, espying in the process his reflection in the mirror over the telephone table. In the swift second during which that was a stranger in the glass, no stranger to a glass, he saw a type he did not like. Neither tall nor short, hair neither red nor brown, complexion the commodious ruddy, an Irish nose, a trace too much, leading the face prowlike, a sad face with merry eyes. When the figure became himself Rogerson went out the front door and sat on the porch step.

It was after five. The traffic on the street was thick and impatient; on the walk students went wearily away from the campus. Noting the general passage of his mortal fellows, Rogerson addressed them mentally. Oh all you who pass by the way, consider if there be any sorrow like unto my sorrow. Forty-four, a faint-hearted fouled-up mediocrity undeserving of the epithet failure. I salute you. I envy your teleological goings and comings, your essential purposiveness, the distraction or busyness or just plain juiciness that prevents your seeing there is nowhere really to go. Once you get there, there you are. As I am here at forty-four on an April afternoon alien alike to the Old Bastards and the young fools in the kitchen.

Rogerson rose, drank, pitched his glass behind an arbor vitae and walked to the street with a bouncy step.

"You said you'd do it," Marge warned, seeking control. Rogerson had just admitted he had not written the play for Barbara's Campfire ceremony.

"I'll do it. I'll do it."

"You've been saying that for weeks. They have to rehearse. It's less than a week away. What am I supposed to tell Mrs. Crease?"

"What the hell is it supposed to be about?"

"The history of the Campfire movement. What it was like when it began. How it differs today."

"Marge, I don't know a damned thing about the outfit."

Marge pressed her eyes shut, opened and closed her hands. She stood in the door of the kitchen. She did not look like the most attractive faculty wife bar none.

"The books are on your desk, Matt. They have been there for weeks."

"I'll do it later."

"Do it now!" Not quite a scream but getting there. Why in God's name had he agreed to this? It was clear Marge would not let him postpone it further.

Rogerson stamped off to his study, followed by a mollified Marge who told him to keep it simple, keep it short, it shouldn't be difficult to do, Barbara would be so proud, she knew he was busy but he had promised and they were his children too, etc. etc.

Fifteen minutes later Rogerson sat at his desk, flicking the pages of the Campfire manual, trying not to retch, the blank sheet in his typewriter accusing, repulsive. God. Rogerson the author. Rogerson the playwright. He rubbed his face with both hands and remembered his dreams of avarice. Sitting at this desk, five years ago, his imagination

fired by the writers' magazines he had purchased. It was
all so simple. Make $15,000 a year writing fillers for the
Plumbers and Steamfitters Journal. Some dazed bastard
whose novel had made the best-seller lists and sold to
Hollywood urged the struggling brethren not to give up;
there was gold enough for all. And the ads of agents. For
a fee they would market your material. Only blinding
venality or rampant vanity could enable one to trust the
car salesman's smile on the face that formed nebulously
against a frieze of publishers' checks. I sold mailman's mem-
oirs to movies; housewife's exposé of sex in the PTA a
national best-seller; three-year-old deaf mute writes science
fiction trilogy. Rogerson had begun reading with smiling
incredulity, then with attention, finally with rapt belief.
Any idiot could make a fortune writing. And who was
better prepared than he? He had swept the magazines
from his desk and in one fell swoop, one punishing five-hour
session, written a story. When it was finished his tongue
was raw from cigarette smoke, his neck ached from scrunch-
ing over the typewriter, but he shuffled the pages with the
exhilarating certainty that he had turned a corner in his
personal history. Warily he reread his story. It was better
than he had thought. He wanted to race through the house,
wake Marge, run into the street. What he did was retype
the story, select a smiling agent, write a check and sit awake
until morning when he drove off to the post office to mail
the beautiful, well-wrought tale that would make his fortune, bring money raining down upon them. It showed
talent, the agent wrote, but it needed work; for a further
fee he would be proud to give a detailed analysis. Rogerson's
ardor cooled. The sonofabitch. He wrote an icy letter, suggesting in Olympian tones that the charlatan return post-
haste his darling story. He crumpled the letter and threw
it away. He wrote another check and requested the detailed analysis. The detailed analysis consisted of a summary of his story, several airy paragraphs of generalities
on the nature of the short story followed by the recom-

mendation that he graft an inane plot onto the story he had written. Rogerson raged and, alone, wept; he endured Marge's abuse when she discovered the two checks among the canceled ones the bank sent back. And burned with a terrible desire to make a fortune without a middleman. For a year he had mailed story after story and for a year they came back with printed slips explaining to whom it might concern that the enclosed material did not meet the current needs, etc. etc. Not even the wild promissory articles in the writers' magazines could restore his hope that he was destined for fame and fortune as an author. It was a great relief when he decided to quit trying.

So now, finally, unconfused by facts, trying for banality, Rogerson wrote a skimpy skit featuring an Indian maid, a member of the first Campfire group and a little girl of today. It was frightening how it flowed. It had unity of place, it collapsed the dimensions of time, it was deliciously and thoroughly awful. It was five pages long. Rogerson went with them into the living room, bathed in a sense of parental righteousness, and delivered the script to Marge. While she read it he actually began to hope she would like it. Nobel Prize winner recalls first play written for daughter's Campfire pageant. Manuscript now in Notre Dame library, the subject of eight doctoral dissertations and subsequent basis for musical comedy that broke Broadway records . . .

"Matt?"

"I know. It stinks."

"Matt, it's supposed to be a *puppet* show. They can't use this."

"A puppet show!"

"I told you, Matt. You never listen."

"For the love of Christ. Well, that's all they're going to get. I couldn't do it again."

"But they can't use this. It has to be a puppet show."

"I'm going to bed."

"You can't! You have to do it."

"I've done it."

"You have not."

Rogerson fled from the room and went raging upstairs; this was worse than that agent. Behind him Marge screamed at him to come down, it's your daughter, you never care about the children, all you think of is yourself, you can't even do a simple thing like this right but by God you're going to, you promised, I refuse to explain to Mrs. Crease, I certainly can't give her this, you knew it was a puppet show, you deliberately . . .

Rogerson slammed the door of their bedroom, wishing Marge would shut up, didn't she care that she was waking the kids? Even the neighbors must hear her. He got into his pajamas, collapsed on the bed and Marge's voice was louder, she was coming up. The door burst open, the light went on and she stood beside the bed. "You bastard, you bastard, you just don't care. Selfish. SELFISH. Your own daughter, I wish I'd never met you let alone MARried you." Her voice was hysterical now, his skin crawled and he wondered, will she hit, will she throw things; he was frightened by the unreason of her outburst and he was tired, he was so goddam tired. He said nothing, ignored her, thought please God make her leave and turn off the light, and then her hand was on his shoulder, tugging, making him look up at her distorted face. Marge, Marge, my God, is she having a breakdown, what the hell, and then I HOPE YOU DROP DEAD, inches from his face, her eyes popping saying each word distinctly as if composing an hysterical telegram. She went then, ripping the blanket from the bed, snatching her pillow, leaving the light out finally and silence.

He could not sleep. He sat in the bathroom smoking. At four o'clock he went downstairs. His script lay in shreds on his desk. He wrote some dialogue for a puppet show. He put it on the dining room table, went upstairs and shaved and at five-thirty drove to school and the haven of his office.

At nine that morning Rogerson was asleep, his head on his desk, when someone tapped on his office door. He sat upright, eyes burning, unsure momentarily where he was. At the door, silence, and then again the tapping. Rogerson rubbed his eyes, wondering if he should ignore it. Who could it be?

"Matthew?" Schmidt. "Matthew?" Tapping, tapping.

"Come in."

"The door is locked."

Had he tried to come in without knocking? Rogerson went to the door, opened it and Schmidt shot past him into the office.

"Close it, Matthew. Close it."

"What's the matter, Reinhardt?"

Schmidt sat and looked mournfully at Rogerson. "That goddam Laplace."

Rogerson closed the door and returned to the chair behind his desk. What had he been dreaming with his head on the desk? He could not remember but he had the sensation of having been wrenched from some unutterable peace by Schmidt's knock.

"What is it now, Reinhardt?" Trying to sound patient made his voice more impatient.

"Laplace says I can be discharged. Is this possible?"

"Everything is possible."

"Please, Matthew. You are my only friend." Schmidt looked as if he actually meant this and Rogerson was filled with something approaching pity. His only friend!

"He exaggerates, Reinhardt. Forget it. Don't worry."

"Has a professor no rights? The girl had a book I needed.

She insulted me on the telephone. And now *I* am in trouble? It is incredible."

"You should have asked Mrs. Larson to get the book."

"That wild woman? And where was she? I knocked, I called. I saw the list of names, the room numbers. I went to get the book. I could not wait until Monday."

"Herb is just teasing you."

"I don't think so."

Rogerson went on, trying to allay Schmidt's fears long after he had lost interest in doing so. Schmidt defended himself in a way that brought out the prosecutor in Rogerson. But he couldn't believe Laplace hoped to turn this crazy event into a serious charge against Schmidt. Reinhardt refused to be consoled. He rolled from side to side in the chair, keening, demanding more reassurance.

"Schmidt, I have to get ready for class."

"Of course. Of course." Schmidt got immediately to his feet, backing toward the door. The magic words, the intellectual life, the preparation of lectures as sacred as Hegel's *Gesammelte Werke*. "Thank you, Matthew. I hope you are right. That goddam Laplace."

The door closed. That goddam Laplace indeed. What was he up to? Call him.

"Matthew Rogerson," he said when Norah answered. "Is he in?"

"Say, you left your books here yesterday."

"I'll pick them up."

"I could send them over."

"I'll get them." Pause. "Is one Dante's *Inferno*?"

"Yes." Silence. My God, that paper in it. "The dean is here. Do you want to speak to him?"

"Norah, what does he intend to do about Schmidt?"

"You're asking my opinion?"

"Yes."

"Nothing."

"That's what I thought."

"I'm guessing."

"Let me talk to him."

A predictable minute went by. It was Herb's way. To answer immediately might suggest he had nothing better to do.

"Yes?"

"This is Rogerson."

"Matt. What can I do for you?"

"Schmidt was in here a moment ago. He's crawling the walls."

Laplace laughed. With the receiver to his ear and his eyes shut Rogerson felt he was in the belly of an obscene whale. "Good. I worked him over a little at the club yesterday. Told him I'm having lunch with Wooley today. He put the two things together." Laughter. Rogerson opened his eyes and it was like being spewed forth into his office.

"Well, you've got him by the umlauts, Herb."

"And I intend to put the squeeze on him."

"Watch those vowels."

After he hung up, Rogerson decided he would skip classes. To hell with them. He wanted to sit here in his office and spin in his chair and do absolutely nothing. This afternoon was Marge's tea. He must remember that and not go home at the usual time. Rogerson got up, made sure his door was locked and turned off the lights. He pulled the blind cord and closed the drapes. Not dark but almost. An ice shack far out on a lake, two-by-fours covered with tarpaper, inside a board seat, like an outdoor john but unholy, he sitting there confined by thin walls and outside an immensity. What did it mean? What did it mean? He wished he kept a bottle here. But he was afraid of that; he always had been. The Irish weakness. He had it. Without Marge's nagging he might have succumbed long ago. He could go out and buy a pint. The thought excited him. A pint. A half pint. It wasn't need, it was the principle of the thing. He felt wronged, grievously wronged. The memory of Marge's contorted face and that I HOPE YOU

DROP DEAD. Almost he could believe a wish like that, once expressed, added some force to the cosmos, a malevolent force that could not be dissipated and which however circuitously would one day expend itself on its original target. He closed his eyes. The walls of the fishing shack were no protection against Marge's wish which whined like the wind, picked up bone-chilling speed as it skimmed the ice and raged against the tarpaper walls. He had neglected to chip a hole in the ice. A clear membrane had healed over the hole; its icy ridges resisted his kicks. He was wearing street shoes. Why did Marge hate him so? Couldn't they find some livable middle ground between love and hate? Rogerson stood as his phone began to ring. He would go out. A pint. Just this once. He would sit here all day, answer neither phone nor door. And fish.

Two o'clock. Rogerson drunk. The bottle of rum he had bought stood empty among the debris on his desk. Yo ho ho. He couldn't remember when he had last drunk rum. And Coca-Cola. The Andrews Sisters, for the love of God. Rogerson aroar. Somewhere Marge was serving tea. An unlit cigarette dangled from Rogerson's mouth; he was out of matches. He did not trust himself to ask a colleague for some. They would know he was drunk. Take care. He formed a mad desire to smoke. He rolled the cigarette in his fingers. Two o'clock. Noises in the hall. The change of classes. People coming and going. Not safe. In ten, fifteen minutes he could get out unnoticed. Where could he get some matches? He would like another drink. Rogerson Rogerson, what are you doing? The club. Harry would be there. He lived there. He didn't open until four but surely this was an exception. Of course it was. Rogerson pretended his cigarette was lit and dragged on it. He crushed it in the tray. Accept no substitutes.

A quarter of an hour later he opened his door stealthily and looked out. No one. He stepped into the hall and quickly with concentrated footwork went down the hall and out the ground-level door and then like a rubber ball bounced over the campus walks, smiling, ignoring the nods and hellos of the young, a middle-aged man off to his club in the afternoon.

The front door was open and Rogerson let himself quietly inside. He stood in the hallway and listened to the silent house. Really quite peaceful. He should have come here earlier. No need to drink alone in a civilized society. Voices. Far off. Where in God's name were some matches? In the living room. Finally. Great billows of smoke, bright lengthening coal. Upstairs. Voices. Harry's room. A radio perhaps. Rogerson looked into the kitchen. No bottles in sight. Everything locked up, no doubt. As it should be, as it should be. Well, upstairs then. Get Harry. He felt like talking to someone now. Or listening. A human face.

On the landing he steadied himself. Drunk. Really drunk. Wonderful. The voices. A woman? My God, it was. And no radio. At the head of the stairs Rogerson sat and listened. Amorous byplay, no doubt of it. The ash from his cigarette fell to the carpet. He had no place to put out his cigarette. The bathroom. He stood. Steady now. Steady. He dropped the cigarette hissing into the toilet. His throat tightened at the uninhibited sounds from Harry's room. At least fifty. Probably more. The dog, the dog. Without thinking, Rogerson flushed the toilet. When silence resumed it was total. A hush in Harry's room. The doorknob turned slowly and then the steward looked out.

"Professor Rogerson! What are you doing here?"

"Thought I'd have a drink, Harry." His voice was thick and there was a little smirk in it.

"It's not four o'clock."

"You're right."

"You want a drink?"

"Do we have rum, Harry?"

"You go downstairs, Professor. I'll be right with you. I'll make your drink."

"Thank you, Harry."

Gotcha. What he should have said when Harry looked

out. Going down now, grinning, Rogerson suddenly felt raw envy. Harry! If Harry, why not Rogerson? Steady, Matthew. He sat at the bar in the kitchen and in minutes Harry came down.

"You say you want rum?" Harry unlocked a cabinet behind the bar and began to remove bottles. He set them in an irregular row and stood on tiptoe looking into the cabinet. "I'm sure there's rum. Not many people ask for it."

"Anything will do," Rogerson said affably.

Harry turned. Rogerson saw that for the first time Harry realized he was drunk. "Bourbon all right?"

"Bourbon's fine."

Harry sloshed a double for him. Rogerson reached for his wallet and Harry raised a staying hand. "That's on me. I mean it."

"Very kind of you, Harry. Tell me." Rogerson settled on his stool. "How do you like your job?"

"Fine. Fine. I like it. Your drink all right?"

Rogerson sipped. "Wonderful." He could hear someone sneaking down the stairs. Harry's eyes were watchful, willing Rogerson not to hear. He began to speak rapidly about the weather. Rogerson turned with elaborate casualness, felt Harry's desperate grip on his arm, the panicky tempo of his voice. A woman went by in a flash, heading for the street door. Rogerson turned to a suddenly silent Harry.

"Congratulations."

A hundred lies leaped to Harry's eyes but finally he smiled sheepishly. "Please don't say anything, Professor."

Rogerson's smile sought a mean between reproval and worldliness. He didn't want to erase entirely Harry's sense of indebtedness. A drunken dream teased Rogerson's imagination. He thought of Marge. I hope you drop dead. Why? Why? Right now she would be smiling at her tea. Rogerson got off his stool and wandered into the living room, bearing his drink. From the windows of the room he looked out at a blurred world. For how long? He came

as if from a trance and went into the hallway. The phone.
He dialed his home. Whoever answered wasn't Marge. His
voice gruff, holding the phone six inches from his face, he
cried, "Tell Mrs. Rogerson her husband is a sonofabitch."

He slammed the phone down and returned to the kitchen.
Harry wasn't there.

"Harry!"

"I'll be right down."

Rogerson put his drink on the bar. He didn't want it.
Coffee. That's what he needed. His office. He went swiftly
to the door and outside.

"Professor Rogerson. Professor Rogerson." From far off at first, then nearing now beside him the repetition of his name and Rogerson turned to a breathless girl. Through an alcoholic haze a note of familiarity established itself. A student in his class but past or present, he didn't know. He went on walking but she kept pace with him. Rogerson smiled in a total way, casting a benediction on this furry April world; around him he could hear life teeming in brittle branches, a first surge of sap, and the pulpy ground assumed the faintest suggestion of green. Rogerson welcomed to the wider womb of the world all nameless and unwanted weeds.

"I'm Maureen Nugent," the girl said.

"We live in a jungle," Rogerson said to her. "There are mice in the library. And bats. Last winter a fox was seen on campus."

"I'm in your American. You didn't come today."

Rogerson suppressed a nasty remark. "I was not up to American today. I have been adrift in the Caribbean." He brought the girl within the range of his smile. She too was smiling. How odd.

"Professor Schmidt told me to talk with you."

"An edifying suggestion."

"He broke into my room last weekend."

"Maureen Nugent."

"Yes."

"The book."

"A library book. Have you heard?"

They had reached the Administration Building and Rogerson sat impulsively on the steps. The girl stood before him as if guarding him from an enemy marshaling out there among the elms.

"I've heard little else since yesterday."

Maureen Nugent sat beside him on the step. "You know how Schmidt is. Professor Schmidt." She took in breath with great concentration and ungloved her hands. Hands in lap she flicked the gloves in a boneless gesture. "He takes out so many books and he never acknowledges requests that he return them. Yet he demands books from everyone else."

"Books," Rogerson mused. "Have you seen the display of paperbacks in the bookstore? Acres and acres of them. I went out for matches."

"I stopped at your office."

"I flushed the club steward from an illicit union."

The girl seemed to be studying his face. I am not making sense, Rogerson informed himself. Why doesn't she leave me alone? Harry, furtive Harry, and the swift passage of the bird no longer in hand, hastily into the street. Harry would have a hell of a time luring her back to his room. Daring devil at that.

"Monday when I heard I called him. I told him what I thought of him."

Rogerson felt his head clear. "Did you swear at him?"

A flick of the gloves, chin up. "Yes."

Rogerson laughed and the world went along with it. The campus turned merry and frolicsome. Passers-by smiled. Maureen Nugent giggled beside him. Wasn't this what life is all about?

"Mrs. Larson hopes they fire him."

Again she giggled. Rogerson urged her to tell him the whole story and she obliged and for fifteen minutes they sat there. For the first time the episode seemed funny to him. How had Schmidt reacted when the girls surrounded him, preventing his departure? And what did he do when she swore at him on the phone? Delicious. Delicious. Poor benighted Reinhardt.

"I felt bad about that. Swearing, I mean. I called him again today."

"To apologize?"

"More or less. Yes."

"Good girl."

"Do you mean that?"

Her face refused to firm under his scrutiny, but he felt her decorum and decency. A splendid gesture. Professor Schmidt, I am sorry. Wonderful girl. Wonderful. "Yes, I mean it."

"That's when he suggested I speak to you."

"What in the world for?"

"Actually I told him I was going to and he urged me to. I'm not sure he meant it."

"Well, you've talked with me. Why?"

"It's something else. Professor Schmidt asked me several times if you had put me up to it."

"Put you up to it?"

"Taking that book. He claims it was on reserve but it wasn't. For some reason he seems to think you asked me to take the book out."

"Did he say that?"

"Not in so many words. You know how he is."

Rogerson began to doubt that he did. What in hell was Schmidt up to? He felt vaguely disconcerted. He remembered Reinhardt saying, You are my only friend.

Maureen had got to her feet and again his name was being called. Behind him. Looking up, Rogerson saw Herb Laplace standing at the top of the stairs. The view from the bottom gave Laplace a regal, triumphant look; a royal arm went out in a beckoning gesture.

"Matt, come on up."

Beside him Maureen murmured something and when he turned she was going away; he was aware of the fetching sway of her walk.

"In my office," Laplace called. "Come on."

Rogerson mounted the steps. He counted as he went
and when he stood beside Laplace said, "Thirty-seven."

"You brag. She looked flat-chested to me."

"The steps."

"Sure." Laplace studied him. "Have you been to the
club already?"

"What time is it?"

"Just four."

"I had a drink with Harry."

"I've been trying to get hold of you. Did you skip your
class?"

"Unavoidably detained. I had a visitor from the Caribbean."

"You weren't in your office."

"Did you call?"

"Norah's been ringing your number for hours. She even
went over there."

"What's up?"

"Come on."

Norah was not in the outer office when they passed
through it, Laplace in the lead, loping along, his left shoulder
lower, Rogerson had not noticed that before; it threw the
suit coat off kilter. Herb compensated by tilting his head
to the right. In the inner office Herb took off his suit
coat, waving Rogerson to a chair. He took his coat capelike
by the shoulders, a veronica and *voilà*, it clothed a stand
in the corner. A faint odor of perspiration invaded the
room. Laplace, when he sat behind the desk, looked agitated.
His eyes dropped to the papers before him and his lower
lip jutted, deepening the lines that ran from his nose and
enclosed his mouth.

"What's the matter?" Rogerson asked.

"Schmidt." Herb groaned.

"For God's sake, forget him, will you?"

Laplace gave him a mordant look. "I'd like to. At lunch
I was with Wooley and Schmidt just crashed in on us.
Pulled up a chair and sat down."

Rogerson laughed. "Well, you're the one who got him worried."

"Matt, wait. Schmidt told Wooley they want him in Munich."

Rogerson lit a cigarette. He knew that story. It was Schmidt's pardonable fantasy, a triumphant return to his university, the vindication of these awful days of exile brought on by the old—and need it be said?—baseless accusation of plagiarism. "Did Wooley believe him?"

"Isn't it true?"

"Ask Reinhardt."

Laplace looked puzzled. "Wooley doesn't want to lose him."

"Lose him? I thought you were going to get him fired?"

"God! Don't you know a joke when you hear one? They want him in Munich, Matt. It's all very hush hush. Wooley didn't like it a bit. I mean, he was grateful to Reinhardt for coming to him. He knew he could simply have accepted and blown out of here. The thing is, Wooley is convinced we need Schmidt."

"Wonderful."

"Look at it from his point of view. If we're going to get into the state system we need a halfway-decent faculty. How many people publish the way Schmidt does?"

"You have a point."

"Right. So the lunch turns into a negotiation session with Reinhardt. He complained about this and that. Wooley promised him the moon."

"Why not?"

Laplace was suddenly angry. "You're not making this easy, Matt."

"I couldn't care less. Give him the moon, Herb. By all means keep him from going to Munich. If Munich wants him, that is."

"He wouldn't bullshit about something like that."

"Why are you telling me this?"

Herb got up and put a hand on the back of his chair. He

looked at the window and then sat again. "You were one of Schmidt's complaints."

"*I* was."

"He's convinced you turn students against him. He brought up that goddam book, I didn't."

"What about it?"

"Did you put that girl up to it?"

"Up to what? All she did was take a book from the library."

"At your instigation?"

Rogerson felt momentarily sober. And wary. What the hell was going on? His afternoon of dalliance now seemed a season away from things. "What are you getting at, Herb?"

"Well, Wooley asked me to talk to you. Get you to speak to Schmidt. You know, reassure him. Make him feel loved. God, I don't know."

"I could apologize to him."

"Apologize?"

"Of course. If I have disturbed Reinhardt in any way, I must apologize." Saying it set Rogerson free. In an unreal world further fantasy was the only defense. His head had started to ache. He stood. "At the first opportunity. Apologize."

"Matt, are you all right?"

"Perfectly."

And he was. All the way to the door. He closed it behind him and then, in the riot of color and muffled sound that greeted him, felt immensely dizzy. He stepped forward and began to fall. Norah caught his arm and managed to ease him to a chair.

At eye level bunched breasts but whose? Norah's. And her hand slapping his cheek and making of his name a plea. Rogerson looked up. He was still drunk. It was no longer pleasant. He wanted to sleep, to sleep.

"Mr. Rogerson, can you walk?"

He looked at her. She seemed genuinely concerned. He saw that he had fainted. He sat now precariously on a chair beside her desk; the door to the hallway was closed. Laplace's door too was closed. How long had he been out? He asked Norah.

"It just happened. Come on, we have to get you out of here. Can you walk?"

Rogerson stood, wavered, got the world settled and nodded. Good she said and took his elbow. In the hallway she released him and they walked together, without speaking, to the parlor inside the main entrance of the building. Norah closed the door behind them and Rogerson looked longingly at a couch. But when he got to it he did not lie down; it seemed important to imitate the sober self he had once been. Norah sat beside him. For a minute they stared at a portrait of Hughes, Wooley's predecessor, hanging on an opposite wall. Rogerson winked at the oiled visage. Hughes had been all right; a washout like the rest of them.

"Feel better?" Norah had removed her glasses. Her eyes looked odd, unfocused, and they were moist.

"Norah, I'm drunk."

"Lucky you. I don't think he noticed. Did he tell you?"

"About Schmidt?"

"The tables turned. Laplace of course is still upright." She put her hand on his arm. My God, she was crying.

"Don't," he said. His arm described a wild arc, his hand alighted on her far shoulder. "Don't."

Norah looked at him, her face sad, almost pretty. Almost, almost. He felt her near shoulder against his chest. His head thundered with the effects of the alcohol and the situation seemed murky. What had Laplace said? The net effect was that he, Rogerson, was getting the shaft. And poor dear Norah knew and was sad.

"It doesn't matter," he said into her hair. "It doesn't matter."

"But it does. They can't do this to *you.*"

"They haven't made me what I am, Norah. That's my work."

"No. No, don't talk like that. You're not—old. You're not."

For several minutes they sat in silence. From a great distance he observed them; he was holding her in an almost embrace. She was a dear kind girl. She had read his poems. If his head did not ache so he could have taken comfort from her.

"How will you get home?" she asked. "You can't drive."

"Coffee. I need coffee. I'll be all right. There's no rush. Marge is having a tea. They never leave."

"Where is your car?"

He told her.

"Give me the keys. Come home with me. I'll make coffee."

He must have assented. He was sitting there alone. From the hallway came a faint susurrus of voices, the traffic of the ordinary world. Rogerson felt permanently parked. He put his head back. He slept. But it seemed only a moment later that Norah was back. His car was outside the building. Come. Thirty-seven, he told her when they went down the front steps.

"Forty-four," she corrected. She smiled. She had his paperback *Inferno* in her hand. First his poems, now that.

Norah closed the street door and they stood in a small area between two doors. Rogerson had stepped back to

permit the closing of the outer door, his back found the wall
and he pressed his head against it, looking up. From a high
ceiling a lamp hung unlit from a gnarled chain through
which serpentine an electric cord twisted. The lamp itself,
rhomboids of pale glass in a metal frame, was mocked by a
faint slice of sun from the street. Along the opposite wall
the sun assumed a variety of colors on the white surface,
refracted by the angled edge of the glass in the door.

"Don't pay any attention to Mother," Norah said. She
faced him, a foot away, her eyes watchful behind rimless
glasses.

"Don't pay any attention to Mother," Rogerson repeated.

Norah came closer. "I left the Dante in the car."

"Serves him right."

Her hand sought his, held it. He looked down at his hand
in hers. He was vaguely moved. Her hand squeezed his and
she lay her head on his shoulder. Rogerson put his head
back against the wall and studied the overhead lamp for a
moment, then closed his eyes. What was he doing here?
Norah had read his birthday note to himself. He was aware
of the smell of her hair, a faint drugstore smell, shampoo, a
bargain-counter aphrodisiac. Harry. Eyes still closed, he
brought his face into her hair. Sleep. Peace. Don't pay any
attention to Mother.

"Come. You want coffee."

He had conferred on her the authority of woman; she
assumed a brisk no-nonsense air. She opened the inner
door, Rogerson stepping out of range of its foreordained
arc; when it was open they went into a dark house. Shadows
and lace. "I'm home." Norah crossed the hall to the entrance
of a darker room, peeked inside. "I'm home."

"I'm here." An old voice from the depths of the room
and the recent depths of sleep.

"Professor Rogerson is with me." Norah's voice a warning, fanfare; apparently reassured, she turned and beckoned to him. Rogerson felt at ease in the darkened house,
found the doorway a good target, aimed and entered a

room where an old woman moved slowly in a rocker which
seemed the petering-out pendulum of ·her personal clock.
Norah repeated his name, said this was her mother and
Rogerson bowed. He sat on the couch across from Mrs.
Vlach. Norah remained in the doorway.

"How was your afternoon?" Norah asked her mother.

"I didn't have my nap." She looked sharply at Rogerson.
"Some days I can't sleep."

"I'm going to make coffee, Mother."

Norah left. White hair, rolled back in a wispy halo,
framed the old woman's face. Rogerson thought of his
grandmother. Like this woman. A dress collapsed on the
collapsed body, breasts fallen, useless, obscene.

"She hates me," the old woman whispered.

Rogerson sat forward, smiling quizzically.

"Norah. I live in fear."

Rogerson looked toward the empty doorway. From the
kitchen he heard water echo as it filled a coffeepot. The
old woman's face was screwed into an elaborate expression
of fear.

"I'm ready to die, God knows. But it's dreadful knowing
your own daughter longs for the day. You have to help
me."

Rogerson nodded, his head aching. Why didn't Norah
come back? The old woman hissed on in the darkened
room, telling of her money, that's what Norah was after,
and they wouldn't let her change her will any more. Suddenly, brightly, "What do you teach?"

"Humanities," Norah said, back in the room. "It won't
be long," she said to Rogerson.

Until the coffee was ready they sat in the room which
grew progressively darker but neither Norah nor her mother
turned on a light. Norah reported the details of her day and
finally the coffee was ready and Rogerson, holding a small
ribbed cup, sipped and sorted his thoughts, memories of
the exchange with Laplace making disturbing sorties into
the forefront of his mind where a small clearing had formed.

He remembered too Norah's sympathy, so tender, but that endorsed his conviction that what Laplace had said had some meaning that wouldn't come completely into view. He felt dull, his body seemed a tremendous weight anchoring him to the couch, making it important to be there in that twilit room with Norah and her mother. On occasion the old woman gave him a meaningful glance and Rogerson smiled. Ah, the mind, mind has mountains, cliffs of fall, frightful, sheer and Norah's mother, weary from years of scaling, was sliding spiderlike down the skein of sanity into a darkness not unlike that of this room, a menacing darkness, busy with danger.

The coffee did not help. When he stood to go Rogerson swayed, caught himself and went unsteadily to the door. Norah came with him. "I could drive you home." She looked at him protectively.

"I can make it."

"I left your book in the car. The Dante." Her eyes concentrated on his chin. She had read the note, no doubt of it. What did he seem to her? The prospect of pity was inviting; he wanted . . . No. He put a hand on her arm and thanked her.

"About Schmidt."

She shook her head. "Tomorrow." It *was* bad. Rogerson felt a surge of feeling for this girl, responding to her concern. They stood there, his hand on her arm. A sad smile played on her lips. From inside the house the old voice called, summoning Norah. Rogerson put his hand on the knob of the street door and turned it. His other hand still touched Norah; he turned to her, turning her. Close. Almost. He couldn't. As he went out to the car her expectant eyes stayed like an afterimage until his lungs filled with a fresher air and his head seemed slowly to expand with the novelty of breathing, the sounds of evening, an everywhere of children's excited homeward voices.

"Where have you been?"

"I stopped at the club."

"You're drunk."

"I had a few drinks."

"A few! Do you know what time it is?"

"For Christ's sake, Marge, it's only ten after six."

"Don't swear, the children can hear you."

"Not with that goddam TV going full blast."

"Matt! What's wrong with you?"

"Nothing's *wrong*. I assumed the ladies would hang around till late so I stopped at the club."

"The tea was over at four-thirty." Marge slumped into a chair beside the telephone table. "What do you want to eat? I've already fed the children."

"I don't care. I'm not hungry."

Marge sighed with noisy resignation and squeezed her eyes shut. "Matt, I'm tired. Do you want me to fix dinner or what?"

"What did the kids have?"

"Soup and sandwiches. I had to clean up and you didn't come. . . ."

"That's fine."

"You should have called. I tried to phone you."

"I've explained, Marge. I thought they were still here."

"Are you crazy? It was a tea, not a cocktail party. You know we eat at six."

"But you didn't make dinner."

Marge stared at him, her face slack. "What does that mean? Do you think I've been lolling around all day?"

"Forget it, Marge. I'll make a sandwich."

"Stop acting like a martyr! Coming home drunk, swearing . . ."

Rogerson went into the kitchen. His tongue felt puffy, his mouth dry. He ran water in the sink, filled a glass and drank. Marge had followed him, her voice was loud, accusations tumbled from her: he had no consideration, he knew she didn't want him stopping at that damnable club and drinking for hours and he could just fix whatever he wanted to eat because by God she was going to sit down. It had been a horrible afternoon, not that he cared. An idiot phone call. The least he might have done was ask how the tea had gone, but all he thought of was his supper ready and at this hour.

She was right. He should have asked. It was too late now. She was gone. Silence asserted itself in the kitchen, accentuated by the racket of the television from the living room. Rogerson did not feel hungry. He was tired. Laplace. Worry gnawed at him. What was going on?

He had another glass of water, the liquid gliding over his tongue leaving it leathery and parched. When he put the glass down he slammed it unintentionally, the counter arriving several inches sooner than his gesture accounted for. He moved toward the racket.

Barbara glanced at him when he came into the living room, her eyes returning immediately to the TV. The children were clustered by their mother. Despite the noise Rogerson felt their silent solidarity against him: a clutch of Catholics vis-à-vis the unchurched heretic. They had heard. The argumentative exchange made no sense; it seldom did. The children were uneasy. Tommy essayed a smile, the one reserved for not-quite-strangers. Rogerson crossed the room and entered his study. He stood next to the desk, waiting for the room to issue its welcome, but it seemed untidy, a mess. He sat at the desk and lit a cigarette. With an open book as prop, assuming a pensive frown, blotting out the living room noise, he sought a mindless suspension, waiting as always to be alone.

When it was time for the children to go to bed, they called dutifully from a distance good night and minutes later Rogerson was aware of far-off upstairs noises. Would Marge come down or go to bed? Either way, either way, he didn't care.

"Matt, *is* something the matter?" Marge stood in the door of the study, her stern look balancing the question.

"No." Suddenly he wanted to tell her about Schmidt, about Laplace, but he didn't know what to say.

"You should have something to eat."

"I'll get something later."

She went away. When she came back she carried a tray with sandwiches, soup, a glass of milk. He cleared a space on the desk and mumbled thanks. Marge avoided his eyes.

"How was the tea?" he asked.

"I don't want to think of it." She sat in the leatherette chair. "Oh, everything went all right. Someone phoned." She shook her head, looked pained. "I feel I've earned that trip to Milwaukee."

"Everyone show up?"

"Yes. Harriet Wooley was late of course."

"Emily Pruitt?"

"Of course."

Marge stood and yawned. "I'm going up."

"All right."

She hesitated in the doorway. "Do you want the TV off?"

"I thought it was."

"Just the sound."

"I don't want it on."

Marge went into the living room. She left one light on. He heard her check the doors and go upstairs. He removed the top from the bronze urn and tapped the ash from his cigarette into it, tamping it to the powdery condition of the rest. Suddenly he was crying. It angered him to feel tears well in his eyes, warm, stinging, fleck his lashes and, when he blinked, wet his cheeks. For Christ's sake, Rogerson thought. For Christ's sake.

2

In the high-ceilinged gym fifty adults on folding chairs moved with their squirming the slats on which they sat, exchanging smiles of shared pain when, turning from the maroon curtain whose promissory ripples had not yet prefaced its opening of the Campfire pageant, their eyes met. The airless room, the ambience of sweat left by years of dutiful exercise, volleyball games, basketball games, wrestling, boxing, the usual ooze of flesh, induced expectancy in Rogerson too. Oppressed by the olfactory vestige of past purposeless movement, he told himself the waiting was surely less tolerable than the program to come. Beside him Marge straightened once more, bringing her back against the chair, smiling defiantly, and then began slowly to sink into her hips toward the nadir from which again she would arise to an erect posture.

"Why don't they begin?" she asked, her teeth bared in a smile.

Rogerson shrugged, descending into a psychic slump, the hips of ataraxy. His puppet show was an item on the evening's bill; he tried to remember it but could not come up with a single line. Author, author, and Rogerson rose before such a group as this, bowing with contrived humility, assuming the lidded look of the creative personality, half frightened himself by the daimon that possessed him, he its instrument. Released by fantasy, he drifted from the gym, from the space-time of his life and the depression of the last few days. Far below him now the recent exchange with Marge in which finally and with unintended brutality he had told her of the Schmidt incident and its significance.

"In a nutshell, Marge, I'm a goddam flop."

"Don't say that!" Written on her face was his own dread

of that simple truth and Rogerson repeated it as if confrontation could soften its impact. How odd that he had never truly admitted it to himself before, meaning it, accepting it. He did not in his guts accept it yet but if Marge could be made to realize it, if she could be led to the acceptance of the fact, he would find it easier to take his defeat by the hand. How little they thought of him to demand that he be obsequious with Reinhardt, apologize, make him feel loved. To be least in Rome would be bad enough, but how much worse to be at the bottom in this outpost of the academic empire. "You're a good teacher," Marge had pleaded. "Everybody always says you're a good teacher." Or did they? Testimonials were suddenly difficult to recall. Hadn't Hughes once said such and such? Perhaps. But Hughes was long since dust, no more material than dreams. And even if remembered accolades had flooded both their minds, there was the fact of Rogerson's own estimate of himself. *He* knew. It was he who had entered those hundreds of classrooms and closed the door on his mediocrity. And he had tried. When research showed itself to be closed to him, he had fueled himself with the hope of being an impresario of the lecture room, a sage substitute father for the flux of students moving inexorably by before him. Yet how many old students had returned to wring his hand and with wet eye testify to his edifying influence?

"Matt, you can't let this happen. When Wooley gets that bill through the legislature . . ."

Or, what will happen when standards are applied? How will you survive on a competitive scene if you fail in the present one? Good questions. Rogerson conceded their cogency, repeated them, granted them the ring of the rhetorical, for they both knew, didn't they? His attitude, however, was not one of acquiescence. He would have liked to fight the oblique verdict Laplace and Wooley had passed on him. Good God. Bad enough to be hanged but by such judges!

"Thank God," Marge sighed and Rogerson looked up to see the curtain part.

The parents leaned forward on their chairs. Mrs. Crease, surrounded by girls in white blouses, blue skirts and beanies, beamed at the audience, eliciting polite applause. Rogerson writhed through the quasi-religious ceremony that followed: a lighting of candles, recital of vows, an Indian mumbo jumbo. Barbara to her credit seemed embarrassed by it all; indeed only Mrs. Crease seemed to be at ease on the stage. Her smile grew ever more benevolent during the distribution of beads, the songs and recitals and, finally, the puppet show itself. The thing was worse than Rogerson had feared and he whispered the news to Marge.

"I think Mrs. Crease made some alterations," Marge whispered back.

Rogerson's annoyance with the woman became hatred. Was even that toothy bitch his mentor? He joined with angry relief in the applause when the curtain closed mercifully over the stage.

"Let's get out of here. Where's Barbara?"

"Matt, we have to linger. Say hello to somebody."

"No thanks."

"Matt." The monosyllable rippled with menace and Rogerson turned from her to face a huge pair of horn-rimmed glasses.

"You're Rogerson." A face formed around the glasses, eyes looked out, a grin of beige teeth established itself. "Baker." A hand pointed abruptly and Rogerson felt an impulse to put his hands in the air. But he shook the proffered one. "I'm Donna's daddy of course."

"Of course."

"You're at the college."

"That's right." Rogerson looked over his shoulder but Marge had gone to speak with Mrs. Crease.

"I taught myself for ten years. Sixth grade."

"English?"

"Everything. I'm in sheet metal now. Couldn't cut it on a teacher's salary. It's different in college, I suppose, but it's slave labor down there in your elementary school."

"What do you do in sheet metal?"

"Sell it, Rogerson. Sell it." Baker smiled the smile of camaraderie and then moved closer, steady eyes level with Rogerson's, watchful. "You don't mind my not calling you Professor?"

Rogerson felt a deferential smile distort his face. "Of course not." He turned once more toward Marge.

"Wonderful program. Wonderful."

Rogerson nodded and walked away, certain he could not hurt this insistent interlocutor. From behind him Baker called, "So long, Professor Rogerson."

"Are *you* Marge's husband?" The woman had reddish-brown hair, rather unkempt, and there was a merry, almost impish gleam in her eye. "I used to see her and the kids at St. Patrick's on Sundays."

"Used to?"

"I'm Fran Heller." She smiled as if to say, Indeed it is so. "We don't go there any more. To St. Pat's. What do you think of that parish?" Mrs. Heller made a sour face and examined him for signs of relief that she too despised the place. "We've switched to the Newman Club."

"At the college?"

"Have you met Marty Hoag?"

"I don't believe so." On the far side of the room Marge was still standing with Mrs. Crease and Rogerson tried to catch her eye.

"Did you know his middle name is Luther? Reverend Martin Luther Hoag. How's that for a priest? Of course Luther was a priest himself. His mother wasn't Catholic."

Rogerson realized she was speaking of the Newman Club chaplain. He had seen the man, of course; Wooley had asked him to give an invocation once but all Rogerson could remember of it was that it had been brief.

"One of the new breed," Mrs. Heller said, winking an

eye and bobbing with approval. "Say, why don't you come to the discussion groups? We're reading Teilhard and it's so exciting."

"I'm sure it is."

"Marty would like more of the faculty to come, but he doesn't want to make a nuisance of himself."

Good for him, Rogerson thought. With relief he saw Marge approaching with Barbara at her side.

"I've been telling your husband of Father Hoag," Mrs. Heller said when Marge joined them. Rogerson put his hand on Barbara's shoulder and she pivoted under his palm, surveying the room. "I'm Fran Heller."

Rogerson moved a few feet off with Barbara and in the swirl of noise in the gym Fran Heller's voice asserted itself, rasping on about liturgical innovations, discussions, *aggiornamento*. Marge had the smile with which she suffered the importuning of a Jehovah's Witness.

"You were swell," Rogerson said to Barbara. She threw him a fleeting smile and adjusted her beanie. Her shoulder under his hand felt bony, her posture uncomfortable. The little felt vest, navy blue, was emblazoned with symbols. Rogerson, not knowing what they represented, feeling his daughter's interests and activities an alien area to which he had not been admitted, to which he had never sought admission, felt uncomfortable too. Public places make members of the same family strangers. That was it, wasn't it? Marge came over, ready to go at last, and the three of them walked swiftly to the door.

"Who is that Heller woman?" Rogerson asked in the car.

"Debbie's mother," Barbara said. Marge raised her brows and shrugged her shoulders.

The headlights of the old Plymouth were weak on the street, making its surface look spongy and moonlike. Marge turned and talked with Barbara and Rogerson envied her rapport with their child. He felt excluded from his own family, mildly wronged, as if Marge's love, soured with him, was directed safely at the children. When he turned in the driveway the ragged border of grass made its edges indistinct; the lights grew brighter as he eased the front bumper to within inches of the closed garage door.

"I'll hurry Mrs. Snow," Marge promised.

Rogerson turned the car around and waited for the baby-sitter to come out. Mrs. Snow had turned out all the lights but one and the house loomed darkly in the night, brooded over by dying elms. The myrtle beside the house was a mélange of green and shadow. The day after tomorrow he would put Marge on the train to Milwaukee.

Under the high-arched roof of the depot a few rows of benches faced one another like choir stalls and on one of them with papers spread for what comfort they could afford a stubble-faced, disheveled man slept, oblivious of the desultory if scheduled arrivals and departures which gave that sooty structure whatever significance it retained in an era of air travel. A cavernlike corridor leading to the platforms opened onto the waiting room and after Marge had stopped at a window to verify the time of departure with a functionary startled at being consulted, they went down the corridor and up a flight of stairs between walls with peeling plaster and out onto the almost deserted platform. A small tractor thumped toward them, weaving among the pillars, pulling a rattling train of carts burdened with two canvas mail sacks and several pieces of baggage. They went to the edge of the platform; Rogerson put down the suitcase Marge would carry and they both looked eastward up the tracks as if wishing would hasten the appearance of the train.

"I wrote everything down for Mrs. Snow," Marge said.

"We'll get along. Just have a good time."

Marge frowned, but only to suppress a joyous smile. When the train came into view and went past them in a diminuendo of roar and crescendo of hissing brakes, Rogerson picked up the suitcase but Marge took it from him immediately, their hands meeting awkwardly on its grip. She thrust her face at him, aslant, and he lay his lips on her cheek. Marge gave out a little embarrassed giggle, said good-by and hurried onto the train.

Minutes later, watching the train diminish down the

track, Rogerson felt only solitary, no elation gripped him, and he turned to retrace his steps to the car.

"Just getting here, Matt?" Felix Freeman intercepted Rogerson in the hallway leading to his office and fell into step with him. "Want to go for coffee?"

"Come in. I'll make some." At his office door Rogerson put his key into the lock. When he stepped inside, flicking on the lights, Felix came in on his heels.

"Why so late?" Felix asked.

"I had to take Marge to the train."

"Forget the coffee, Matt. I just came from a cup." Felix made a smacking sound with his mouth. "Now I know why they call that thing in the lounge an urn. Where's Marge going?"

"To visit her mother."

"How long will she be gone?"

"A week at most."

"A week! Matthew, you are a favorite of the gods. Seven days' reprieve from matrimonial bliss. I imagine you have an adulterous riot planned?"

"An absolute orgy, Felix."

Felix regarded him with mournful envy, then stood. "I mustn't tire you. You'll need your strength."

When the door closed behind Felix, Rogerson picked up his coffeepot, sloshing its cold contents, and rose to go down the hall with it. A cup of coffee, solitude, an hour before his class. What more could a man ask?

When he entered the lavatory Dowlet at a sink banked his eyes from the mirror to look at Rogerson. "Good morning, Matt. Did Reinhardt find you?"

"Was he looking for me?"

"He asked if I'd seen you." Dowlet turned off a faucet and ripped a paper towel from a dispenser and began to dry his hands with it. Blot, don't rub.

"Thanks for the warning."

"Say, what's Herb going to do about that business in

the women's residence hall?" Dowlet pitched his wadded towel into the basket beneath the dispenser, turned to the mirror and smiled lovingly at himself.

"Tell Reinhardt to keep out of his territory."

Dowlet laughed and began to comb his hair. Rogerson, having cleaned his coffeepot, filled it with water. When they left the lavatory Dowlet held the door for his senior colleague and they went down the hall in opposite directions. Back in his office Rogerson spooned coffee into the aluminum entrails of the pot, ignoring his ringing phone. It was still ringing when he had the pot plugged in and he answered it. It was Norah.

"I never see you sober."

"Thanks for helping me that afternoon."

Some seconds of silence intervened and then Nora said, "Felix tells me you're a bachelor this week."

"Marge wanted to visit her mother." Rogerson closed his eyes, trying to summon an imaginary Norah, someone sultry and sexy who might breathe, "Alone at last," into his ear. But all that came was the real Norah, the woman in Laplace's outer office, the harassed daughter of last week, someone lonely and unattractive.

"Who's fixing your meals?"

"A woman comes in during the day."

"Darn it. I was going to offer to cook for you. Could I persuade you to come to dinner, Matt? Say tonight?"

"I couldn't put you to that bother, Norah." Rogerson groped for the words that would enable him kindly to turn her off but none came.

"Don't be silly. Why don't you come?"

"But your mother . . ."

"That's just it. She loves guests. Someone to tell what a terrible daughter I am. Come at five-thirty for drinks. All right?"

Incredibly he agreed. When he had replaced the phone, he poured a cup of the now ready coffee. Remembering Felix's inquiry about his adulterous plans, Rogerson groaned.

Whatever nymphs his orisons dwelt on, the best the real world provided was Norah. There seemed a message there, of sorts, but Rogerson was not in a receptive mood. He had to get ready for class.

The Arts Building had all the warmth and character of a public toilet and through its yellow-tiled corridors past indistinguishable doors leading to homogeneous classrooms, Rogerson went with an odd shuffling walk bequeathed to him by Phillip Morgan, a revered teacher of long ago, dead these many years, survived by his professorial gait. For it is into the past that Rogerson heads when he goes to class. He entered his room on the peals of the bell and no matter the pastel walls, the pocked acoustical ceiling from which futuristic fixtures dangled, the daddy long-legs of the technological age. The blackboards were greenly indifferent to etymology and the kidney-shaped writing arms of the chairs where his waiting students sat were filled with ballpoint graffiti engraved against boredom: Sandy, Pat, Alice, a pendulant pair of breasts, the plaintive repetition of the monosyllable of procreation, dark exhortations to darker deeds, a penis perhaps. The penis mightier than the sword, Rogerson, beginning his lecture, mused. Than the mind. The emergence from Plato's cave is not easy in these bright rooms dedicated to number theory, the inch of history, the pulse of politics, the measured aspiration of poet and sage. The Ideas beckon from the front of the room, the elevated desk under a clock whose blood-red second hands revolves in the perfect purposeless motion, but in the lemon-colored chairs, their seats molded to the standard shape of buttocks—the national average ass, the median bottom?—there the loins seem master, the students adrift in reveries of sex. No matter. It is not to them that Rogerson speaks. He looks from the front of the room with the perennial hope of surprising himself expectant in the audience. His seeking has the force of the Ontological Argument, his wanting projects its object and his slow pace from window to door and back again, his fifty-minute walk stitching the walls of the room begun, Rogerson speaks to an earlier version of himself through the code of a lecture.

How odd to have lived his life in classrooms, caught on the threshold of life, aging among the young. The faces fuse and drift, boyhood friends sit side by side with his actual students, but seeing is not the sense of teaching; Rogerson, tactile, moved across the front of the room, a piece of chalk in his hand, rubbing the ball of his thumb on its smooth column, the taste of its dust in his mouth, its powder on his clothes, despite appearances inhabiting the paradigmatic classroom, the basement room where Morgan taught. The garden in the court was flush with the bottoms of the windows and in spring, with the windows up, the moist green smell was one with the business of Morgan's class, Rogerson's new world, a world of essays, of books, of hopes encouraged by his patron. How easy at fourteen to see life in terms of an inkwell and pounds of paper awaiting his incisive thoughts, anything but the strident world through which his father moved with the natural grace of a native. Rogerson senior had had the vulgarity to see life in terms of money and Rogerson, with the indifference to the practical security permits, had dismissed the interpretation. His father's question pursued him through school: What can you *do* with it? In college Rogerson retained a seraphic other-worldly smile to go along with his condescending explanation that the beauty of it was that you couldn't do *any*thing with it. Except perhaps teach. Unwittingly he had thrown his father a bone. He's going to be a teacher became the explanation and though he hadn't liked it, had grimaced when he said it, Rogerson senior was clearly relieved to have some slot in the real world to which his son belonged.

Thoughts of his father made Rogerson more conscious of the dual performance his teaching had become. He had said nothing new in years; the words spilled from him and would until the bell rang but he sank within himself. Now, thinking of his father, he remembered his surprise a few years ago when he first realized how much he had come to resemble his memory of his father. The resemblance had since increased, as if his face, after years of trying for its own contours, had settled with relief into the waiting visage of his father. His father had had more hair at forty-four; his nose, which had been broken and healed badly, had been more prominent, but standing before his mirror Rogerson could, with a minimum of squinting to fuzz the reflection, imagine he faced his father. Almost, he could find in his own eye the authority glinting from his father's, the authority conferred by the peaks of his career. The modest fortune made in the twenties as a plumbing contractor, lost in the Depression, had been eclipsed by the pile made in the windfall of the war. Declaring himself a general contractor against the background of a decade of desultory WPA work, Rogerson's father had won cost-plus contract after cost-plus contract. He had died in the same month as President Roosevelt and Rogerson, when he received the news, found himself wondering if he were mourning the dead President or his father. By the time he had been discharged and returned home his mother had been swindled out of most of the jerry-built empire by the partners. She had gone down in a sea of gin; for a year or two she had been periodically washed ashore at one sanitarium or another and when Rogerson visited her they sat in silence, each uncomfortable with the memories the other stirred. She went down for the third time the spring he took his master's degree, the spring he met Marge.

Rogerson plucked his watch from the desk and began to strap it to his wrist; no glance at it was necessary to tell him the period was drawing to an end. Up with

his bulky manila folder to the accompaniment of the bell
and toward the door, his step cautious, he never knew
any more whether students would give way or race him
from the room, elbowing aside their professor.

Eschewing the lounge in the Arts Building, into the out of doors, Rogerson filled his lungs with air and surveyed from the promontory of the stairhead the slice of campus on whose walks students sluggishly moved in the to-and-fro of class changes. Most of the campus elms had already been removed. Last fall, for a week, the air had been filled with the angry whine of chain saws, the plunk of trunks onto the grass of the mall; now he had to hunt for where they had been. New sod and saplings disguised their absence. Interchangeability is the mark of the member of a species, but to have a whole species drift out of the present filled Rogerson with no Darwinian sense that all is for the best. What survives is not the fittest but the darling of the laboratory.

"Good afternoon, Matthew." Schmidt, his smile wet and apprehensive, took up his position beside Rogerson and followed his gaze onto the campus as if to an event of great importance.

"Good morning," Rogerson corrected, causing Schmidt to consult his watch. From beyond the campus, factory whistles went off in a noontime blast and the phony chimes in the tower of the Administration Building sounded a few safe intervals. "I had a little chat with Laplace the other day, Reinhardt."

Schmidt made a gesture with his hand, plam down, an away-from-the-body dismissing gesture. His face was overcome by a magnanimous frown. "Please, Matthew. Please."

"Is it true you're leaving us, Reinhardt?"

"Leaving? I?"

"Everyone's talking about it, of course. Students, teachers, everyone. Munich, isn't it? Good God, I hope it wasn't supposed to be a secret."

Schmidt, turning, moved his face closer to Rogerson's. "Laplace told you that?"

"Herb mentioned it, yes. Anyway, my congratulations. What a relief it must be to know your days here are numbered." Rogerson extended a hand and snapped his fingers at the campus. "Colleagues with questionable qualifications, students who despise a true scholar. But fie on it, eh, Reinhardt? Soon you'll wing away to one of the great Continental universities. How I envy you."

"Laplace said I was leaving?"

"Aren't you?"

"Certainly not. Nothing is settled. I intend to stay here."

"Come, come, Reinhardt. You can be candid with me. I know what you think of this place. Why should a man of your caliber tolerate the treatment you receive?"

"Treatment? What treatment?"

Rogerson started down the steps and Schmidt kept to his elbow, his face straining toward Rogerson's. "Frankly, Reinhardt, you should consider the students' estimate of you a compliment. What can they know of academic excellence? Their *praise* would be an insult."

"Matthew, what is all this, what are you saying? What students? I am not going to Munich. You understand? I am staying right here."

Rogerson stopped and looked incredulously at Schmidt. "You're turning down the Munich offer?"

"It's not that . . . Matthew, you must understand." Schmidt's glance flew past Rogerson, returned, left and, having found what he sought, came back in a less agitated look. "After all, there is my contract here."

"Ah. I see. And Laplace is holding you to that?"

"Would it be fair for me simply to break it?"

"Perhaps not. But certainly understandable. And when your contract expires? What then?" Rogerson gave off a conspiratorial laugh and dug Schmidt in the ribs several times, rather sharply.

"Laplace should not have told you this. It was a confidence."

"Fear not, Reinhardt, Herb is a perfect confidence man. And your secret is safe with me. Still, the students should know you're staying. This will come as a great relief to them."

"Relief? But you said . . ."

"That they despise you? An exaggeration to make your departure easier. Don't worry, Reinhardt, they love you."

They began to walk again. "Incidentally, Reinhardt, I want to extend my apologies to you. I assured Laplace I would be pleased to do so. I apologize. Do I have your forgiveness?"

"Apologize for what?"

"Why, for turning students against you, of course. Put it down to the envy of a provincial pedagogue, Reinhardt. I should not have harassed you, trapped you in the women's dorm, caused you to make a goddam fool of yourself. That was wrong of me and I'm sorry."

"But those things . . ."

"My work, Reinhardt, all of it. Jealousy is a mysterious thing. Here am I in the autumn of my life and what am I? Nothing. But you, hardly more than a boy, well, look at you. Can you blame me? It is an old story. If the midget can fell the giant he is as tall as anyone."

"I find this difficult to understand, Matthew. This isn't like you."

"That is my essential danger, Reinhardt. I am such an improbable assassin. But it is true. Ask Laplace. You really should discuss the matter with him. You'd be quite within your rights to demand I make amends. Though how anything I might do could save you now, I don't know."

"*Save* me?"

They had reached the library. Schmidt's hand gripped Rogerson's sleeve as if for support, as if he feared Rogerson

might escape before this conversation achieved some measure of meaning.

"It's all water over the dam now, isn't it?"

"Matthew, what did you mean, save me?"

"Curry favor with Herb, Reinhardt, and salvation is yours.
I promise you."

"I don't want to talk about Herb. I want to talk about . . ."

"Yourself? Another time, Reinhardt. I'm going to have
to run. Are you going into the library?"

"Yes. Yes." Schmidt began tugging him toward the building.

"I'll be leaving you then. I have some errands to run.
This has been very pleasant, Reinhardt. Good day."

And the day seemed good indeed as he walked away
from Schmidt. He would stroll about the campus, have
a bite of lunch, return to his office later. How good re-
pentance is for the sinner's soul. When he did get to his
office, when he was sipping the cup of coffee unfinished
before class but now brought to a tepid potability by the
addition of more from his constantly simmering pot, the
thought of Norah's invitation eclipsed the enjoyment he
had derived from apologizing to Schmidt. He had to get
out of that dinner. What had he been thinking of? What
in God's name was Norah thinking of by asking him? But
when he dialed the dean's office Laplace answered.

"She took the afternoon off," Laplace said in reply to
his airy question as to where his secretary had fled. "Goddam
it, Matt, what did you say to Schmidt this morning?"

"Has he been there already?"

"No, he hasn't been here. He's been to Wooley and
Wooley called to chew me out."

"What I did was apologize."

"Oh, come off it, Matt. Look, I'm laying it right on
the line. Whether you or I like it doesn't matter. Wooley
wants Schmidt happy. You have a knack for making him
unhappy. You're going to have to lay off him and that's
final."

"What can I say after I've said I'm sorry?"

"For Christ's sake, Matt, quit clowning around. This is serious. Do you want to be out on your ass or something? Don't think it couldn't happen."

"All right. I'll be careful."

"I'm sorry, Matt. But it isn't a joke any more."

"Or it's really become one. Don't worry, Herb."

Afterward he sat there numb. The depression of two days before was heavy upon him once more. Could Wooley really be such a complete ass? Was he taken in by Reinhardt Schmidt? Obviously he was. And Laplace, of course, was not likely to disabuse him of his presidential misapprehensions. Rogerson pulled open the bottom drawer of his desk as a prop for his feet and saw the rum bottle he had emptied on that memorable day. He picked up the bottle and jiggled it; it was quite empty. On his feet, he started for the door. With Marge gone he could drink at home. He would devote the afternoon to it, then call Norah, tell her he could not come. An image of his mother assailed him as he went down the hall, he tried to summon the disgust he had felt at her drinking years ago and was filled with an odd sympathy. Why not? Why not indeed?

Mrs. Snow peered out at him for a moment as if she did not recognize him. When he had found the door locked, he decided against using his key, not wanting to frighten her. Now, opening the door for him, she stood back sheepishly.

"I've been cleaning the upstairs."

"Go right ahead. I've decided to work at home this afternoon."

"I haven't cleaned your study."

"Don't," Rogerson said. "There's no need. Mrs. Rogerson never touches a thing in there. It's an agreement we have."

She shrugged and pushed the sleeves of her sweater back on her ebony arms. She wore lime-green slacks that stopped abruptly in mid-calf, giving her outfit a truncated look. She seemed to be waiting to be dismissed and Rogerson assured her he would keep out of her way. When he went into the kitchen he heard her go slowly up the stairs and a minute later the vacuum cleaner started.

Rogerson found a bottle of bourbon hidden behind the boxes of cereal and took it and a glass into his study. Having poured himself a drink, he opened an examination booklet, uncapped his pen and stared at his Rembrandt print. He put down the pen, picked up his glass and toasted his guardian angel. The liquor contracted the inside of his mouth as if it were citric, it burned in his throat, it began a small warm glow in his stomach. Rogerson lit a cigarette and ignored the blank page before him.

"I made them with vodka," Norah said, handing him a martini. "Tell me if that's all right."

Rogerson sipped, closed his eyes in an appraising way, opened them and nodded. "Where's your mother?"

"I'm afraid she won't be joining us. She's upstairs, out like a light. She's had a bit of a day." Norah, in a sleeveless black dress, a strand of pearls at her throat, her hair rigid with spray, settled back at her end of the couch and sighed. "So you've been left to your own devices?"

"Free as a bird." And he felt it. The slow drinking all afternoon had induced a protective numbness at the center of which his mind guarded an essential clarity. He felt as if he housed wit and charm, was capable of a conversational gamut running from wild erotic humor through subtlety to profundities he could clothe in the lightest of language. Happy in this certitude, he sat in silence, smiling across an intervening cushion at Norah.

"Does the woman stay in?"

"No. But she's baby-sitting tonight." Mrs. Snow had not been happy with the news that he had a dinner invitation, but her manner became more receptive when he explained that her duties this evening would be an extra. He was not clear when he had decided to accept Norah's invitation, when he had decided not to phone her to say he couldn't make it. It hadn't been a moment of time so much as a slow alteration of mood. The realization that Marge was not in the house, that she was indeed away, had turned his thoughts to the possibilities of the evening. He could drive to Morton, a town twenty miles away which was reputed to be wide open. But there was a risk of encountering students there. Morton's bars were a constant topic

of talk on the campus, among the students and, conse-
quently, among the faculty. One Sunday afternoon, with
Marge and the kids, Rogerson had driven along its strip of
nightclubs, shut for the day, their gaudy exteriors inviting
to revelry. There were strip shows and B-girls and watered
drinks and Rogerson would have liked to look it over but
his habitual caution, strengthened by his conversation on
the phone with Laplace, vetoed the trip. The mounting
languor brought on by the bourbon made an evening with
Norah seem less improbable, then faintly attractive, until
finally he found himself consulting his watch to see how
long he must wait before setting out. The children took
the announcement that he was going out with a noticeable
lack of interest. With Tommy between them, Barbara and
Bobby went on watching television.

"Well, how was your day?" Norah asked.

The question was jangling, bringing thoughts of Schmidt
and Laplace; moreover it had an uxorial ring to it he did
not like. "Dry," he said, draining his glass. Norah leaned
forward for the pitcher, the scooped neck of her dress
revealing the pinkish swell of her breasts, the dividing
inclivity. When his eyes lifted they met hers, warm behind
the lenses of those glasses. As if sensing his reaction, she
took them off after refilling his glass and adding a dollop
to her own. Her eyes when she looked at him over a
toasting raised rim seemed slightly unfocused.

"*Gesundheit,*" she said.

"Please. No allusions to Reinhardt. À *voltre santé.*"

They drank. Rogerson was aware of succulent odors from
the kitchen; the phonograph insinuated a muted music
into the room. Two lamps were lit but it seemed almost
as shadowy as it had the afternoon he had had coffee
here with Norah and her mother. Norah went off to the
kitchen and when she returned sat not quite so far away.

"We're in no hurry to eat, are we?"

"Not while these last," he said, making a gesture with
his glass.

She laughed approvingly and Rogerson wondered how
long it had been since he had had a drink without antic-
ipating Marge's wrath. The realization that Norah actually
enjoyed having cocktails with him, that she was making
dinner for him, that they had the whole evening together,
filled him suddenly with an intense gratitude.

"There's no rush. I've turned everything low. Would you
like me to mix another pitcher?"

"Why not?"

"All right." There was a girlish lilt to her voice and
he went with her into the kitchen, looking up the darkened
stairs when they passed through the hall. In the kitchen
Norah moved from the cupboard to the drainboard, then
back to the refrigerator to draw out a tray of ice cubes
and Rogerson seemed always to be getting out of her
way.

"You stir, will you, Matt? I want to peek at the meat."
She stooped and drew forth the broiler and once more
Rogerson found himself staring at the tops of her breasts.
When she stood their eyes did not meet, but he knew
she had felt his eyes on her. The evening seemed electric
with promise and when they returned to the living room
couch they sat on contiguous cushions, their knees deliberately not touching.

Without her anachronistic glasses Norah's profile had a
distinction he had not appreciated before; the warmth of
the drinks, the promise of the evening, transformed her
into a woman and Rogerson, putting down his glass, taking
an hors d'oeuvre from the plate she extended, had a sense
of *déjà vu*. This was a scene, though Norah had not figured
in it, that he had imagined a hundred times over the
years, throughout a marriage marked by a fidelity that
was less a tribute to his virtue than a result of lack of
opportunity. Adultery had been the object of his whimsical
velleities for years and Rogerson, finding himself for the
first time in a situation where it did not seem unlikely,
dismissed the thought by assuring himself that Norah must

regard the evening from a virginal vantage point that
excluded anything beyond a remote teasing of the possibility. Turning to her, he realized he didn't know her
at all. Out of her native habitat, at least for him, she was
simply a stranger. The recognition seemed to neutralize
the setting but it aroused his curiosity as well.

"Tell me about Norah," he said, putting an elbow on
the back of the couch, his body receptively toward her.
Even as he said it the full effects of his drinking that
day made themselves felt. Space seemed as spongy as the
cushion he sat on; Norah's face became slightly ectoplasmic,
and he addressed it with what he took to be a paternal
smile, aware that he had triggered off with his question
the recitation of a manifesto. It broke softly on his ears
in paragraph waves, survived their eventual transference
to the dining room, where, trying to clear his mind, Rogerson concentrated while he listened on a wall fixture over
Norah's head, a lamp in the shape of a candle, its bulb
flamelike, simulated wax running down its side. The table
wine was tasteless to his numbed palate. He became aware
of this at the same time that it dawned on him that Norah's
autobiography seemed to contain an unusual number of
references to himself. Putting his glass down, running his
index finger along the back of his fork handle, he tried
to concentrate. She was speaking of the summer course
she had taken from him, of his poetry. He felt called
upon to make a diffident remark but this only increased
her praise and he saw that she too seemed to be showing
the effects of drinking. When they left the table she disappeared for a moment and when she returned she was
carrying a looseleaf notebook. On the couch they were
cushion to cushion now and not pretending otherwise, but
when she opened the notebook he saw with horror that
it contained his poems. She had made copies of them
all; she wanted him to read to her. He excused himself,
asked directions and went to a washroom off the kitchen
where as he urinated he examined in a mirror his wavering

countenance. All those lousy poems, for the love of God! He felt like a fourth-class lover foisting on the object of his attention his own imitative verse. She had actually copied them all. Yet the thought got to him, warmed him, filled him with tenderness. Who before had ever cared for his poetry? Once he used to show it to Marge, but she found it depressing; of course she didn't care for any poetry but he had counted on her being impressed that this, poor as it was, was his. So he had adopted the pseudonymous ploy, quoting himself in class. He knew the poems were no good—perhaps a phrase here, a couplet there—but as wholes they were imperfect. Now the quality of the poems seemed unimportant; he was overwhelmed by Norah's interest. Zipping up, rinsing his hands and dashing water on his face, he succeeded only in reminding himself how far from sober he was. He took a deep breath and buttoned his suit jacket. When he came into the living room again he assumed a professorial aloofness he was dying to be argued out of. She patted the cushion beside her. The notebook lay closed on the far end of the couch. On the coffee table was a bottle of brandy.

"An impartial observer would say you're trying to seduce me," he said, pouring the brandy.

"Could it be done?"

"Marge had me welded into my chastity belt, of course. Do you have a good file?"

"Perhaps if I chucked you under the chin it would melt."

They laughed. They drank. They drew on seduction scenes from a hundred novels. His arm on the back of the couch became more like an embrace and Rogerson was transported back to movies where as a boy he had over a maddening twenty minutes maneuvered his arm around his girl only to have it shrugged away. Norah did not shrug it away. He felt her nestle against him, her hair on his cheek, his fingers moved along her collarbone. Objects across the room were indistinct and Rogerson closed his eyes. How long had it been since he had made love to anyone like this, sat on a couch and begun tentatively the ritual leading to . . . He opened his eyes. He rubbed his face against her hair and she looked up at him, close, so close, this dear girl who had such a surprising devotion to him. With the ardor of Narcissus he lowered his mouth to hers, felt her arms come about him, drew her closer. My God, the sheer joy of a woman's body warm against him, given, not conceded, her answering kiss as passionate as his own. An odd anguished sound formed itself in his throat and he brought her more closely against him; his left hand slid up her rib cage, seeking her breast, and now she moaned.

"Norah! Who is this man?"

They swung in sweaty confusion, still embracing, to the door, where Norah's mother stood looking like the wrath of God. Her wispy white hair stood out from her head; she tugged a maroon bathrobe tightly about her. Her eyes sparked with triumph.

"Mother! What are you doing up?"

"I asked you who this . . ." Mrs. Vlach came into the room and peered at Rogerson, smiling, nodding her head in recognition. She turned to Norah. They were all standing now. Rogerson held Norah's hand in his sweating palm, held it loosely, felt it begin to slip and let it go. "Thought you had me knocked out for the night, I imagine. Well, it didn't work."

"Will you please go upstairs?" Norah's voice was an attempt at command but she was clearly shaken. But not so shaken as Rogerson, who felt suddenly sober, who was aware of perspiration running down the sides of his body, who felt his legs weak, who wanted to run for the door and get out of there. For God's sake, caught with his hand in the cooky jar at his age.

Nodding her head up and down, the old woman looked at the two of them. "Well, this *is* a scene. This is cer-tain-ly a scene."

Norah grabbed her mother's arm and propelled her from the room. The old woman gave out a feeble scream. There was scuffling in the hall. It sounded as if Norah might be carrying her mother upstairs. From above, a hissing quarrel went on and Rogerson, in sober embarrassment, stood in the center of the room whose inadequate light seemed to add to the ludicrousness of his position. Should he have said something? Madame, I assure you my intentions are honorable. I have here in my hand letters of recommendation from my wife and three children. How insane to have come here, to arrive half loaded and then add to it the quantity he had, to succumb to the flattery of her interest. He wanted nothing more than to get out of the house but he had to wait for Norah, had to say good night, had to thank her. He waited in the hall for her to come downstairs.

But she fled past him, covering her face with her hands, into the living room. Rogerson followed. He would wait for the tears to stop, make a graceful exit . . . Her hand came up to his, pulled him down beside her on the couch. He didn't resist. Anything that speeded his exit he would do willingly. He put his hand on her shoulder, patted it as if to indicate he regarded the whole episode as the merest bagatelle. She misread the message. She flung herself at him and Rogerson, flustered, took her once more into his arms. Nuzzling against his chest, her voice breaking, she told him she couldn't stand it any more, she would put her mother in an institution, she didn't care what her brothers and sisters said, they didn't have to live here with her. It was always like this. He had no idea. "I can't do *any*thing," she cried, drawing back and staring at him, her eyes swimming in tears. "I have no life of my own." He took her face between his hands, brought his lips paternally to her forehead, but she twisted and brought her mouth to his, churning against him with an ardor that both frightened and repelled him. When he broke free, when her cheek was against his, she moaned lightly in his ear and her behavior seemed suddenly unexplainable simply in terms of passion. This whole evening made no sense. The invitation, the elaborate preparations, the mother strangely abed, the notebook with his poems. He could half believe now that she had made a copy of the note she had found in the Dante. He asked Norah why her mother had gone to bed so early.

"I put sleeping pills in her tea. I was sure she would sleep through till morning."

"How many?"

"Oh, three, four. And she suspected! She's uncanny, she really is. She poured out her tea and had been lurking up there in the dark waiting to spring on us."

"But why?"

"I don't know. I just don't know. Oh, Matt, Matt!" Once more she sought solace in his arms, made the mewling sound, dug her fingers into his back.

"Well, it's been a wonderful evening nevertheless." His voice sounded like a cheery newscaster's announcing traffic fatalities on Memorial Day.

"You don't have to *go!*"

"I really should. The baby-sitter."

"At least finish your brandy." She handed him his glass and when he took it, cupped his hands in hers, bringing the glass to his lips. Rogerson drank as if from real need.

"Good?"

He said it was. "You haven't finished yours."

"I don't need liquor when I'm with you." Her eyes took on a meaningful expression. She traced her finger along his lips; he lifted a hand to stop her and she brought her mouth to his hand, filling his palm with wet kisses, her tongue flicking at the weblike conjunction of thumb and index finger. Rogerson felt his loins stir. But he could not forget the old woman standing in the doorway like some mad angel of judgment. He finished his brandy, leaned forward to put the glass on the table, got somewhat abruptly to his feet. Norah looked up at him forlornly.

"I'm so sorry the evening turned out badly, Matt."

"Nothing could spoil it, not even . . ." The polite remark, so bravely begun, had nowhere polite to go.

"Nothing except Mother."

That called only for a studious pause. "Well," he said a moment later.

Norah nodded but remained on the couch. He moved toward the door slowly, then stopped. After a strained silence she sprang to her feet and came rapidly to him, crushing against him, hugging one arm with both of hers. She went with him into the little area between the outside door and hall door and, the light out, he took her once more into his arms, willing to pay for his freedom now. He kissed her with great intensity, pressing his whole body against her, felt her pliant reception. Blood churned in his head. God, how he wanted it. But the situation was impossible. Better to get the hell out of there. Which is what he did, by inches, with a dozen more kisses, withdrawing from a series of clutching delays.

On the sidewalk he had to make an effort to walk slowly to his car. Behind the wheel he looked up at the house, saw Norah, in the darkened areaway but vaguely silhouetted against the light from the living room. So their prolonged farewell would have been visible from the street. Rogerson started the car, put it in gear and slipped away from the curb; with belated prudence he did not put his headlights on until he had driven half a block from the house.

Ad seipsum:

Could I have gone through with it even if the circumstances had been different, if that crone had not put in an appearance at the crucial moment? I don't know. I really doubt it. What is difficult to grasp now, two hours later, home, Mrs. Snow gone off in my car in which she can return in the morning, what is difficult to grasp is that it was Norah I held in my arms, Norah I kissed. Laplace's secretary! Plain little Norah with glasses that were the latest thing in the forties. Kay Kyser. That's who she reminds me of wearing those damned things. But I wanted her. She seemed attractive, very attractive, with her breasts pushed flat against me, her mouth busy on mine. Christ, she was as hungry for it as I am. No, it wasn't the fact that it was Norah; it wasn't because her mother showed up like Rochester's wife. I couldn't have gone through with it. Unzipped, there would have been the humiliation of *ejaculatio praecox* or, worse, an inability to cut the mustard. Even here I fail. A Don Giovanni *manqué*. The possibility still existed after she hustled the old witch upstairs; Norah was still game. Wasn't I relieved rather than dismayed by the interruption? Scared shitless, of course. All she lacked was a camera. Aha. Then, pow. The flash bulb blinding us, the mandatory scene in every B movie starring Lee Bowman, seen from the balcony of the Nokomis Theatre. The hero staggers toward the cameraman, impeded by his dropped trousers which hobble his ankles. Home now in the familiar context of my unhappy marriage, feeling unclean, how much worse it would be if I had gone the distance, had put it to poor little Norah. What next from her, for God's sake? Phone calls, impassioned messages, a demented call on Marge. I love him, you see. Drawing back. Oh for a fur piece to bring flipping across the throat after the delivery

of that line. An uptilted chin, emphasizing her defenseless-
ness. Or, my God, nine months hence, Norah at the door
with the telltale bundle in her arms. No, no. Fear not. Norah
will forget it as I will forget it. Why should I succeed at that
dream when I have failed at all the others? Be thorough.
Sitting here, I am actually tempted by righteousness, as if
what explains this disastrous evening is my resolution to
save my body for my wife. God. God. Would Marge even
care? Of course she would, not because she wants me, not
because some seed of mine were sown elsewhere than in her.
My balls are an escrow account, gathering no interest from
her, but legally untappable by another borrower. Fie on it.
Pee on it. Sleep on it.

"Matt, I have to see you."

"Norah?"

"Where can we meet?"

Rogerson floundering, for the love of God, it was worse than the worst possibility he had conjured up in his study the night before, sipping cups of instant coffee that had kept him awake half the night, tossing between shallow sleep and sodden wakefulness. Norah's voice had the crisp, nervous intensity banality demands. Ridiculous, incredible, yet her urgency communicated itself to him.

"I don't know."

"Should I come there?"

"No." His voice sounded like a slap and there was silence on the other end of the line. "Let me think."

"You're through with classes for the day." She would know that. There was no point in pleading class as an excuse.

"The Faculty Club."

"Matt, that's crazy."

"No one's there at two o'clock." Except Harry perhaps and he didn't count. Tit for tat.

"Not there, Matt."

"Yes. It's best, believe me."

He took the sound she made for assent. When he had hung up he rose immediately and started for the door and stopped. He should have put her off. This was crazy. She had no right to call him and demand a meeting. He should have said . . . He looked longingly at the phone, wondering what he should have said. Well, it was too late now. Perhaps he should call Harry and ask him to lock the door and admit no one. Without a rendezvous they could postpone it and, in the meantime, he would think of an excuse for not seeing her. Her reputation. What else? Look, Norah, this isn't fair to you. What might people think? There, there, my dear, no tears. Please. I understand. You're lonely. You crave affection. Someday the right man will come along—no one quite so exciting as me, of course, but a personable chap nonetheless—and, well, things work out, Norah. They really do. Calling Harry was out. No point in making waves. When Rogerson opened his office door he looked stealthily up and down the hallway before stepping out.

Norah stood at the corner, at the bus stop, her forced air of casual waiting wholly unconvincing. When she saw Rogerson coming up the street she walked swiftly toward him, her body bent forward, her eyes on him as if she were a long-distance runner and he the terminal tape. He stopped and she drew next to him; her hand fluttered out and then returned to her side. She wasn't wearing her glasses and she looked pleadingly at him, waiting for him to say the perfect thing.

"Let's go inside," he said.

"Please, Matt. Not in there."

"Don't be silly, Norah." He started up the walk and reluctantly she came along. But a couple of jiggles indicated that the front door of the Faculty Club was locked.

"It's locked," Norah said. "Let's go. We can talk in your car."

As they stood there Rogerson's back felt like a target a hundred eyes were reaching with unerring accuracy from the street. They had to get out of view. He took Norah's hand and they followed the walk around to the back of the house. But the back door too was locked. On impulse Rogerson ran his fingers along the ledge above it and came upon a key. It was not relief that shone in Norah's myopic eyes when he showed it to her.

"I've never been in here before." Norah went ahead of him into the converted kitchen, her hands clasped behind her, her purse bouncing off her buttocks, her head describing appraising arcs.

"Whisper," Rogerson urged. In the hallway he cocked his head toward the stairs, listening. "Just a minute." He went rapidly up the stairs and knocked at the closed door of Harry's room. There was no reply and he knocked again. Turning the knob, he pushed the door open and looked inside. The room was empty. Satisfied, he started for the stairs to find Norah on the landing, looking up at him with dread. "The steward," he explained. "He's out."

Her mouth formed an oval of comprehension and she nodded. He joined her on the landing and she came close to him, laying her forehead on his chest. With the feeling that he was delivering himself over to an unjust fate, Rogerson put his hands on her arms. Her face tipped upward, eyes closed, her lips quivering. He placed his lips on hers chastely. Her hands were still clasped behind her and the stance made her seem at once indifferent to his attention and pathetically defenseless.

"Are you angry with me?" She had drawn back and they started down to the first floor.

"Angry?" He laughed a brief incredulous laugh.

"I had to see you. After last night."

"Forget about last night, Norah. Things like that happen. . . ."

She gripped his arm tightly. "But nothing happened, Matt. Nothing. Damn her anyway. What am I going to do? I can't go on like this. I just can't."

They sat in a room off the bar. "Why do you have to live with her?"

"She can't live alone is why. And there is no one else. My married brothers and sisters either have no room for her or wouldn't have the time."

"You mentioned an institution."

"Oh, sure." She groped in her bag for a cigarette and when she had it, posed until he lighted it for her. She blew out the smoke without inhaling. "On what grounds? That she's a pest?"

"Aren't there boarding homes for old people?"

"That's been vetoed by the family. Too expensive and Mommy needs the love of relatives now. That's me."

Rogerson nodded, his look encouraging her. At least this visit was not what he feared it might be; she wanted only to talk about her troubles with her mother. He settled back in his chair. Go on, my dear. Tell me, how long have you hated your mother?

"Everything was so wonderful until she came down and spoiled it." Norah stared at the end of her cigarette; Rogerson too looked at it, let his eyes drift with the smoke. He agreed that the evening had been nice. And she *had* to say how wonderfully he had reacted when her mother came down; his quiet authority, his untroubled calm. Rogerson listened, trying to make his memories match her description of his comportment. The paradox of the outer and inner. How did others read the signs of his selfhood? From within he was a blundering idiot, but did that get through to others? And if it did not, was he still a blundering idiot? Norah's eulogy went on and Rogerson felt himself without resources. It was soothing to listen to her, though he felt self-indulgent allowing her to continue. But he had learned the night before that trying to stop her had the effect of prodding her onward. He would change the subject. But what was there to talk about with Norah? The young stranger in the chair across from him seemed no one he might come to know.

"What explains it, I suppose, is that we're both unhappy."

"Unhappy," Rogerson repeated. Was that an adequate label for the sullen depression that dogged him?

Norah crushed out her cigarette and armed herself with a new one. She lit it herself. Rogerson could not remember if he had ever seen her smoke before. From a blue-white cloud she developed the theme of their common unhappiness and Rogerson grew vaguely angry. He could not himself catch in words the feelings he had about his life and he resented the airy facility with which she failed at the same

task. He was none of her business, by God; he refused to
be drawn into any consolidated wailing with her. He said
little, however, only enough to keep Norah safely in her
chair. Her words occupied the room, hung above them
like sunlight, burdened with that slight dust permeating
everything like an omen, invisible save for moments of
lucidity. Norah was explaining to him why a man of his
caliber had to be a failure at a school like this, why it was
impossible for him to get the recognition he deserved. The
familiar ground was not welcome to Rogerson. Explanations
he had given himself sounded false and whining coming
from Norah. Failure. Failure. The word itself failed to name
what he felt, what he was. Who had invented the standard
according to which he was found wanting? Did he resent
the standard or his failure to measure up to it? The thought,
amorphous, teasing, absorbed him and he tried to settle
into it despite the insectlike insistency of Norah's jabber.
Then he heard other voices. Norah did too and they were on
their feet, staring round-eyed at one another. Someone was
putting a key into the lock of the front door.

"Come on," Rogerson said hoarsely. He grabbed her hand
and ran into the hallway and up the stairs. They had turned
the landing and were out of sight when the inner door
opened and voices filled the hallway below. Tiptoeing, two
steps at a time, they continued to the second floor, moving
away from the railing. Rogerson felt Norah's hand gripping
his painfully, heard Felix's voice, Dowlet's. What the hell
was going on? Some meeting of the club's officers? Laplace's voice became audible over the others after the door
slammed. Rogerson looked at Norah. His eyes went on to
the door of Harry's room. He nodded toward it and Norah's
brows lifted questioningly. Her expression was dazed. He
led her to Harry's door, eased it open and stepped inside.
Norah stood in the doorway, looking around the room, her
mouth slack, her eyes lusterless. He pulled her inside and
closed the door, turning the key.

Rogerson sighed and sat on the unmade bed. Norah remained standing, a few feet from the door, her head turning slowly as she looked at the nudes pinned to the walls. Horror crept into her eyes. The voices from below were still audible.

"Norah, I could go down there. Distract them . . ."

She turned to him. "You can't leave me *here*."

She was right. He couldn't. Even if he could think of a way to explain to those downstairs how he had got in, he couldn't leave Norah cowering here in Harry's room. She came to him, stood before him. He got off the bed and then she was embracing him, crying in deep sobs she tried unsuccessfully to muffle, and he was soothing her. For God's sake, she had to take it easy or they would hear. He put his arms around her, moving her like a clumsy dancer away from the door, maneuvering her around a stack of girlie magazines, to the window. Over her shoulder he looked out at freedom, at people moving along the walk without apprehensions. Norah sobbed against his chest, less noisily now, but with less control too. He tried to push back, to look at her, but she felt boneless and limp. Her face, when he saw it, was ravaged, twisted with a grief that seemed out of proportion to the admitted absurdity of their plight. They stood there for fifteen minutes.

"Let's sit down, Norah."

She shook her head violently but permitted him to move away. Her face was white and expressionless. She stared at the window as if it were opaque. Rogerson sat once more on the bed, listened to the rumble of voices from below play against the muted high-pitched sound Norah made crying. He felt as detached from the one as from the other, a prisoner of his indifference. Why had he agreed to meet Norah? Why had he brought her here of all places? Norah should have known Herb was coming to a meeting at the club. A vague resentment took possession of him but dissipated as his eye roved the walls, receiving the bovine semi-sultry looks of a platoon of nudes who displayed their impossibly pink, airbrushed bodies.

Norah had grown silent, but remained standing, her body rigid now, her hands making white-knuckled fists. She kept looking at her watch as if the slowness of time surpassed her understanding. Rogerson could not quite make out the debate raging below and then downstairs too there was silence. Norah looked at him and he shook his head. "They're probably voting." She swung away. Voices started up again below, more restrained. Rogerson went to the door and pressed his ear against it. He could hear Laplace then, and Dowlet.

Half an hour later Rogerson slipped downstairs. There were two or three men in the kitchen, but the door was closed. He went back for Norah and led her through the hallway and outside; she came along as if she were an automaton, her eyes closed until the street door shut behind them and the sound of the afternoon traffic assaulted their ears like music from the promised land. They parted there. When he offered to drive her home, Norah shook her head once, looked at him in silent stupor and hurried away up the street.

Barbara ran from the house to the car when he pulled into the driveway, her eyes frightened, Marge's set to her shoulders as she hurried to him.

"Tommy's hurt," she said. The accusing tone too was her mother's.

"Hurt? What happened?" He clambered out of the car and started for the house. "Where's Mrs. Snow?"

"Inside."

In the hallway he called and was answered from upstairs by Mrs. Snow's calm voice. He went up the stairs to find Tommy lying on the floor of the bathroom with a washcloth on his forehead. His son looked up at him with wide, steady eyes. He seemed all right. Mrs. Snow, who had been kneeling beside Tommy, stood.

"What happened?" Rogerson asked.

"The boy cut his head. He slipped on the bathroom floor and hit his head on the sink here. The bleeding seems to have stopped."

Rogerson knelt and removed the washcloth. The wound had not stopped bleeding, it gaped open, red-lipped, angry. "Come on, Tommy." He put one arm under Tommy's head, the other under his knees and raised. "He'll have to have stitches."

"You taking him to the hospital?"

"Yes, of course." He stopped and looked back at her. "You'll stay, won't you?"

She pouted, studying the floor, and then shook her head in assent. To hell with her. He could take the other kids with him if the woman had to go. But when he told her this she said she would stay. Rogerson carried his son to the car and made him comfortable on the back seat and while he was backing down the drive asked Tommy how he felt. Tommy said he felt fine.

He parked against a railing a few feet from the emergency entrance of the hospital and when he carried Tommy inside, felt his son's body go tense and turn against him. Standing before the glassed-in reception desk, Rogerson looked through a hole in the glass at a middle-aged woman with frizzy red hair who did not look up. He cleared his throat, waited a moment more and then spoke impatiently. "My son has been hurt."

"Name?" He hurled his name at her indifferent head. She pulled a clipboard in front of her and copied the information. Finally she looked up at him. "Would you wait across the hall?"

Rogerson stared at her in disbelief. "Is this the emergency ward?"

"That's right." Her smile suffered the obtuseness of wounded hordes descending on her sanctuary. Rogerson became aware of a young man, scarcely more than a boy, lounging in a pale green pajamalike costume in a corner of the office.

"Then what the hell do you mean wait? Is *he* a doctor?"

"You'll have to wait. Others are before you."

Rogerson swung and looked into the reception room: couches with dented leather cushions, flanked by tables bearing mounds of magazines. The room was empty.

"I asked if that fellow is a doctor. Hey, *you!*"

The young man looked up laconically, his eyes rested briefly on Rogerson and then dropped to the red-haired woman, conveying a message.

"Send him into 3," the intern said, addressing himself to the receptionist.

"Emergency room 3," she relayed to Rogerson, indicating the direction with a nod of her head.

A black plastic plaque with the number 3 engraved in

white above the door and Rogerson stepped inside with Tommy. The dominant color was green; there was a cabinet on the far wall filled with bottles containing a clear fluid, topped with aluminum clasps; in the center of the room, a table covered with a sheet on which a bright spot of light glowed. A fat nurse leaving by another door looked over her shoulder at them as they entered and then was gone in swish of swinging door. Tommy, looking around, was rigid with fear now and he coiled in his father's arms.

"I don't want a shot."

"You won't get a shot," Rogerson lied. On the wall a clock read ten to eight; Rogerson sat Tommy on the edge of the table, staying close, his arms still about his son, staring at the door and waiting for the nurse to reappear. The minute hand crept toward twelve; Tommy, more at ease, looked around the room. His wound had stopped bleeding, but it had to be closed. Good God, if all it required was a Band-Aid!

"Is the doctor going to come?" Tommy asked.

"Yes." He'd better by God come soon. Rogerson went to the door and looked out. Across the hall a woman, wrapped in a sheet, sat on table with a mask strapped to her face. Her eyes studied Rogerson. From the brink of the grave? Trying to look away, Rogerson found himself fascinated by the woman. Her dark hair was matted on her head, her complexion white, one hand gripped the mask though it was held to her face by head straps. It might have been her one link with the world. Was she dying? Her exiguous face, those staring eyes, almost coquettish, held Rogerson and the anger drained from him. That intern could be tired not bored, emotionally numb from death and injury, a constant influx of casualties from the humming city. There were voices behind him and Rogerson turned to see the nurse and intern come in by the swinging door.

"You'll have to wait outside," the nurse said. She put a hand on Tommy's chest, as if holding him down, and the doctor bent over the boy. Tommy began to scream, to kick his feet, and the nurse's expression grew stern. "Outside, please," she repeated.

Rogerson stepped into the hall, trying not to look into the room where the woman gripped her mask. He started toward the waiting room as Tommy's crying grew more shrill. "Hold still!" A shout, impatient, angry, a male voice, it had to be that intern. Rogerson turned in fury, slamming his hands against his legs; he didn't care how tired the fellow was, that was no way to talk to a frightened injured child. He became aware of the woman's eyes on him once more, wide, dry, drained of color. Wasn't anyone looking after her? She was alone in the room. Was she trying to signal him for help? Rogerson moved to the door of the room and stared in at her. Her eyes crinkled, a hand went to her hair, fluffing it, and on the edges of the mask her smile made itself known. Rogerson fled to the waiting room and flipped savagely through a magazine, not even looking at the multicolored glossy pages as they fanned from his thumb.

He saw the nurse emerge from number 3 and he went down to find Tommy sitting alone on the high table. Several stitches had been taken in his forehead. At the sight of his father he began to whimper and Rogerson took him in his arms, soothing him.

"We gave him a tetanus booster," the nurse called in to him.

"What is that doctor's name?" Rogerson asked.

"His name?" The nurse came into the room, looking puzzled. Rogerson glared at her name tag. Miss Grosset. She smiled as if having the first premonition that an award might be coming her way. "Dr. Rush."

"Thanks."

"We always give a booster. Just to be safe."

Rogerson nodded. The nurse fussed with Tommy now, patting his head; she settled on one foot and rested her thigh against the table.

"Can I take him home now?"

"Oh sure. All done. Your own doctor will remove the stitches."

"You're goddam right he will."

He left her there, stunned, speechless, and went out to his car.

It seemed the evening of more than one day when Rogerson sat later in his study. The kids were in bed. Mrs. Snow had gone. Darkness invaded the house; he had turned out the lights to let it in and now a vagrant grayness emphasized the cornered, recessed blackness. An occasional car sent the windows along the walls, swift distorted parallelograms. Laplace had called to say in a thick half-drunk voice that Wooley appreciated his placating Schmidt, that Reinhardt was definitely staying.

"My day is complete," Rogerson murmured.

"Who would have thought he'd turn down Munich?"

"Who indeed?"

Herb filled the phone with a noisy sigh. "Just when I thought I had the bastard he comes up with the trump of another offer."

"Did you check with Munich, Herb?"

"He had letters." Laplace's voice dropped. "In German."

Meaning Herb couldn't understand them. Some Bavarian henchman might have purloined stationery and pled with the émigré to return. A paragraph from Nietzsche would have sufficed to fool Laplace and Wooley. Dear, ingenious Schmidt, Rogerson felt a grudging admiration.

"Reinhardt *über alles*, Herb."

"Yeah."

When he had hung up, Rogerson sat at his desk in the darkened study making an inventory of his failures, as husband, as teacher, as father, as friend and colleague. As lover. On all fronts the enemy was in hot pursuit of the deployed Rogerson, driving him toward his diminishing center. Look at it this way, Matthew, you might have succeeded. He lit a cigarette, pulled the Mexican silver urn toward him, cleared a place for it on the desk top. He removed its cover and stirred the ashes with his mortal finger and thought of his father. Success. Success. Excel. Succeed. Ever upward. To what? Where was he meant to go pell-mell and panting, hot-eyed after what prize? He had not escaped his father's categories after all. They had pursued him into this supposed haven, turned it into a hell. He had tried so hard for so long, unwittingly wanted on this stage to do publicly well. No mordant humor could conceal the fact that he had wanted to be a good husband, but what verdict would Marge pass on his efforts? He had wanted to be a good father, but he knew what Barbara, his little Campfire girl, and Tommy, his injured son, would say to that. A good teacher? My God. And now poor Norah had felt the sting of his inadequacy. Could he have done worse if he had set out to fail?

That question, seeming at first the summary of his litany of woe, gained with repetition a programmatic clarity. If he had set out to fail. He examined the thought through two cigarettes, turning it and the burning stub he held over and over, allowing a funny fancied sequel to form in his mind. Why not? Why not indeed? Rogerson smiled, he got to his feet. On with the lights. Inaction. Still camera obscura, but by God an Augustinian O felix culpa too. Rogerson strode from the study to make himself a drink. To jump or be pushed, his choice seemed as simple as that. In the kitchen he popped the cork from a bottle of bourbon, his smile grimmer, made himself a drink. Back at his desk he toasted the great globe itself, man's fate, Marge, the kids, his job, Reinhardt and Norah. And finally himself, himself and the chosen nadir to which he now aspired.

PART TWO

Fall

1

Down the hallway between tiled walls, lavatory walls, Rogerson went and up the gray stairs because the elevator moved with slightly more than gravity and above the bank of buttons someone had corrected a split infinitive in the officialese of the printed inspector's chart. The righteousness of grammar. Some pedantic prick advancing on the world like a correcting pencil, freshman compositions a prissy synecdoche for the whole flawed world. Above that professorial correction Rogerson had written, as if to redeem his kind or separate himself from the rest, ROGERSON IS A SON OF A BITCH. In ink. The next day a line through it, then several, finally the whole thing blotted out because it embarrassed the others to ride in the elevator, with or without him, and try to ignore that scrawled judgment on an esteemed colleague. Damned embarrassing. Only faculty had access to the elevator, admitting themselves with keys. For a week there had been an air of accusation in the lounge. Felix, as if fearing he was under suspicion, asked Dowlet point-blank if he had done it. There was a new warmth in the reception for Rogerson whose long-suffering dignity was more than a match for such a cowardly smear. Would life be possible with truth inscribed on every wall? •

On the landing he halted, one elbow on the slate ledge of the narrow window giving on the yellowing October grass below, and looked at the walks athrong with doomed foreshortened students on foot or cycle being belled to their third-rate higher education. The alienation of the modern student. Title of editorial in this week's student newspaper. More pretentious dry rot written by some goddam goateed kid whose credentials were two decades adrift in mindless

affluence. Eager for *angst*. The power structure of the college. Conceptual frameworks. Rogerson lit a cigarette,
drawing the cancerous caress of it deep into the cold cage
of his breast. He would get it in the prostate, like his
father. One way or the other in any case. The morality
of breathing. Mustn't be too flip in class; a constant risk of
popularity in amusement or instruction. Dullness was more
difficult when you have ceased to care what cargo you
jettison into the chromed corridors behind their staring
eyes. Mixed metaphor penciled on Rogerson's forehead,
teetering on a carat between his brows. Be dull. Be awful.
The Rogerson Code. Go swift and willing into that dark
night.

Onward and upward in the Arts Building he continued
to the faculty lounge. Slowly, exercise not punishment,
squeeze and release of the red fist, flushing the essential
juice. The roar from below, beasts in the corridors, their
noise and stench rising even to this retreat of coffee in
paper cups and leather chairs releasing artificial farts
through porous metallic buttons. Whoopee cushions. Fool
your friends. Advertisements on the backs of comic books
rolled into the pockets of a lost youth. Mandrake. Get with
child the round earth's imagined corners. Big Little Books.
His father reading one once on the porch swing, pulp paper,
huge print, illustration on facing page. Oddly embarrassed.
Goddam the young, himself young then with a loathsome
conceptual framework, now at forty-four coming undone
into the haven of the lounge.

Sitting with his head wreathed in the leaves of spring
in the four-seasons mural some summer school student had
perpetrated on the far wall, Felix Freeman in this building
of grafitti released a noisy mote of greeting through squared
air which graphed the elusive rise of smoke. The others in
the senior corner turned with fake conviviality to mark his
entry. James scattered ashes on self, on limewood veneer,
even with aimless accuracy into the ceramic tray on the
table, a tray ringed by stained cups with more lightly

stained napkins puffing like scarves from their rimmed headless throats. Son of Roger not of bitch at last, cried Felix. At the urn, two cubes of sugar cast rattling into his cup, its handle unimpacted from the sides, Rogerson drew coffee and pronounced a general curse on this municipality's college, its minions, mentors, victims and nameless bene-factors. Crossing the room, he settled warmly into the ap-preciative laughter of this grievously sinned-against gather-ing. He shoved his fat manila folder, emblazoned with the greasy smudge of his palm, onto the table, pushing before it the clicking discarded cups.

"What in God's name do you have there?" James reached and got a firm rap on the knuckles from Rogerson's ball-point for his pains.

"Wisdom. Keep your foul hands off it. It could ruin your life."

"Ann Landers in Academe."

"The intellectual life, James. Surely you've heard of it. Beyond dollars and cents, over and beyond your base fleshly desires, a shimmering eudaemonistic telos moving with metaphorical motion the tangled hierarchy of appetites to a quietus no bodkin could purchase."

"Bodkins being what bishops wear," James explained.

"But bare bodkins for the laity." Leahy, devout Catholic, professional anticleric, scowled; his elbows angled over the bloated arms of his chair and he pulled on his stinking pipe.

"The end all men seek."

"Please!"

A bell up the tiled throat of the stairwell, beckoning, beckoning, and all but Felix slid dutifully away, left the caught seasons of the mural to descend once more into the winter, the Friday, the unwanted birthday time of the class-room. Felix rolling in a complaint of leather, wedding art and nature, broke wind and eyed Rogerson's manila folder with disdain.

"You're after that award, Rogerson."

"Merely a Guggenheim, Felix. A year in the South of

France to complete course notes in undergraduate ethics. Any foundation would be proud."

"The student thing."

"I lust after it, of course." Rogerson dropped a hissing match into the viscous coffee, expelling smoke contemptuously.

"You're in the running, Matt. James was just telling us. The Student Senate is down to four names and yours is one of them."

"Bullshit." An actual flush of pride, goddam it, a fleeting vision of Sinclair Lewis thumbing his nose at the Pulitzer, of Sartre raising a phallic existential finger in the direction of the Nobel committee. "Who could survive their praise?"

"You're on the way up, Rogerson. You were not meant for failure. Too bad. Raises. Promotions. Crowded sections. You poor bastard."

"Fear not, Felix. It can't happen. I blue-pencil their quizzes unread, flunk twenty-five per cent on principle. I am magnificently dull in class. I insult them." Fifteen minutes ago he had glared at a sea of fetal faces and told them they were easily the least gifted mental delinquents he had encountered in a long and less than illustrious career.

"That's it, Matt. You've found the key to their masochistic little hearts. Now I know you'll get it. You'll have no friends of course. Merely success. I can see you sitting on that stage with the other dignitaries."

Rogerson, serious, leaned forward. "That nonsense should have been discouraged from the start. Where will it end? Students assessing the faculty! My aching ass."

"These are dark days, Rogerson."

"Absolutely ecumenical. It all goes back to John XXIII."

"We're all smirched with it."

"There should be a faculty pact. No one to accept it. Hurl it back at them."

"How many do you think would agree to that? Any of the young ones would love to have it. For the rest of us it would be an empty gesture." Felix smiled slyly. "We agreed it would be fitting for you to get it. One up for the Old Bastards."

"It would be the definitive blow."

"We'll see."

Could he really have been currying favor with his students, wooing them, wanting their esteem? Rogerson refused to accept this. He had no doubt of his hatred of students, of teaching; he despised the whole process and he was determined to do magnificently badly. After twenty years of chalk dust, one eye squinting against the windowed wall of the room, building in the airy void the period sentences freighted with insightful fact, wanting to awaken the minds before him, he had despaired of success. That dream had been replaced by another, one whose subtle intense attraction he would never again doubt: the dream of failure, the deliberate, willed plummeting before the same audience that had witnessed his hitherto unwilling descent. Now he would expose his wax to the sun, welcome the molting of his fake defiant wings. His lectures were spoken for his ears only, a solipsistic exercise on which students eavesdropped. Despite them he would continue the fallacious flow of words. He had easily acquired the art of ignoring the tentatively raised hand that hitherto would have drawn him like a bee to pollen, learned not to encourage the infrequent glimmer of inchoate thought in the eyes of the beholder.

After a recent class Maureen Nugent, a two-time loser, high-cheeked face and green eyes bracketed by thick brown hair, ever so slightly sericeous upper lip, asked if he would devote a class to birth control, there's so much talk nowadays and wouldn't it be relevant really since he'd mentioned existential ethics and no, lashes furiously fluttering, she was not married, nor engaged. Rogerson in the role of nasty old man regarded in a distracted way the pearlike protrusion of her young breasts, allowing that he would consider the matter, delicate topic, you know, opinions divided and he had no wish to offend the religious sensibilities of anyone. Or had he? Could the new Rogerson Code encompass that ridiculous academic taboo? We shall see, we shall see. Thinking the while, dear nubile Miss Nugent, flee with me to my dreary office in the basement of the library and under my surprising importunate kiss hoist with overcome reluctance that plaid skirt that I might discover the pleasing plumpness of thy thigh and try with my forty-four-year-old finger the sanctum of your private parts.

"I really like this course, Professor Rogerson. Better than last year's."

"Well." What in the world for? Why in hell didn't more of them skip? He refused to call the roll; there was no need for them to be there. He had told them as much, told them ethics had nothing to do with the classroom and even if it did he was quite sure he had nothing important to say on the subject. Predictably, perhaps, they had laughed. But his deed had matched his promise. Couldn't they see that he had sedulously avoided the subject of the course, that his lectures were random illogical essays into which absolutely no thought had been put prior to stepping into the classroom? The folder he carried was filled with scrawled pages on which he had written *ad seipsum* essays. Talking with Maureen Nugent, Rogerson had felt a cold sweat, had feared her single voice of praise, and no longer because popularity would bring the scorn of the Old Bastards— he wanted their scorn too. Besides, he had suspected what Felix now revealed: the denial of interest in student response was a mere pose by the Old Bastards. They were old bastards indeed; they would take vicarious pleasure in any accolade given to one of their own. No. Students be damned was Rogerson's personal motto, part of his code and creed. Woe to him who prepares for class, whether he takes a seat under the four-seasons mural or elsewhere in the lounge, off with the ambitious upstarts with their goddam Ph.D.s and eternal applications for grants and their contributions to learned journals and earnest talk of faculty-student relations. Twenty years of this drudgery permitted reality to seep in along with the images of alumni rich and poor, pink and gray, hustling for a buck, their minds mercifully purged of three credits of this and three of that, though sheepish in their occasional return, mumbling they had not known, had not taken advantage. And the alumnae, God love them, spirit of City College intercede for them, supine in suburbia catching the urgent seed in their baccalaureate wombs, eyes moist with fugitive pleasure or the ammonia from the diaper pail. Faculty-student relations, for the love of Christ!

Miss Nugent pensive, then in a rush said, "It's the very first class here I've found truly relevant."

"Relevance is my watchword. I admit that." Rogerson shuddered.

"It's your examples more than anything."

My examples? Whatever he said had been purloined and plagiarized over the years, smoothed and trivialized by repetition, perhaps thus had become his own. "I think of my approach as existential." Sartre, the Boul' Mich, *les mouches*, Rogerson on the prowl in the city of lights.

"Other teachers are so dogmatic. You make us think."

Oh, God, God. But Rogerson said, "Action is difficult." And thought is fleet, oiled, lubricious, Miss Nugent. You are deflowered in imagination's moment though leadenly in time I take my leave, head modestly bowed after your irrelevant praise, down the hallway between tiled walls, lavatory walls, and up the gray stairs.

Now after this more alarming exchange with Felix the two men went out of the lounge and Rogerson left Felix inserting his key in the elevator lock and once more on the gray stairs downward and finally outside into the haunted October air. High above him the wind was a vehicle of lost cries, the lament of this suddenly deciduous day; the crisp coin of leaves spent themselves over the campus, their brittle points scraping as they scudded across the walk tak-

ing Rogerson to the squat ivy pile of the library. He went
through the door under the main steps and along the linoleum hall to Room 212.

> *Professor Matthew Rogerson*
> *Humanities Department*
> *By Appointment Only*

Beware of the dog, the *cave canem* of that by appointment
only, take heed you young bastards full of juice and life,
devoid of this feeling that does not deserve the name despair.

Rocking in his desk chair, coffeepot plugged in, he turned
to the cloudy window, pooh-poohing Felix Freeman's ominous prophecy. How that meaningless endorsement by the
unwashed rabble would kindle the licking flame of hope in
Marge. It couldn't happen, not to him. A special meeting of
the AAUP? Should call Dowlet immediately. But Rogerson
hadn't paid his dues this year, not since the chapter had
been taken over by the new men who spent their time draft-
ing resolutions on administration-faculty and faculty-student relations. They had started this alienation horseshit.
The anonymity of the school. Why couldn't they understand that that was the saving feature of this disastrous
life? Dowlet, pricky Dowlet, the local Renaissance Man,
was moderator of the student paper too, filling the editors'
as it were minds with tripe.

Write a letter in Kierkegaardian anonymity, the alienation from his true self, occupy say the lightly hirsute skin
of Miss Maureen Nugent. An old universal instantiated once
more. His second year of teaching, penciled in the bluebook
of a final exam, that effusion from her whose wide eyes
had watched him into eloquence and fierce lyrical flights
until his class had been a fifty-minute tryst with her en-
raptured gaze, penciled Mr. Rogerson, this semester has
been torture, you remind me so much of my fiancé it's uncanny. So for the first time went the hope that the pupils

of his pupils were avenues to mind. The not so funny laughter, ho ho, that what he said had not been heard, the stand-in for her partner in a cleft bedded paradise. A note, a letter, Miss Nugent pray for me, nymph in thy orisons, and into the trusty Underwood an untraceable sheet, addressed to the editor of the college paper.

Dear Sir,

In a time of aggiornamento and the need for relevance, it seems to me that a searching look into some of the courses currently being offered has much to commend it. The arid, aloof and sometimes downright sterile approach in courses whose titles would lead one to expect a discussion of the more vexed issues of the day is something most students notice and lament. A case in point is the ethics course offered by the Humanities Department where insinuating and bawdy examples make the course a real threat to student morals. Couldn't the Student Senate look into this and if feasible make suitable recommendations to the administration?

Sincerely,

Maureen Nugent '69

P.S. For obvious reasons I must ask that my name be withheld.

But only Rogerson teaches ethics. Hmmmm. Uncanny. That pimply gangly delivery boy at Herman's Grocery years ago living for Friday when with whitewash or whatever it was he could paint the bargains on the front windows, the special grace of his number 5, a calligrapher of talent who in another time might have earned some immortality on more lasting glass, saying have you heard of the ten-story building without any toilets isn't that uncanny? An authoritative turn of the wrist, thank God for 5s and this doomed art. Do we indeed protest against the ravages of time? Into an envelope with your folded note dear disloyal Miss Nugent, preserver of my honor. Next class a surprise quiz to count

fifty per cent of the final mark will send them snarling away
to curse him and see with new eyes what a fake he was, the
course a pastiche of trivia and they cruelly mishandled by
this academic tyrant. Down with the tyrant.

"Come in!" to the knock on his door, shouted, a dare.
Reinhardt Schmidt fresh from without within still wearing
his corduroy cap, off with it, into his gnarled Teutonic hand,
looked with obsequious eyes through the copious forestra-
tion of his brows at Rogerson. His eyes darted to the empty
chair, getting the lay of the land. "Well, what in God's
name is it, Schmidt?"

"You are busy?"

"Busy? We are professors, Reinhardt. Professors by defi-
nition sit on their dimpled ass and fix the eye of the soul
on eternal truths, those changeless entities of a better world.
Contemplation, Reinhardt, not work; leisure, not busyness."

"But who sees it such?" Schmidt, coat unbuttoned, cap in
hand, rolled his eyes in resignation. The analogy of Europe,
the sinecure of a professorship in his native land wracked
his malodorous body. "We should have the assistant, the
typist. How can one write under these conditions?"

Rogerson shoved the letter to the editor out of sight
under the rubble on his desk, the grade book girdled by a
green rubber band, the *ad hoc* ashtray with *Photostat* on
it, papers, journals, junk, junk. "Or teach, for that matter?
With all these goddam students and classes, how can anyone
possibly teach?"

Reinhardt wary. Best to think of him as a Nazi, Rogerson
decided. An old SS man come this way from South America,
rather than directly by plane three years before, bagged by
a touring trustee drunk in Munich who thought this seedy
Privatdocent, discredited by his discredited master race,
was an academic find. God save the mark, the franc and
the insanely inflated college credit won now in abundance
by listening to this wretch slaver about *Sein* and others of
his transcendental friends.

"Matthew, do you have any offprints of your paper on the concept of obligation?"

"Not a one. Suppressed by the bishop. All copies collected and sent to Rome; burned in St. Peter's Square while cardinals snake-danced around chanting the litany of Blessed Heraclitus, patron of Auschwitz, Dachau, wienie roasts and burnt books."

Reinhardt abject. Too bad. He had read it, of course; perhaps he would have a microfilm made from the library copy or Xerox it. The sly sonofabitch. Rogerson's only publication, yellowing in the bound volume of a minor journal, the thing accepted when the chief editor was ill. For a year and a half afterward there had been unanswerable refutations of it published in the same journal. It had become in its way a minor classic.

"I'm working on a sequel to it," Rogerson said, commencing with that remark his work on the sequel.

"You are?"

"The response to that article was tremendous, Reinhardt. You may know that. Some negative reactions, of course. But I believe all serious criticisms can be handled. As I see it, though, the task threatens to mushroom."

Reinhardt closed his eyes, nodding in ecstasy: labor, research, wet armpits in a dry library, mounds of notes written in a small hand and clipped according to subjects, perhaps potential chapters, visions of a multivolumed work. Watching his colleague, Rogerson found his imaginary labors take on broader dimensions.

"Amazing you should mention that article today, Reinhardt." Rogerson took his letter opener from the drawer and ran its sharp tip under his thumbnail. "I am considering applying for a grant to underwrite the necessary research. As you know, such presentations have to be ingeniously drawn up and, I am afraid, foundations do not smile on the solitary scholar. Fortunately, this problem would lend itself to the team approach. With a principal researcher, of course."

"A team?" Reinhardt's eyes ascended until only the yellowish whites showed under his brows. "As you say, it is a large, unwieldy problem."

"I don't suppose your own work would permit you to consider . . ."

"My work is moving precisely into this area. That is the cause of my interest in your article. Matthew, I have never applied for a grant because I was afraid the committees would not, well, smile on a poor immigrant."

Good God, didn't he realize what an overwhelming advantage his foreign birth was? Broken English fairly dissolves the bowels of the dispensers of the fortunes of dear departed robber barons. "I'd be happy to cut you in on this, Reinhardt. If you're free."

"Wouldn't it be months before it was certain?"

"At least. Reinhardt, here is what I will do. I will draft a proposal. Then we can go over it together."

"Excellent, Matthew. Excellent."

Rogerson dropped his letter opener into the drawer with a decisive clatter. "Done." Humming meditatively, he stared at Schmidt. "Incidentally, Reinhardt, have you heard . . . But, of course, you must have."

"Heard what?"

"Surely they've informed the finalists?"

"What are you talking about?" Forward on his chair, eager, fearful, hopeful, pure-hearted Schmidt.

"The Student Senate best teacher award."

"I have never heard of it."

It was possible. Schmidt did not read the student newspaper. "I can't believe they haven't told you."

"Tell me what?" A gray tongue worked spittle from the corner of his wide chapped mouth.

"It's not definite yet. But I'm told they're down to four names."

"What does it mean? A popularity poll?"

"Quite a lot, I'd say. A plaque presented to you at the December convocation."

"I had no idea. Truly."

"It's amazing they wouldn't have let you know."

"But, Matthew, my teaching . . ." Schmidt displayed his hands like a child showing he had washed.

"You're too modest, Reinhardt. I've heard reports." And such reports. Half the students could not make sense of Schmidt's English, his mouth frothed while he lectured, he made constant references to articles in German journals which were not in the library even if his victims had been inclined to seek them out. But he was a merciful marker so that, in the end, they forgave him.

"It would be an honor to have it come to our department," Schmidt said, taking the high ground.

"We shall all share in your triumph."

"But it is not definite?"

Rogerson smiled reassurance, felt no remorse at the gleam of hope in Schmidt's eye, could not believe the benighted bastard actually believed him and then, blanching, wondered if Felix had been pulling *his* leg. Get rid of Schmidt! A quick consultation of his watch and on his feet saying "Good God" and Reinhardt up and out and the door locked, that goddam Felix, of course. Splitting a gut going down in that elevator at his gullibility, his diffident dismissal of the richly deserved if despised honor. God, God, I do deserve that filthy award, it would serve me right. Matthew Rogerson, M.A., best of breed, best of show in this byway, this fetid fading flirting-with-bankruptcy excuse for a college with its faculty of near misses and rejects, the 4Fs of academe, and its students at best turned down by the college or colleges of their choice, at worst too stupid to aim higher than this four-year harbor for the mental basket case.

Rogerson poured boiling coffee into the unwashed cup, coffee sterilizes, cursing Felix and himself. He was no better than Reinhardt really. Rogerson is a sonofabitch. Up with the phone, he dialed the extension of President Wooley's office, click, fizz, pause, then ring once only and the dusty

aloof virginal voice of Grace, actual Grace, and he in a
false voice yelling, "Professor Rogerson is a sonofabitch!"
Her high-pitched prolonged *What* and into the cradle with
the goddam thing. That would show them. He had integrity,
by God, more than anyone knew. A sip of coffee and then
coatless with the now stamped envelope Rogerson loped
down the hall and outside to the mailbox in front of the
library. Red, white and blue. He remembered when they
were green, when everything was green and this a way
station, temporary, not the only groove his slide into the
waiting dark would ever know. Down the chute with it,
there, *la chute*, the fall, the declension of the proper noun
called Rogerson.

That evening his spouse and *Kinder* ringed the television, off in the elsewhere of dental hygiene and whirring depilatories and the orgiastic possibilities of soft drinks and cigarettes. Marge, when he told her he had to go back to the office for an hour, perhaps more, merely nodded. Her new attitude, one she had been able to sustain for a day or two in the past after an argument, he had managed to consolidate into a permanent plateau of noncommunication between them. It dated from Tommy's injury. When Marge returned to find her son in stitches, literally, she was not, figuratively; Mrs. Snow managed to convey the impression which was half fact that he should have been home at the time it happened, that it was his responsibility not hers, and Marge had grasped the opportunity to correct any imbalance there might have been, any gratitude due him for her week away from the salt mine. Rogerson did not, as he always had in the past, seek to ride out the storm and then take advantage of dimming memories, weather influences, the ebb and flow of emotional tides, to bring them back to their usual less choppy course. He drifted out of range, did not choose to call her back. Throughout the summer they had tried this new limbo of their marriage and found it not distasteful. Did this follow from the Rogerson Code or did the Rogerson Code follow from it? The sequence must be left to those who easily read the logic of events. Rogerson had written indelibly on his consciousness, I am a lousy husband and father. It was a challenge he intended to meet. He parried all suggestions that they take a trip, vacation as they sometimes had in a cottage at the lake, until Marge, rising almost happily to the lash of martyrdom, fell into the habit of taking the kids to a local pool. During the summer session Rogerson practiced the art of unteaching but could not put it to a fair test. Summers he taught a course in the philosophy of education, his students were teachers returned to pick up the credits on which promotion and salary increases depend, and they were so numb from previous summers of nonsense that no idiocy could possibly stand out from the boring backdrop of inanity. Rogerson felt as if he had crawled out on a ledge, made the required preparatory and threatening moves, only to discover that the spectators he had attracted were one and all afflicted with some swift and terminal disease. Freed from the hazards of a true test, he perfected his method with impunity—like a suburbanite hacking away at a driving range with any measuring par of his efforts an imaginary one easily attained. Between the end of the summer session and the beginning of the fall semester he had avoided his home, spending the hot August days in his office in the library, attended by a cheap fan whose twisted blade clacked against its wire enclosure and sent a constant wave of heat over a perspiring conspiring Rogerson, his mind aflame with the ideal of a magnificent failure. After months of preliminary inconsequential skirmishes and imaginary losses Rogerson fairly lusted for the beginning of school once more. With the return of the students in September, his campaign had begun and the results to date were ambiguous.

Rogerson left the house, a can of rustproof paint and a stiff brush in his briefcase. Outside he got into his ten-year-old car and drove down a street lined with dying elms, into their ultimate autumn and would the city stand the expense of their removal, to the campus. On the walk in front of the Arts Building he crouched and with uncanny stroke painted the ineradicable truth. ROGERSON IS A SEX MANIAC. He went quickly, furtively away, with the imagined sound of pursuing footfalls to his car and the library, to his office where still plugged in his coffeepot filled the room with an electric stench. He went down the hall to the head with it—rinse, hiss, fill with cold water, pitch the grounds grandly into the basket of twisted paper towels beginning a moist sifting noise while he rinsed the entrails and then back to his office to see if it would still make coffee. In with the plug and soon the syncopated slurp began.

To such disfavor come at forty-four and why? That would have been his question last year, the year before that, adjusting for age and rage, going back to the commencement of his tenure here. It had been difficult to dislodge the thought that life is meant to be a rising curve, that our days inch to a destination which will give retrospective meaning to this pale, flat unprofitable duration. Maturity. Clarity. This is it, no more, just this. Why not? He deserved no more. Honesty. Honesty. A piss-poor school and he no teacher nor one who had wisely chosen the better part. He had reacted against an avaricious father and had come secretly to long for affluence in the bourgeois soul he still retained, wanting his wife and children decked out indistinguishably from the rest. Fat chance. Teaching is better than working and that is all. Recognizing this, he could have decided to expend the minimum of effort, be loose, withdrawn and survive. That would have been one way to avoid the hollow successes of his unchosen field. But Rogerson had resolved to react definitively against his father, against the memory of the man and the vestiges of his influence that rode in his son's blood. He would no longer be an inadvertent failure, a moaning loser. Away with inadvertence, down with moaning, hasten the *Gotterdämerung*.

Why sex maniac? Why not? That too was true. Bottom drawer on the right of his desk, locked, packed with glossy magazines and pornography that would arouse even Harry's jaded soul. Had Wooley heard from the firm specializing in 16-mm. dirty films? Grinning, Rogerson had filled out a blank in the president's name and mailed it off some months before. Now Rogerson unabashedly lusted after them all as they sat in his class, sitting on a fortune, legs crossed, one foot jiggling up a minor landslide on the Mount of Venus, smiling in an autoerotic daze before him. But mustn't touch. Fatal, instant death. That was the maxim of his profession. Poor Regis, years ago, had been certain a coed was throwing it at him but she went screaming down the hall bringing them all out of their offices. Regis stood there crimson with horror. Gone the next day. It's there in the contract, not even the AAUP made a *pro forma* demur. Prudence counseled keeping it in the realm of imagination but prudence was a virtue of the unwilling loser and Rogerson, if he were to keep to his code, could not for long be the unsung stud of these hallowed halls.

Remembering his conversation with Reinhardt Schmidt, Rogerson ran a sheet of paper into his typewriter and typed "Being, Having and Behaving" across the top and then "by Matthew Rogerson." In a parody of Schmidt on those occasions when he cornered Rogerson with a spiel about his phenomenological professors back in the Fourth Reich, Rogerson felt the keys take on a manic Ciceronian rhythm under his fingers as with polysyllabic obfuscation he rang the changes on trivia, invented etymologies, issued a flood of promissory notes in an opening paragraph he carefully failed to redeem in the sequel. It flowed. A modest heap of pages formed beside his machine. As he wrote, a resolution formed. Every other week he would compose an article for a learned journal, the off weeks to be spent removing any clarity beyond the minimal surface clarity, typing it up in a clean copy and putting it in the mails. He would send off a barrage of tripe and when it came sailing back would make Schmidt the messenger of his defeat. The plan had the double advantage of national and local self-destruction.

The following day was Wednesday, no morning classes, which was why the night before, going home, he had stopped at the Faculty Club and had four doubles at fifty cents apiece, only advantage of the place, keeping his lines out to Harry, he had plans for Harry, but now morning and emergence from the red aching warmth to consciousness and Marge tugged urgently and strangely without her usual matutinal malice. The president is on the phone. Instantly alert and, admit it, fearful to the roots of his proletarian soul, an image of Regis, brief, repressed, then barefoot down the stairs to the hall table smelling freshly of wax.

"This is Rogerson."

"I'm sorry to interrupt, Mr. Rogerson." Grace, just Grace. Rogerson wore a relieved smile. One hell of a note to have to speak to Wooley half awake; undeniable disadvantage. But interrupt? Did she for God's sake think they were tearing one off at nine-thirty of a Wednesday morning? Ah, the intricacies of the spinsterish mind.

"Nothing that can't wait, Grace." Scratching his groin. A thousand and three in Spain alone. Leporello, take a letter. French, of course.

"President Wooley would like to see you today if it's convenient." Tone conciliatory, deferential. Everything okay or being sly as shit.

"I'm free at eleven."

"Mmmmmmmm. Yes, that will be fine."

He hung up and turned. Marge stood poised and curious, still on the stairway, cursed as always with hope. "Are you going to see him?"

"At eleven."

"What does he want?"

"Probably going to fire me." The possibility was remote now but it did no harm to lay a few preparatory hints across Marge's path. She had no idea how close she was to the end of her bondage to him.

"Don't be stupid. You have tenure." The hum that accompanies her calculations. "Harriet was especially nice to me two days ago at the president's reception for faculty wives."

"It's nothing, Marge. Not a goddam thing. Is there coffee made?"

"I told her about those terrible postcards."

Cheerist! Rogerson had printed those out during a faculty meeting and mailed them at irregular intervals for a week. Nothing she didn't already know. Your husband is a prick. How is he in bed? He's lousy in class. Scared the hell out of her though. Was he teaching as well as he could; it wasn't wise, was it, to become unpopular with the students? The consumer is always right. Why had he done it? Why did he do anything? Why was he? "What did she say?"

"She was shocked, of course. And very sympathetic. Some demented boy, that's her theory. Things like this happen and I shouldn't concern myself."

"I still think Wooley sent them."

"Matt!"

"The lecherous type. Fat lips. That gives them away."

"Can't you be serious? What can he possibly want?"

"Perhaps he wants to send me off to a convention or to raise funds for a student clinic. Any pretense to have you here alone and defenseless."

A moment of silence and then moving from cold fury to screaming rage, Marge went through her whole repertoire of denigration, all of it lacking in imagination and rhetorical punch. Rogerson put in toast, lit the fire under the tepid coffee and wondered himself what Wooley wanted while Marge's screams assaulted the periphery of his at-

tention. Later when shaved and scented he came downstairs again an icy truce obtained and he bade Marge
civilly good-by.

At her desk Grace gave him a facsimile of a cordial
smile and lapsed into solemn busyness while he waited
and then a beep and in he went with Wooley bouncing
across the room toward him, pink hand extended, leading
him to one of the chairs facing the desk. Once more in
his own chair beneath an ectoplasmic painting that swirled
toward a center of realism where a vague lady bared
a nippled mound (aha!) at the addressee of the president.

"I understand Miss Press caught you at home."

Rogerson nodded. As I was rounding the dining room
table the damned wench grabbed my ankle, grounded me
and worked her evil will on me. Sordid.

"Do you have Maureen Nugent in class, Matt?"

"I believe I do, yes," having judiciously paused. "Why?"
Rogerson's wet palms slid to the knuckled ends of the
chair arms. Wooley was in his fifties and even if he did
have fat lips he was president and beyond reproach and
would have no compunction about giving the faithless
Rogerson a premature heave-ho.

"A number of bits and pieces are fitting together."
Wooley's fingertips met, his eyes lifted to the stippled
ceiling at which his steepled fingers pointed, his mouth
working. Portrait of a man wondering how to put this.
"Harriet told me of those cards your wife received and I
understand there was something scrawled in the elevator
of the Arts Building."

"What has this to do with the Nugent girl?"

Wooley smiled as gods must smile at mortals and went
on. "This morning there was something painted on the
sidewalk in front of the Arts Building. I don't know how
we'll get it off."

"What was it?" Neither smiling nor frowning, receptive,
deep in his heart uneasy, stepping on stage in a play of
his own.

"Someone seems to think you're a sex maniac."

"I've tried to be discreet," Rogerson said, the words escaping, feeling right as they went. "Perhaps I went into class with my fly open."

Wooley popeyed and then, suddenly, laughing. Ho ho. Rubbing the purselike opening of the pouches from which his eyes invisibly looked out. Deep breath now, a toothy smile for envoi. "It is serious, Matt. And I think we may have the answer."

"I'm to be sterilized?" By God, weren't they old buddies, though? The sonofabitch, the fat bastard, look at him ho ho.

"Dowlet has come up with a clue." Pause. One reminiscent laugh. "A letter arrived this morning at the office of the student newspaper. A veiled attack on you. Signed by Maureen Nugent."

"Covered with painty fingerprints?"

"I've had her records checked. She has a mental okay but of course they all get that from their family doctor. It doesn't mean a thing."

"Look, I couldn't pick her out of a group of six. I don't even know the girl." Lies, lies. Only yesterday I committed adultery with her in my black heart.

"The odd thing is that this goes back into the spring semester. She was harassing Schmidt then, if you remember, but she managed to drag you into that too. Told Schmidt you had put her up to pestering him."

A bink from a gray and chrome instrument, Grace's voice. She excused herself for all eternity for interrupting but could the Student Senate committee see him today? They could. The machine soothed, Grace no longer audible, Wooley looked seriously at Rogerson. "Another thing. Grace got a call yesterday. Someone shouted an obscenity about you. Grace thinks it was a girl trying to sound like a man."

"Miss Nugent again?"

"Do you have any other ideas who it might be?"

"It could be anyone, of course."

Wooley shook his head sadly in assent. An imperfect universe. In the best of colleges. Damned shame, really. Well, you know what we all think of you, Rogerson. God knows you're well liked by the students generally. This on the way to the door; Rogerson protested, his honor at stake. But he was outside then and past Grace and it was only himself he could assure that he was rightfully despised by every goddam student he had, that he could not abide, would not accept their acceptance, the final seal on his failure to fail.

In his office Rogerson felt an unfamiliar remorse, agenbite of inwit, thinking of poor little busty Maureen Nugent on whom would shortly be visited such incredible accusations. It was no part of his plan to ruin her, to be the cause of such injustice. But who knew the underside of another's soul? Might it not just possibly come as the objective correlative of sweetly secret schemes troubling her mind while she whiled away his class? For didn't the bifurcation of the race into sexes entail that each of us at least fleetingly speculates about the amorous possibilities of anyone of the opposite gender we even slightly know? Surely Miss Nugent had daydreamed of a venereal tussle with him and then despised herself and him. Consider for your edification, brethren, the case of Miss Norah Vlach.

How fitting that Emily Pruitt had been the bearer of news the significance of which must have been wholly lost on her. In July, at the checkout desk on the main floor of the library, she had adapted herself to the protective angle of Rogerson's elbow and roughly to the tune of *Dies Irae* hummed her necrology into his unheeding ear. Until the name Vlach twanged his inner ear and he turned to the self-appointed chronicler of local deaths and listened with silent dread. An overdose of sleeping pills, the poor dear too impatient to wait for the Lord's summons, her daughter had found the body. A long history of previous attempts, though Norah, she works in the dean's office, you know, Rogerson knew, go on, go on, well, Norah had concealed the previous attempts and a person could understand that, family pride, and now she is left alone in that great house.

But Norah had not stayed. Rogerson had surprised Marge by going to the wake; he had joined the little line going

up to Norah and the older brothers and sisters and when
he took Norah's hand and mumbled his condolences he
stared into her dry, watchful eyes and knew. The day
after the funeral she had phoned him to say she was
leaving town, perhaps for California, perhaps New York
eventually; she was going first to Chicago. Her statement
curled in his ear like a question and after a moment he
said he understood, that it sounded like a sensible idea
to him. The reply had released her and when she said
good-by it was good-by and if he had had any doubt
about the Rogerson Code at that point, all doubt and
hesitation would have been removed. Norah, with her mother's blood on her hands, would move on to the next rung
of freedom. Rogerson wanted to retch. He began to thirst
to be accused of wrongs he had not committed; he longed
for a Socratic, a Boethian fall, as well as the one he deserved.

There was a knock at his office door. A pause while
Rogerson glared at the offending panel. Another knock. A
minute went by and still no departing footsteps. A third
knock and Rogerson went swiftly across the room, pulled
the door open and there stood a startled Maureen Nugent,
girl of his dreams. Sweet Jesus, what is this? Come in,
my dear. Wooley couldn't possibly have talked to her yet.
Rogerson had himself been sifting ways of summoning her.
Coffee, Miss Nugent? Thank you, sir, but a tremble of her
lower lip. What are they trying to do to him?

"Is something the matter, Maureen?"

"I don't know." A hurt, moist-eyed stare. "I don't know.
I just had the strangest conversation with Paul Swenson,
the editor of the paper."

"That coffee is very hot. Be careful."

"He accused me of things."

"I leave it plugged in and it keeps reheating. I can't
stand that paper any more. It's become a continuous whine."

"It concerned you."

"Those of us who have been here any length of time are a special target."

"Oh, not you, Mr. Rogerson. They like you. I like you. But Paul accused me of writing a nasty letter and and and . . ." Honest-to-God tears, suffering Christ, he had to get her out of here. Shades of Regis. I'm being framed and I won't have that. The condemned gets his choice of weapons. Cunning, diabolically cunning, but it won't work.

"Pay no attention to it, Maureen. The whole place is unhinged."

"And now President Wooley wants to see me."

"Be careful there. I've never trusted that man."

Maureen shuddered, still crying. "He looks so soft and pasty."

"Bad type. It's common knowledge. Scandalous to have him here with young people."

"Mr. Rogerson, I'm worried sick."

Around the desk, hand under elbow, upsy-daisy, that's right. They are pear-shaped. Lovely, lovely. Rogerson is a sex maniac. Memories of his erotic dreams here in this office assailed him, dreams of just such a nubile girl pressing against him like this, his arm slipping around the small of her back to pat her nether curve, and, my God, Maureen, eyes brimming with, can that be, and her lips, moist, plush, I will, I must. And there contrary to every maxim of professorial prudence on the one hand and, on the other, not consciously implementing his carefully drawn code, stands Matthew Rogerson, M.A., feasting on the lips of a girl, a student, a mere child a quarter of a century his junior. Who quivers, who oddly seems to struggle, who breaks from his arms and, good God, her eyes are wide with fright, she is opening her just kissed mouth and she is screaming. What have I done? What crazy toll is being exacted for my months of feverish abstinence from Marge's grudging thighs? Maureen raced to the door, went still screaming into the hall and Regis, Regis, where did you go after you too stepped from your office looked at the retreating back of a wronged girl while the heads of colleagues came out of doors and swiveled from girl to you, from you to girl?

"Stop her!" Rogerson shouted, authority capturing his voice. "Stop that girl!"

But she was gone and Dowlet came down the hall to Rogerson smiling with grim knowledgeability. "That was the Nugent girl, wasn't it, Matt?"

"Is that her name? I have her in class. She burst into my office . . ."

"I know, Matt. I know. Go back inside. I'll explain to the others."

Dowlet went off, whispering discreetly, moving down the hall, eliciting understanding nods and Rogerson went once more into the sanctum of his office, poured coffee, sipped, sat at his desk and realized that he was perspiring freely, his knees shaking. And in his head all in capitals a surprising sentence formed. I DO NOT WANT TO LOSE MY JOB. Incredible thought, but that was a sobering episode, the imagined event become real, the future fiasco nudging its way into the honest-to-God here-and-now present. Rogerson, his head spinning, spun in his chair, seeking equilibrium by multiplying his levels of imbalance. I hate myself, my job, this life. And echo says: It is all I have; I am all I have and what am I apart from this?

A delicate thing, the human mind, and the female model surpasseth understanding, even presidential understanding. This from Wooley later, going on five, left profile over left shoulder as he busied himself at the bar sprung full blown from the wall at the twist of a key. Rogerson not bothering to nod, settled in the womblike warmth of official approbation and did not dislike it as he ought, responding nobly as he had to Grace's arched brows over upward-rolling eyes when he came in. Accepting the drink, he tried it; a castinet of cubes accompanied the placement of the glass on a table, men of the world they, bound by a droll episode.

"I asked her what she thought of you, Matt."

"What did she have against me?" Was Judas offered a drink? "Once I reminded a girl of her fiancé."

"The Nugent girl claims she thought very highly of you. Until today. You'll be happy to learn that today you attacked her in your office."

"A flattering charge."

Wooley's fat lips twisted in a smile, the slits of his eyes healed to a lashy atrophied blindness. "What did go on over there anyway?"

"How did she describe it?"

As it happened, as it happened, but of course they knew her feverish mind, the history of erratic behavior. What had prepared him so perfectly for this hypocrisy? The girl had sensibly agreed to withdraw from school, had seemed relieved to escape, in fact; the whole thing would be smoothed over. Just let her try to get a letter of recommendation though. Ho ho. Poor little Maureen. Perhaps he has done her a favor. What fate worse than this life?

Socrates quoted by the sophist Rogerson. Why are survivors so sure they should thank their rescuer when they know not what he has preserved them for, what more hideous hurt awaits them in a future so seemingly golden now? Something to think about there, Maureen. You may have the last laugh, shaking your pear-shaped breasts, tossing your thick brown hair.

"The Student Senate committee assured me you're a strong candidate for the best teacher award, Matt. That could be particularly opportune now. To balance things for you. And for Marge."

Yes, yes, it was true. This to Rogerson's moderate explosion of surprise. Wooley delighted by his remark that he wasn't sure he wouldn't prefer being known as the faculty lecher. Lecher in residence as opposed to visiting lecher. Ho ho. Funny things happen in the profession, Matt. Somehow Wooley himself had gotten on every pornographer's mailing list. Unbelievable what gets through the mails. His pink tongue licked the fat lavender lips. Wouldn't do for him to make a public complaint, of course, too easily misunderstood. He had taken the liberty of phoning Mrs. Rogerson, incidentally, to reassure her, news like this travels so fast, and in the light of her upset over those postcards, well, there's no harm in her knowing about the Student Senate possibility. The strong possibility. Oh the ending is Aristotelian, Rogerson thought, a veritable catharsis of the emotions. Pity and fear. Respectively for Maureen Nugent and himself.

Rogerson's apprehension for himself increased when, drink done, hand wrung, he was going across the campus; the walks, the trees, the dim ivied buildings were ominously unchanged. And menacing. A little self-pitying mockery would preserve his seat under the four-seasons mural but he would no longer be just one of the Old Bastards again. He was, as Felix had warned, on his way up. If he didn't watch out. Like the man who had crossed the Atlantic three times on the same girl, Maureen was the vehicle of his arrival. Success. Success. Rogerson housing unwanted his father's hopes, laughing nervously, quickened his pace, wanting to get off this goddam campus where for the first time in years he feared he truly belonged.

2

Sap receded, leaves fell, the globe tipped slightly and Rogerson, under the campus trees, scuttled along the walk to his office in the basement of the library. The Maureen Nugent fiasco had been a lapse, no more, the predictable wavering of the novice. Rogerson nodded, dragged on his cigarette, felt a zing in his blood that was wholly new. Say it in whispers, but there were days when he actually enjoyed teaching.

He went under the steps leading to the main entrance of the library, gripped the handle of the basement door with his free left hand, canted his weight onto his left foot and drew the plunger from its socket. Through the door he went to the faint hiss of the plunger pressing its caught air, easing the door back into its frame. He stopped. The hallway contracted by its bordering walls seemed bent on refuting the parallel postulate but was defeated by the wall at the far end of the corridor. Without that truncating wall would those planes meet in perspective somewhere this side of infinity? The linoleum floor was a pattern of squares, yellow and green, and Rogerson like a king in checkers took the green-squared route, a stagger of diagonal moves, to his office door. Going inside, he kicked ahead of him in the still unlighted room the mail that had been slipped under his door. The door clicked behind him. The blinds were drawn, the drapes pulled, but the October day asserted itself despite these impediments.

Rogerson snapped on the light, threw his books on the desk, hung up his coat, stooped to gather his mail and sat behind the desk. A postcard topped the pile. He turned it over. It acknowledged receipt of his manuscript; he would be informed of the decision of the readers as soon as it became available. Rogerson, pinching a corner of the card, flickered it toward the wastebasket as toward his magician's top hat. Woe unto those readers.

The rest of the mail followed the card into the wastebasket. Most of it was junk. Dear Educator . . . Flip, into the basket. Dear Subscriber . . . No more, no more. Away with you and your seductive four-color brochure reproducing the most famous Renaissance Madonnas and *au verso*, autographed photos of pitchers who had thrown no hitters in World Series played in odd-numbered years. I will not renew my servitude to your weekly newspicture magazine. Dear Professor. Dear Colleague. Publishers, associations, journals, deans . . . A mimeographed note from Laplace announcing a faculty meeting the following Friday. Into the basket with it, make no note of it. Ignore all meetings and committee assignments. Away with all communications from whatever sector of the academic monolith. The card on his door now read *Do Not Disturb* in lieu of *By Appointment Only*.

Rogerson lifted his coffeepot. Its heft indicated some of yesterday's brew remained; he plugged it in. A cigarette. Excess. Caffeine. Nicotine. Maureen. The girl still bothered him. He remembered last spring, during the Schmidt business, sitting with Maureen on the steps of the Administration Building. There was the more recent memory of his lips on hers. Insane. Incredible. That would be one way to go, surely, but too soon, far too soon. His had to be a many-faceted, glorious descent: Rogerson as Kamikaze flaming downward in the western sky. He would write a note to Maureen. Clearing a space on his desk, he took a piece of college stationery, consulted the student directory for her home address and began. Dear Maureen. He told her he was deeply sorry that anything he might have done, might not have done or said, had in any way contributed to the misunderstanding that resulted in her withdrawal from school. He assured her that if there was anything he could do in the future, a letter of recommendation, perhaps, she must not hesitate to ask yours sincerely, Matthew Rogerson. There. His crippled conscience was partly salved. The coffee hot now, he poured a cup and lifted it in long-distant toast to Maureen returned to the family home in Morton. Her father's home.

He thought of his own father and the few attempts the elder Rogerson had made at camaraderie before accepting their inability to be father and son according to the stereotype he cherished. Once they had gone ice fishing, taking over shacks already standing on the ice, no need to build one's own or have it built. Little Matt went into one, his father into another and it was an odd togetherness on the frozen lake. Confined by his own thin walls, Matt dropped his line through the hole, shivered, not wanting to be here, waiting for he knew not what to rescue him from the frigid duty of trying to coax through ice the trophies of summer. His feet, layered in socks, laced into boots, were numb with cold and when he stamped them on the ice there was a delay before the shock got to his swaddled feet. He was asleep when his father came for him, three fish dangling from a gloved hand, disappointment sullen in his eyes as he shook his son back to consciousness. They drove for miles in the car before the heater deserved its name; the windows had clouded with their breath, frosted, closing them in on their silence.

But back to work. Rogerson shook away the memory. There were articles to write. And the proposal to be prepared for submission to a foundation, a pointless research project in tandem with Reinhardt Schmidt. But first an article. "The Logic of the Comma in Ordinary Discourse." The spoken as opposed to the inscribed comma, the hiatus in ordered noise, silence as gesture, etc. etc. Involuted, interminable, dreary sentences relieved infrequently by the most desiccated imported British humor, the essay crept in dense dark paragraphs to a final noncommittal list of questions for others to answer. Perfect for *Mind*, not inappropriate for— well, for any number of journals.

Reading it over, Rogerson had the strange sense that it was not completely a parody, that it was really rather good. He shrugged away the feeling with a minor effort. He had to be careful his joke didn't end by being on himself. While the spirit was with him he went on to a penciled draft of the research proposal. Emily Pruitt had secured for him everything the library had on foundations; his requests for forms were in the mail. He scribbled away, laboring with urgency. In slightly more than a month the winner of the Student Senate's best teacher award would be announced and that was a disaster Rogerson had to avoid. Before that day arrived he wanted to be eligible only for a booby prize.

Dowlet sat in Rogerson's living room, the small of his back on the cushion of the couch, his crossed legs like a barricade before him. He tasted the cocktail Marge had brought him and complimented Rogerson's skill. Rogerson bowed and perversely poured a plain ginger ale for himself. Let Marge and Dowlet drink the martinis he had mixed, only a thimbleful of vermouth and an onion disturbing the purity of the gin. Marge had laid in a supply of booze unprecedented in the house except for out-and-out parties and their only guest was Dowlet.

"I didn't have a thing to offer him," Marge had said the week before when Rogerson came home from Wooley's office, the fate of Maureen Nugent settled. "Bottles I could find, but they were all empty. Why don't you throw them out, for heaven's sake? Finally I gave him a cup of warmed-over coffee."

And why not? But she had been grateful for Dowlet's reassuring visitation, crowning the president's call. Dowlet had come in his capacity of president of the college chapter of the AAUP. Student rights are indistinguishable from faculty rights in the final analysis, he had opined, doubtless running his assessing eyes over her body as he spoke, but the chapter would not sit still while a professor was being slandered. She had shown him the postcards she had received. ("*All* of them?" Rogerson asked and, "Yes," she had replied, with a blush.) Dowlet too had spoken with Wooley; they were all behind Matthew on this. Chances are they had the offender already and she would be expelled.

"A girl, Matt?" Marge had asked him, her eyes full of wonder. "I can't believe a girl would send cards like that."

"The flesh is no respecter of sex," he had said. "Did Dowlet try to goose you?"

Her answer had been a cold, lidded, contemptuous look, a fastidious glimpse of a sewer by a passing princess clothed all in white who had never had gas on her tummy let alone indulged in a bowel movement. But now, with the three of them sipping in the living room from which the children were absent ("Can't you take the TV up to Barbara's room, Matt? They'll be out of our way and happy"), Marge was moving from her acquired neuter back into her superseded feminine gender. Her lips were moist from her drink, her eyes sparkled, her laughter came to Rogerson like a ghost from earlier days. Marge's company manner made him see that she was attractive, even beautiful, and it amused him to think that Dowlet might actually envy him Marge. Hadn't he once called her the most beautiful faculty wife? Would he assume that Marge lay pliant and eager in her husband's arms at a snap of his fingers, that she radiated vitality and interest when he was her only audience and directed at him that throaty laugh he had not heard in years? Sipping his ginger ale, he half closed his eyes, recalling her laughing like that in the dark, the bedclothes tenting their conjugal play, when they had been lovers and friends as well. Marge's performance now bore no relation to the wife she had become, a truth that only he could know. And Marge herself, of course.

"Is that just ginger ale you're drinking, Matt?" Dowlet asked. Marge, when she turned to him, retained for a moment the bright smile of pleasure on her face; then their eyes met and hers clouded in apprehension that he was in fact not drinking.

"I've never been much of a drinker," he explained. "I can't handle it. Normally Marge admits liquor to the house only as a last resort."

"Matt, you're exaggerating." Marge laughed warningly. "But it's true that you tend to overdrink when you drink at all."

"Not at the Faculty Club," Dowlet said cheerily. "We seldom see you there, Matt. You're there less often than old Felix."

"My parole officer isn't as permissive as Harry's."

Marge took the ball and ran rapidly away from this risky line of talk, sitting forward in her chair and demanding of Dowlet when he was going to get married; it was scandalous to find him still running around free and untrammeled when there were so many lovely girls available. Dowlet, welcoming this turn in the conversation, laughed and confided that no girl could bear him once she got to know him, waited for and got Marge's dismissal of that nonsense, drifted on into a murky insincere eulogy of marriage and allowed that he was in quest of the girl, the right girl, for him, and just hadn't had the luck some others had had. A grin at Rogerson, who was in process of refilling Dowlet's glass; Marge twirled her empty glass by running its stem between her palms, did not quite blush and held out her glass almost defiantly when Rogerson asked if she'd like more. Their conversation swirled up behind him as he returned the pitcher to the cart; when he sat he looked across the room at them. He had never really noticed before, never before having chosen the role of onlooker, that even one drink causes a subtle change, an animation, chatter, a heightened bonhomie. Marge and Dowlet, more Marge than Dowlet, acknowledged his presence now with half turns of the head, their eyes for one another, their kidding conversation moving on from the subject of Dowlet's freedom to Maureen, the postcards, the painted legend on the walk in front of the Arts Building. Yes, paint, Dowlet assured her; a rust-red paint. "The color of our swing set," Rogerson intervened, unheeded, for Marge was saying that, my, girls have certainly changed, and Dowlet wondered if that was really true and Rogerson settled back as they tried to match their memories of the good old days. Their pasts did not make a set, of course, Dowlet was almost a decade younger than Marge. Marge offered for his consideration a portrait of the girl of yesteryear as scrubbed, clean of heart and body, for whom boys were a somewhat fearful mystery and Dowlet countered with a composite sketch of the girls of his youth. Rogerson watched his wife become a woman there in the living room, encouraged it by keeping her glass replenished, surprised that she had retained the ability after so many years of little or no practice. Was it because responding to Dowlet was safe, that sexuality was merely verbal and she wouldn't have to deliver on the faint promise her tone came to convey, to prove anything what-soever to him? Until she had finished her second drink, her eyes when she glanced at Rogerson held the look of a liar discovered.

When he had four drinks in Dowlet, Rogerson, perfectly sober, engaged his younger colleague in discussion, ques-tioning the goals of the AAUP, asking his opinion of various foundations, mentioning the joint proposal he and Schmidt were considering. It was amusing to receive in return Dow-let's slow-motion, slow-witted replies, his voice getting louder as his thoughts grew less coherent. The sober world seemed a strange one to Rogerson, almost an unfair ad-vantage, and he felt the attraction abstinence must hold for the self-righteous. He was relieved when Dowlet stood to go, uneasy when Marge asked him to stay for dinner, relieved again when Dowlet had the grace to refuse.

The domestic front provided the least demanding task, Rogerson came to think, calling only for an alteration in his own assessment of the situation rather than any change in the situation itself. Marge was clearly convinced he was a washout as a husband; the children were polite to him at best and, as a rule, ignored him as if they had been in long strategy sessions with their mother. Not that Roger-son believed they had; their behavior was spontaneous, he was sure. All that was required of him was acquiescence on his part to a home that fell short of whatever measure was applied to it. It was surely not the ebullient television family Marge and the children seemed never to tire of,

whatever its cast of actors, a family run like a scout troop
with many powwows, much consultation with the tribe and
general joy all around when the story's half hour faded
into a scarcely less insipid commercial. Nor were they the
kind of family Marge's faith demanded, though how that
failure could be laid at his door Rogerson was not sure.
What mattered, from his own point of view, was that it
fell short of any ideal that had been operative in his own
mind. His wife did not love him, she did not even like him;
he could have accepted her as a daytime enemy if she were
his nighttime lover, but since her indifference and hostility
had a round-the-clock consistency, since the children were
instinctively on the side of his enemy, their mother, he had
to concede that his home essentially excluded him. But so
what? Here was the application of the Rogerson Code. To
expect otherwise was visionary at best and, if amelioration
seemed possible, one had to push on to question the criteria
of betterment. What real difference did it make? How easy
to regard Marge and himself as a mistake, an aberration,
unlike the millions upon millions of husbands and wives
whose marriages were happy. That had to be ridiculous.
A bad marriage is the best there is. Success in marriage
consists in concealing from others how awful it really is. As
Marge, with Dowlet in the house, must play the role of
woman, become faintly coquettish, suggest that marriage,
being something she had found so ecstatically satisfying,
was a joy which Dowlet must cease denying himself. In
short, the criterion of a successful marriage is found outside
it, in the opinions of others. The trouble was not with Marge,
nor with himself; the fact was there was no trouble. Not
really. Trouble arose only when one compared the reality
of his marriage with the presumed judgment of others who
were not in possession of the facts; then one noticed the
discrepancy between reality and the fancy and cursed reality rather than the phony standard for assessing it. As for
the fulfilling acrobatics depicted so graphically in marriage
manuals, could anyone seriously believe that expertise and

variation led to happiness? It was a patent attempt to stave off the encroachment of a jaded appetite. Only imaginary sex can seem the answer to our heart's desire, Rogerson assured himself, writing it all down in examination booklets, sitting at his desk far into the night. The sex we know, being real, is judged to fall short of imagined bliss, but what is imagination's warrant for reducing humans to their genitalia?

Armed with such monkish thoughts, Rogerson considered the home front secure and permitted his mind to turn to the campaign abroad. In July and August the way had seemed clear, what he intended to do easy, a matter of a falling man's ceasing to clutch at air to arrest his drop and giving himself willingly to the descent. As autumn progressed he came to learn that it could be as difficult to repudiate the ideals of a lifetime as it had been to acquire them. To fail became no easy matter, a truth borne in on him first of all on the academic front.

Maureen Nugent, exiled to her home by Wooley's stupidity and Rogerson's weakness, became a sign of contradiction. Her supposed attack on Rogerson, the wild legend painted on the walk in front of the Arts Building, brought Rogerson a prominence he had not hitherto enjoyed. Even without taking roll, he could see in the following days that his class was in full attendance; the delinquents of before were curious to observe the object of such interesting vituperation. Rogerson lectured on the truth of the maxim that the end justifies the means, asked facetiously what moral law was threatened by the hydrogen bomb and noticed with dread the first advent of auditors. He turned to the morality of genocide but switched in mid-hour and with no fanfare to a wholesale castigation of today's college student and proved with six syllogisms that premarital sex is criminally absurd. He spent two class meetings reading the dullest sections from Bacon's *Novum Organum,* raising his face from the page only to point out that the passage being read had nothing to do with the course, and they kept coming. There were standees along the back of the room, drawn by a student reporter's lyrical account of the pedagogical miracle daily performed in the classroom of Professor Rogerson. He tried coming fifteen minutes late, five minutes after they were legally permitted to assume the class would not meet, but sentries had been posted, his circuitous, time-consuming approach from the library tracked, and they were all there waiting for him when he arrived. He spoke for twenty minutes on the atrocious prose in the student paper which compounded the crime of campus journalism. No person under thirty can be assumed to harbor a single interesting or informative thought, he

assured them, and there was a smattering of applause from
a back row. It came, he later learned, from bitter individuals
who had lost out in the elections for posts on the student
paper, but the applause caught on and he had to contend
with that now too. Like the third little pig, he arrived
early for the next meeting and was standing at his desk
lecturing to an empty room when the first students wandered in. Eyes half closed, speaking *recto tono*, he fili-
bustered almost inaudibly on what he could remember of
the news in the morning's paper, nor did he stop when the
bell rang, but droned on, past the second bell. He was ten
minutes into the following class hour when he stopped but
the room was still half full of students. He decided to skip
the next two meetings and did so; he would have skipped
a third but a group of students came to his office to see
what was the matter and they made so much noise in the
hallway it was like a demonstration. Rogerson did not answer their knock. He extinguished his light, made sure the
door was locked and sat at his desk in the dark filled with
the beginnings of dread. His phone would not stop ringing
and he refused to answer it. Later, when the students had
gone away, Laplace knocked on his door, calling in to him,
demanding that he open (his voice dropping) this goddam door. Rogerson opened it, having pulled the drape
cord and then the blind's and turned on the light. Laplace
was admitted to a sun-filled, brightly illumined room.

"For Christ's sake, Matt, you're turning into a recluse."
He sank into a chair, put Rogerson's phone briefly to his
ear and replaced it. "It works. Why the hell don't you
answer it?"

"Have you called?"

"You're kidding."

"Perhaps I was down the hall."

"If you were you have an historic case of diarrhea.
I've been ringing you for hours. Wooley has had his secretary calling you. I told him I'd come over here to see you."

"What's the problem?"

"No problem, Matt. We're moving your class to the auditorium. Unlimited auditing, no registering. What the hell
are you doing, unzipping in public?"

He told Laplace he lectured in the nude, zippers no
problem; he also told him where he could shove the auditorium. To no avail. It was Wooley's idea, not Laplace's.
Laplace himself thought it a screwball idea. What was the
point of credits and registration if they were going to let
teachers perform like wandering minstrels, that's what Laplace wanted to know. Rogerson agreed. Laplace said
Wooley was adamant. "This is tied up with the damned
Student Senate award, Matt. As far as he's concerned, you're
the man for it. This hullabaloo confirms his judgment." Laplace grimaced and looked curiously around the room;
when his eyes came back to Rogerson they contained a
look of agonizing reappraisal. The dean looked as if he
doubted that that many students could be wrong. Rogerson
got rid of him by agreeing to meet his class in the auditorium. With the door locked once more, the lights out, blind
and drapes pulled, he sat at his desk, hands flat on its surface, eyes closed, wholly unamused by this turn of events.
He felt like an atheist who had defied the Lord only to
have lightning strike inches from him. What he had dreamt
of for years, longed for, wanted, came unbidden now and
he hated to think of the effect of this on Marge, on his
colleagues. Irony. Irony. But irony is no answer to the
question life is. And what of his students? My God, he
couldn't go on filling their ears with tripe simply because
they seemed to thrive on it. The joke seemed less and less
something he was perpetrating on others.

He heard the mail slide under his door, turned on his
desk lamp and went for it. Shuffling through it, he separated a blue envelope from the rest and, when he saw the
postmark, opened it first. It was from Maureen Nugent.
He read it quickly and then went through it again slowly.
It was short, hardly more than a note, written in a firm
hand, the strokes perpendicular to the bottom of the page,

no slant at all. She was happy; she was glad she was no
longer in school; she did not think she wanted to continue
her college education. Her job as receptionist for a doctor
was not demanding, paid well enough and it gave her time
to read, even during the day. It was a joy to read for no
particular purpose. She had come to think that there was
some meaning in her being asked to leave, though she
wasn't sure what it might be, wasn't even sure she wanted
to brood about it. But she *was* happy and wasn't that what
he had wanted to know? Maureen Nugent.

The letter, which might have consoled him, served to
intensify his dread. He read it again after looking through
the rest of his mail, among which was the news that the
first article he had sent out was accepted for publication.
The serenity of Maureen's note was accusing. Why hadn't
she referred in some way to his kissing her, to her flight
down the hall from this office and his shouting that she be
stopped? Had he inadvertently conferred on her some
knowledge he did not himself possess, rendered her in some
way wise by his foolish effort to fondle her? He told himself
to forget it; he threw her letter into the wastebasket and
tried to gloat over the acceptance of his absurd article but
in a minute he retrieved the blue envelope, studied it for
clues, removed once more the thin sheet and pored over it
as if he had missed its message before. Dear Maureen, he
began his reply, dictating to the inverted coolie hat which
was the shade of the ceiling light, Dear Maureen, what
have you been reading or thinking that permits you to
forgive me without mention of my fault; where have you
learned this gentle graciousness . . . ? Why couldn't she
have cursed him, told him what he was, condemned his
lust? He ended by writing her a paternal note. He was
happy to hear that she had survived the misfortune of having her education interrupted, that she realized that most
of what she might have sought by coming to college could
be gained more expeditiously on her own. If she liked he
would be interested to hear what she was reading. In the

meantime, with every best wish, etc. etc. He read it over, lay his letter side by side with hers, blue by white, girl by man, victim by executioner, and wondered if she would discover beneath his bland phrases an inadequate apology.

She answered immediately. At the sight of the blue envelope among his mail, Rogerson plucked it from the pile, sat at his desk, poured coffee, lit a cigarette, studied the address, his name in her hand, the postmark, postponing opening it until he couldn't stand it any more. It was a longer letter, quite impersonal. She was reading Plato. Did he remember saying once in class that the real argument for the immortality of the soul in the *Phaedo* is not what Socrates says, but the way he behaves in the face of impending death? Rogerson winced. Had he put that out as his own idea? Thief, thief, the constant oral plagiarizing of teaching. But, my God, was that slight girl actually occupying herself with Plato? Years of experience had taught him to be skeptical of claims students made for their reading, the claims usually patent attempts to influence his marking, but Maureen had nothing to gain from him now. The remark she cited was one he must have made last spring and he was amazed that she should remember it now. In replying, he asked that she keep writing, keep him informed, and she did; her letters came twice a week, then every other day. They seemed filled with her memories of what he had said in class. Rogerson rocked in his chair as he read them, moaning, sighing aloud; he had never had a student like her before and he had not known it when he had her, had not recognized it. The pain he had felt remembering his stupid attempt to make love to her in his office was doubled now. It did no good to tell himself that she was well out of this. He wanted her here now.

Lecturing in the auditorium, looking out at his students, he asked himself if there was another Maureen among them, but he couldn't believe that there was. Yet it was to her he spoke now, everything directed to her and when he fled to

his office from the lecture, he would type up what he had
said in the form of a letter, wanting her to read it, would
await desperately for her reply to see how she reacted. The
students who crowded the auditorium did not notice the
changed quality of what he said. He had become a fad,
their presence was no tribute to him; it was a trick of
campus gossip. His one concession to his previous manner
was to speak almost inaudibly. One day he came to find a
microphone affixed to the lectern and, unable to find the
switch that turned it off, he tried to avoid speaking into it;
but the students, rather than settling back and napping,
strained forward. There was less noise in the auditorium
than he was used to in the smallest classroom.

One day, twenty minutes into his lecture, he stopped
and stood there, shoulders drooping, eyes downcast. "I
have nothing to say," he told them, speaking into the
microphone. There was utter silence. "You may leave. Go.
That is all for today." But they waited for him to leave.
He had to go out up the aisle and as he went through
the hushed place, his eyes on the pale green carpet, he had
to constrain himself; he wanted to stop and shout at them,
ask them to leave him alone, stop this nonsense, find some
other goddam fool to pester with their attention. For it was
a trick, he was certain of it now, though not perhaps
conscious on the part of the students. They, like himself,
were being employed in a grisly joke. It made no sense,
but he began to feel it was a joke Maureen was perpetrating,
some revenge she was wreaking on him for the way he had
treated her. Her letters informed him that she did not
really care for Kierkegaard nor for Camus; they struck her
as strained, overly dramatic. She was reading Blessed
Henry Suso now and had he ever, she found it fascinating,
extremely satisfying, though she didn't want to comment
on it, just tell him that that was what she was reading now.
Rogerson read the admission over. Of course. That explained it. She had to be a Catholic with that name. The
girl had got religion. He got up from his chair and paced

his office with a relieved smile on his face; he left and went down the hall to Schmidt. He could tell him now, show him the reply from the foundation that had come two days before. The research proposal had met with a favorable initial response at the first foundation to which they had sent it. Nominees would be informed much later, of course, but they had cleared a first hurdle. Rogerson could treat it as a joke now, could share the joke with Schmidt by treating it seriously.

Reinhardt was jubilant. He would clear the decks in preparation for their joint labors. He waved a pile of slips at Rogerson. "Books the library must order if we are to proceed, Matthew. Should I turn them in now?"

"Better wait, Reinhardt. Those would come out of our budget and there's many a slip twixt cup and lip, you know. What do you know about Suso?"

Schmidt with nettled brow. "The American musician?"

"No. No. Henry Suso."

Schmidt's eyes searched, found, glowed, his frown left him, the face of a student who has just remembered the answer. "But of course, the German mystic." He went on, telling Rogerson all he knew of Suso and when Rogerson went upstairs to consult the encyclopedia, he had to give Reinhardt high marks for accuracy. The Teutonic talent for amassing trivia had some redeeming features after all. But there was no Suso in the library. He mentioned this to Emily Pruitt.

"We could order it for you."

"That would take too long. I want to see it now." He explained to her the kind of book it was.

Emily worked her mouth, adjusting her denture. "Have you tried the Newman Club? They have a library there."

When he telephoned a girl answered, said she'd ask Father and dropped the phone with a clunk on some surface where it picked up the sounds of what must have been the recreation room. Conversations, noises, lacunae of silence, people going by the phone, their voices coming into range,

swelling, receding, being replaced by others while Rogerson, his phone to his ear, grew impatient. Someone picked
up the phone and asked if anyone was there.

"I'm waiting for the priest to come to the phone," Rogerson said evenly.

"I'll get him. Who's calling?"

"Matthew Rogerson." He had to repeat it. Once more
the phone was put down but almost immediately there was
a click and a boyish voice said, "Yes."

"I want to speak to the priest," Rogerson said.

"This is Martin Hoag. Just a moment." He shouted for
someone to hang up the extension in the other room and
then came back to Rogerson.

"This is Rogerson from the Humanities Department. Mrs.
Pruitt in the library suggested you might have a copy of
Henry Suso in your library there."

"Suso," the priest repeated. He might have been saying a
student's name.

"A fourteenth-century mystic," Rogerson said.

"I see." He didn't think they had it. He would check; he
would call back. At the least, he would get what information on it he could. Rogerson thanked him, detecting or
thinking he did a disguised jump in the priest's voice. An
inquiry for such a book from Matthew Rogerson? Aha. Or
has he ever heard of me? Rogerson wondered, after he had
hung up.

He drove to Morton one afternoon, drove along the street
lined with nightclubs, then sought out the address where
Maureen worked. It was an office building downtown, gran-
ite, tomblike, four stories high, and he could find no place
to park in front of it. He drove on until he found a place
and then walked back, entered the building. He found the
name of the doctor on the directory in the lobby. R. K.
McNaughton, M.D. An elevator opened, half a dozen people emerged and went across the lobby and Rogerson,
suddenly fearful that Maureen might come upon him there,
fled the building and went back to his car.

When he tried to write to Maureen about what he took
to be her religious interpretation of the surprising turn in
her life, he found he had nothing to say. Should he warn
against an invented consolation, the projection into an airy
elsewhere of some symbol of human kindness, a great transcendent breast on which we can nuzzle for our comfort?
He shared the time's suspicion that religion was an interim
solace, the refuge of the bewildered and weak, but the
critique had bite only if one had a reasonable replacement.
If this is the age of reason, welcome absurdity, Rogerson
thought, pulling a scarcely begun letter from his Underwood. Rejoice in clarity; substitute unambiguous signs for
the mythical symbols of transcendence. Bullshit. Seek mental health. But where, where? If there is only void beneath
our hopes, why go on? But we do go on.

Another tack. He would explain to her precisely what
had happened. Fine. Another sheet into the machine, ad-
justment of margin, the date affixed, new cigarette lit. A
meditative puff, cigarette balanced on the fat lip of his
Photostat ashtray, Rogerson smiled at the blank page, his
fingers arched over the keys. What had happened was
that, first, last spring Reinhardt Schmidt . . . He paused.
And what did that explain? Last spring Schmidt had
wanted a book Maureen happened to have taken from the
library, had sought it in the women's residence hall, had
been caught there in a compromising situation and and
and . . . Secondly, Rogerson said aloud, addressing the
dusty blinds at his window, secondly I used your name
in writing an insane letter to the editor of the student paper for reasons too complicated to go into. Then, Wooley
thought . . . He tore the page from the machine. The
facts were inseparable from some interpretation of them.
He did not know what neutrally had happened; the one
clear thing was that, as the unpredictable consequence of a
series of improbable events, Maureen had been booted out
of school. He didn't know the why of that in any way he
could convey to her any more than he knew why his most

earnest efforts to besmirch his own escutcheon had the exactly opposite effect he intended. He felt toyed with, a pawn in some game he did not comprehend. Better to address himself. What precisely did he mean by pawn? I don't know, he told himself. I don't know. But I am frightened by what is happening. I do not understand the play. What he finally wrote to Maureen was that from time to time he went to Morton and perhaps someday he could come to see her, at the office, any place she thought best.

"Call me Martin," Father Hoag said, grinning impishly but with sheepish overtones. "Everyone does." When Rogerson nodded the priest added, "Fran Heller has mentioned you."

"Fran Heller?" Rogerson said blankly.

"The students too, of course. You've never been here before, I think. Want to look around?"

"I'm afraid I haven't much time." He wanted to grab the Suso and run. Hoag had phoned him that morning to say he had found the book, had borrowed it from a fellow priest.

"I understand. My office is this way."

He pointed down the hall and waited for Rogerson to go ahead. As he did, passing a number of doors along the way, Rogerson remembered the rectory in Milwaukee where he had gone with Marge to make arrangements for their wedding. Unlike Hoag, that priest had worn a cassock and it had seemed odd to see the man, his broad American face and gray groomed hair atop the Roman collar, wearing the skirtlike garment with its line of buttons running from throat to shoe tops. Did Catholics realize how bizarre their priests seemed to others? Marge, he remembered, had been oddly subdued, answering the man as if she were once more a school girl, her tone piping and apologetic. Rogerson suffered through the little homily on marriage, its responsibilities, the Church's position on this and that, the whole talk circling, circling until it arrived at its point. Birth control. None of that, now, do you understand? The priest regarded them sternly, particularly Marge, and her eyes fell as if she had a diaphragm in her purse, as if condoms peeked from her fiancé's pockets. Rogerson was relieved to sign the agreement that the children would be

baptized and raised Catholics and get the hell out of there.
It had taken Marge an hour to become again the girl with
whom he'd fallen in love. But it was as though a pall had
fallen over them with that visit.

At the end of the hallway Rogerson entered Hoag's office,
a pleasant, well-lighted room with a wall of windows which
overlooked a courtyard surrounded by the U-shaped building. Opposite the windows were rows of bookshelves, more
shelves than were required by Hoag's library; there was a
small desk, several chairs and Hoag waved his guest to one.
He took another and settled back and Rogerson groaned
within. He guessed Hoag to be thirty; his doughlike face
seemed cheery despite the paleness, his yellow hair was
thinning but faintly curly. The smile seemed never to go
away, revealing little chipmunk teeth, reducing his eyes to
squeezed apertures from which his eyes glinted like the
lost marbles of youth.

"You didn't seem to remember Mrs. Heller," Hoag said.
"She met you once, I believe. The Hellers are in the same
parish as you."

Rogerson remembered her suddenly, the woman at that
Campfire ceremony, but first he had to set Hoag straight.
"My wife and children are Catholic. I'm not."

"You're not?" His smile grew warmer and he slid forward
to the edge of his chair; there was nothing predatory about
it. "So you're one of the separated brethren." More teeth
appeared, correcting slightly the chipmunk look.

"I suppose so."

"The phrase is in vogue since the Council, you know. I
imagine you're following the sessions in the papers?"

Rogerson nodded, sensing he was making a mistake, remembering Mrs. Heller more distinctly now. Hoag offered
him a cigarette, took one himself, lit them both with a
preparatory deference and when he settled back in his
chair said, "Frankly, I'm more at ease with Protestants
than I am with most Catholics. Just as, generally speaking,
I prefer the laity to the clergy." He waited for this revelation

of his hierarchy of values to draw a surprised and/or appreciative remark from Rogerson but Rogerson passed, nodding, drawing on his cigarette, looking along the shelves behind the priest to see if he might discover the Suso for which he'd come. Undaunted, Hoag went on. It seemed a set speech but its content clearly meant much to the priest. He began with a rather vicious remark on Maritain's version of Luther ("I'm Martin Luther Hoag, you know"), expanded that to a wholesale dismissal of Thomism, spoke of the Church's ghetto mentality and of the need to bring the Church into the world. Hoag's white wrists emerged from French cuffs, lay on his knees and his long hairless fingers dangled over his shins, splaying for emphasis, lifting to score points, seemed to be ticking off victory after victory until Rogerson had to wonder who this cheeky ass conceived his opponents to be. He's like a teacher, Rogerson thought sadly, so goddam used to a captive audience that it has probably never entered his head that I haven't the faintest interest in his grand designs. Bring the Church into the world.

"What do you mean?" Rogerson asked, if only to stop the flow. "Where is it now?"

"Good question," Hoag said with unwearying condescension. Well, he couldn't tell Rogerson where it was, exactly—only where it wasn't. It wasn't where the people are. It had cut itself off, by its ritual, by absurd doctrines ("Rulings, really." Hoag paused. He seemed to find the distinction important) having nothing to do with the way people live.

"Take birth control." Hoag consulted the window, a pained frown on his pasty face, and Rogerson smiled. At last. He felt on familiar ground now, this was what Hoag had been aiming at all along, like the priest in Milwaukee. They are still obsessed with sex. But Hoag was off and running, his flicking fingers dismissing the laughable distinction between mechanical and chemical devices, the traditional barnyard conception of the end of marriage. His eyes ecstatic slits now, he discoursed on love with the empathy of Havelock Ellis, who, according to his wife, had been unable to get it up between the sheets and so, presumably, had retreated to the safer ground of sexual theory. Thus Hoag, a eunuch for the kingdom of heaven's sake, an other-worldly Henry James, but with fewer inhibitions, essayed an inference or two about what married people really expect from the Church on matters of sex.

"Things are as they ought to be." Rogerson grinned with complicity as he said this, scooting forward to the edge of his chair. "The rule is to be found in the situation." He gulped for air, knowing the jargon, and said with an appropriate tremulo, "The *existential* situation."

Hoag might have been having an orgasm he was so delighted to find that Rogerson was indeed a kindred spirit.

"I don't know if you've heard of our lecture series," Hoag said when Rogerson looked at his watch and stood. "Wednesday evenings. It's been fairly successful."

Rogerson cautious now, moved toward the bookshelves. Would the man have to be reminded that he had come to pick up a book? "The reason I mention it . . ." The reason was he wondered if Professor Rogerson would be interested perhaps in developing his views on, say, the new morality. Rogerson, without turning, said he was flattered but couldn't commit himself just now, would think of it, perhaps they could discuss it later. He kept any coyness from his voice, not wanting to prolong it and, when he turned, said, "But you found a copy of Suso?"

"It turns out that it's two volumes. But I suppose you knew that."

"No, I didn't. I've never read him before."

Finally he had it, two volumes indeed, handsomely bound, a new translation, new edition, an abrasive sackcloth binding. Rogerson rubbed his hands appreciatively over the covers and thanked the priest.

"Keep them as long as you like. The fellow I got them from received them as a gift."

And hadn't read them, Rogerson observed, sitting in his car and leafing through the virgin pages. The type was a delight too; he found himself eager to read, as much to be able to refer to the work when he wrote Maureen as for what it might contain. A mystical union, he thought, smiling, as he started the car. Driving back through the campus, to his parking place behind the library, he hoped there would be a letter from Maureen waiting.

There was. Wednesday morning might be the best time, she wrote. She worked but the doctor made no appointments that day, simply made his hospital visits, so they could talk if he wanted to. In replying Rogerson wrote of his visit with Hoag, sticking to the facts since that seemed more damning than any lampoon. He could tolerate the thought of Maureen getting religion, but it would be something else again if she were taken in by a vacuous ass like Hoag. Religion is too important to be left in the hands of priests, he wrote, taking little joy in the echoing phrase. It sounded too much like something Hoag himself might want to say. As for the laity, he added, their incompetence in such matters is too obvious for comment. Where that left it, he didn't know. He told her he would come to see her the following Wednesday.

"This is the waiting room," Maureen said when they entered it. She closed the hall door with its pane of rippling, not quite opaque glass. McNaughton's name, backward, faintly visible, seemed more negative than before. Rogerson turned from the door, having watched it close, and surveyed the narrow room. The maroon carpet, the off-white walls on which hung Woolworth-caliber prints, the patient arms of the many chairs which faced at odd angles, made boredom and dread seem part of the furniture of the room. At one end was a windowlike aperture whose deep sill invited a weary forearm or casual elbow. "I sit back there," Maureen said.

"How do you get there?"

"This way. Come." She opened a door and they came into a narrow hall. He followed Maureen past a number of examination rooms, she opened another door and they could look through the receptionist's window into the waiting room. Below the window was a desk. "That's mine," Maureen said.

"What do you do here on Wednesdays?"

She pointed to another desk against the far wall on which a typewriter stood. "Bills."

Rogerson went to that desk, looked down at the machine, punched the tabular key and caused its carriage to shoot from right to left in an alarming lurching movement. He sat at the desk, pushed at the carriage, centering it, and wondered why he had come. Maureen sat at the desk beneath the window, turning the chair toward him. She wore street clothes, thank God. He had wondered if he would find her done up like a nurse. Loafers, brown skirt, olive-green coat sweater out of which a prim white collar showed. She looked younger than he remembered her and, thinking of their exchange of letters, he lit a cigarette, trying to look aloof and stern. She did not seem to be wary of him. That above all he had feared, that she might think he had come here with the crazy hope of going on with what he had attempted in his office on that dreadful day.

"It doesn't seem like the same place on Wednesdays. Usually, on the other days, we're very busy. If there's a lull you can hear them out there, snuffling, turning the pages of magazines. So many are deathly afraid. Some of them have reason to be." She said it sadly, as if she saw her role here as that of some latter-day Charon, waiting to take the terminal cases across the Styx, which in this context meant sending them in to McNaughton. He told her of taking Tommy to the hospital last spring, his tone savage; in the interim since that night his memories of it had become more vivid.

"If I were ever in an accident I wouldn't want to be taken to an emergency room. I would have thought that would reassure an injured person. At last, the hospital. That's when I would begin to worry."

Maureen had followed his story attentively but when he had finished she said, "I understand how you feel. But I understand that doctor and those nurses too."

"They didn't feel anything at all," Rogerson said.

"It's dangerous to become involved with people. Haven't you ever wanted to settle down inside yourself and be untouched by anyone, by anything, pain or joy, hope or disappointment? To be free?"

"That sounds like being dead." They were moving toward it, weren't they? What he had done, what he had meant to her. "Maureen, I could never say it in a letter. Maybe I can't say it now. That day in my office . . ." He had been studying the tiled floor of the receptionist's room, at once assuming an awkwardness he did not fully feel and wanting to avoid her eyes. When he did look up she gazed at him placidly, no hint of a smile, no hint of a frown, just gazed, her eyes *seeing* him, it seemed, and not much else. She did not give him the help he sought. "It was a stupid thing to do. I don't know why I did it. I'm sorry." He found he meant it more that he would have guessed.

"You startled me, of course. I couldn't believe it." Staring at him, she seemed to be having difficulty of remembering it. "It wasn't very smart to run into the hall screaming like that."

Her eyes continued to hold his, not with an accusation but with the shared knowledge that that had happened; when he permitted his to move away he looked out into the waiting room. "I've been reading Suso," he said.

"Have you?"

"Yes." He watched her push the sleeve of her sweater back and grip the exposed arm with her hand. Her wristwatch seemed to hang loosely. "It's a beautiful book." When she indicated agreement he said, "Where did you get it?"

"I saw it in a bookstore."

Rogerson smiled. At least no Hoag had figured in her finding it. "Have you finished it?"

"Oh, no. I read just a very little at a time. I really don't know what to make of it. Mostly it frightens me. He treats life as something—oh, I don't know, something like a game. No, that isn't it." She got up and walked to a corner where a file cabinet stood; she returned and leaned against her desk. "I guess it's just strange to have someone speak of living as something we should be good at it because everything is a test, every minute counts for something far more than it actually contains. I mean, what do I do all day? I sit here and I check people's names when they come in; I tell them when they should go into an examination room. I suppose what happens here is important, it's certainly important to those who are sick, but what I do really isn't important. Not the fact that I'm doing it. Anyone could do it." She smiled wryly. "I guess that's why I got the job. Anyway, when I read that book I think of what I do here, think of doing that well and what does that mean? What would I do differently? Can thinking of something in a different way make all that much difference?"

"I haven't read it yet. I just got it the other day. That is, I haven't read very much." After inspecting the book he had been unwilling to sit down with it. As he flicked through it, reading a line here, a paragraph there, the strangeness of the contents made him realize it was not just another book. He had been anesthetized to the philosophers: from the beginning of his studies their texts had been objects of analysis; the point finally was the argument and determining whether it was valid, whether it sustained its point. Suso, like Scripture, seemed simply to say, this is how it is; this is what you must do. Gingerly, Rogerson had put it aside, unsure whether he would want to approach it with casual skepticism or docile receptivity. Perhaps any book is what it is because of our antecedent attitude. Books are like mirrors, if a monkey looks in, no angel looks out. Kierkegaard, wasn't it? Kierkegaard. That's who Suso was like. He had been surprised when Maureen said she disliked Kierkegaard. Rogerson had once tried to read the *Edifying Discourses* and couldn't; it was the same with *The Works of Love*. They were closed books to him, unopened ones. Why? It is dangerous to get involved with books too, some books, those that like people go for the heart rather than the head.

Rogerson began to rummage through the drawers of the desk at which he sat, came upon some of McNaughton's stationery, took a sheet and ran it into the typewriter. Dear Professor Rogerson, he wrote. I must see you at once concerning the X rays we had taken a week ago. Without wishing to alarm you, I feel I should say that the possibility we discussed is not excluded. I have tried unsuccessfully to phone you, trying only your office as you asked. Hence this letter. Will you please call my office immediately? Sincerely yours. Rogerson consulted the letterhead and

typed McNaughton's name. "Do you have a pen?" he asked
Maureen.

"On the desk. Behind that box of envelopes. What are
you writing?"

"Just a memo." *Memento mori.* He pulled the pen from its
holder and inscribed McNaughton's name with a flourish.
Folding the paper, he said, "I suppose your parents were
disappointed that you left school."

"Yes. At first. It helps that I'm working, though; they
really couldn't afford to send me and I couldn't earn enough
during the summer to help much. Things are better this
way. I really don't mind. I'm not just saying that."

"It's not much of a school."

"That isn't it. I've lost interest, that's all."

"So have I."

"What do you mean?"

"It's a long story. I've become popular since you were
there."

"Students always liked you. Some students."

"This is something quite different. Maureen, it's like a
punishment."

"For what?"

He looked at her. She was so young, yet he felt comfortable with her. She was undemanding, uncomplicated;
if he didn't know her he would think she was stupid. He
had to tell someone. He stuffed the letter he had typed into
an inside pocket. "For you. For lots of things. Maureen,
things were bad for me last spring. That's not an excuse.
But they were bad. I've taught nearly twenty years." He lit
a cigarette. It should be clearer to him than this. "I wanted
so many things. I never got them, not really. I decided that
if I got nothing when I wanted something, then I would
want nothing. I did want it too. But now all the things
I thought I wanted threaten to come my way and . . ."
And what? She didn't understand. Why tell her that he
was afraid? It would make no more sense to her than it
did to him. What portent was there in the absurd fad

his teaching now enjoyed, in Marge's thawing, in everything that was so different now from what it had been just a season ago? Success, if you wanted to call it that, is surely no less absurd than his failure had been; it was a heightened failure, that was all. He had failed at failure too, so at least he was consistent. "It doesn't matter," he said abruptly.

"Mr. Rogerson?"

"Yes?" He was on his feet now and she got off her desk and they stood facing one another in the little room.

"Were you worried that you had ruined my life? You haven't, you see. I'm not bitter. I'm happy enough. Don't worry about me. If you have been."

He smiled at her. "Thank you, Maureen."

"I better get at those bills."

She went with him down the hallway and into the waiting room. When they said good-by he felt pardoned. He went past the elevator and down the stairway that went in right-angled turns round and round the elevator shaft and brought him into the lobby. Driving back, he tried to explain to himself what he had been unable to tell Maureen. On either side of the road the fields were bare now, awaiting winter, and at irregular intervals, far back from the road, he would see a farmhouse surrounded by a protective copse of trees.

3

He was informed by Wooley on the telephone and when he had hung up, Rogerson took the cigarette that had smoldered in his tray during the brief conversation, got another drag out of it and crushed it out. *Sic transit ignominia mundi.* He had been voted the award by the Student Senate. Wooley had relayed the news in fulsome tones as if he himself were somehow vindicated by the vote. "This makes up for a lot of things, Matt. You know what I mean." Rogerson said that he knew what Wooley meant. It seemed unsportsmanlike to sound as melancholy as he did. You can't win them all. The truth was that he was no more surprised than Wooley. Absurdity seemed to have an inexorable logic. This had been coming like the punch line of a bad joke for so long and so obviously that the event had insufficient socko to inspire any thoughts he had not entertained far too often already. So he sat there waiting the arrival of the Senate committee Wooley had told him was on its way.

Their spokesman was named Litzner. When Rogerson yelled "Come in," Litzner led the trio into the office with a momentum that should have carried him to the window, but he drew to a stop before the desk and the other two, Pebblocz and Flaherty, bumped against the elbows he angled back to brake them. Litzner, a tall bony type, horse face, nose slightly askew as if aiming at the part in his hair, brown as an August fairway, had in his eye the glint of self-assurance that convinced Rogerson he was one of those who would repeat in all seriousness that Salesmen had built this country.

"We bring you good news, sir," Litzner said, smiling away

the suggestion that they sit. There was only the one chair available.

"The Administration Building is on fire."

A dutiful laugh. "I was warned you might say something like that."

"By whom? President Wooley?"

"My fellow senators, sir. We're a delegation sent to inform you . . ."

Rogerson recognized the look in Litzner's eye: a parent's watching a child unwrap a Christmas gift. "I really don't know what to say," he said when Litzner had finished. "How would I go about declining it?"

"Declining!" But Pebblocz laughed a smirking laugh and Litzner, remembering, looked less startled. "I'm afraid you can't do that, sir."

"Very well. Now I appoint you my delegation to the Student Senate." They were to tell their peers that while he found it insufferable to be assessed, let alone rewarded, by young whelps like themselves, he supposed that what they had in mind was the situation at the University of Bologna in the thirteenth century where students had hired the faculty and dismissed them at will. Perhaps this was a step in the right direction, it wasn't for Rogerson to say. At any rate, they could go back and tell the others they had found the Messiah. Standing, Rogerson bowed and, addressing them as Caspar, Melchisedec, and Whatchamacallit, bade them good-by.

Before they could close the door Dowlet stuck his head in. "Congratulations, Matt. C'mon, we want to treat you at the club." Others joined him in the doorway and Rogerson, determined to be a good loser, went with them.

Bracketed at the bar by colleagues, the young, the Old Bastards, Rogerson watched Harry draw the beer he'd asked for. The glass foamed, Harry watched it into submission and, with a flourish, placed it on the bar before Rogerson. He was ready for other orders now and, as he filled them, as on both sides of him it was agreed that

Rogerson was the best choice for the award, it occurred to Rogerson how remarkable it was that Harry had survived so long at the club. Trussed up in his starched white jacket, the happy obsequious menial, Harry was probably robbing them blind. And bringing women to his room. Rogerson lifted his glass in a toast to Harry, catching the steward's eye and winking. Harry winked back. Thick as thieves.

"I'm really glad you got it, Matt," Felix said to him later. They had moved into the hallway, to get away from the press at the bar. "You're doing the Old Bastards a lot of good. I hope you know that."

"Isn't this the sort of thing we're against, Felix?"

Felix lay a finger alongside his nose. "In the lounge, maybe. In the lounge. Let's not kid ourselves, Matt. If we were starting out now, we'd be right in there with Dowlet and the others."

"My God, Felix, what a horrible thought."

"Ah, but it's true, Matt. But I should be telling you? You are adapting. You'll survive. I admire you for it. The place is changing, sure it is. But everything changes. So change with it. It's the only way."

"Felix, you're depressing me. Let's have another drink."

But Felix had to run. When Rogerson got back to the bar it was no longer crowded. Dowlet shook his hand, congratulating him once more, then he too was on his way. Harry kept a small clock behind the bar, shoved discreetly back among the bottles, and Rogerson saw that it was after five. He should go too. Home. To Marge, to the children, to supper and then to his study . . . No. Besides, he no longer dreaded being late. He had been leaning against the bar and now he stood straight. "Another?" Harry asked, taking it for a signal. The man was like an auctioneer. But Rogerson nodded. He reflected that Marge no longer nagged him as she had; some remote semblance of peace had descended on their marriage, doubtless a fringe benefit of his crazy popularity on campus. For she had heard of it; she had mentioned it. Dowlet kept her informed too, he supposed. Dowlet had agreed to stop by one afternoon to meet the daughter of a friend of a friend from Milwaukee who, for reasons never clear to Rogerson, was working in town. Rogerson had stayed away from the house that afternoon, had come home to a slightly tipsy and irate Marge. As he was raising his mental defenses he found that he was not the target of her wrath. "The young snip never showed up. Didn't call or anything."

"Maybe she forgot."

"Forgot!"

"People do. I forget things all the time."

She gave him a brief glance, comment enough on his audacity at assuming he was a paradigm of intelligible behavior. "She couldn't have. I told her about Peter, what he's like. I thought she was dying to meet him, of course. Well, that's the last time I try to do anything for her."

She had seen Dowlet at the Faculty Wives Study Club too, where he had held forth on Willa Cather for an afternoon. He must have been impressive. Marge waded through the whole Cather canon and the green volumes of the standard edition formed little piles around the living room. Sometimes in the evening she would come into the study to read, the television in the living room regarding her with a sullen gray eye.

Harry placed the beer before him and wiped the bar around it, picking up the glass, putting it down again, casting the rag under the bar. There. "What's the celebration, Professor? You get promoted or something?"

"Pulitzer Prize, Harry. Or its local equivalent. How have you been?"

"Can't complain, Professor. Can't complain."

"I trust no one else has surprised you during an afternoon of dalliance." Rogerson lifted his eyes to the ceiling, dropped them and smiled meaningfully at Harry. The steward glanced down the bar where several instructors were treating one another to reports of what they had said in class that day. "I really appreciate your not saying anything about that, Professor Rogerson. I thought I'd really got my ass in a sling that day. Wow. You scared the hell out of me, I guess you know that."

"How about the young lady?"

Harry leaned forward, putting his elbows on the bar. "I'm lucky she didn't go out the window. She nearly flipped when I opened that door."

"A shy virgin, was she?"

Harry grinned. "Shy she was, but that's all." He retrieved the rag from under the bar and made a few *pro forma* swipes with it. Bending toward Rogerson, he whispered, "You wouldn't believe me if I told you who she was. Or did you recognize her?"

"No. No, I didn't. Was it someone I might know?"

"You would have known her all right."

"My wife!" Rogerson cried. "That was no lady, that was my wife."

But Harry was not to be put off; he seemed suddenly eager to confide. "The dean's secretary. That's who it was."

"Norah Vlach?"

Harry nodded. "That was the first time, I'm sorry to say. And, of course, the last. She wouldn't even talk to me on the phone after that day."

"How did you meet her?"

"In the Administration Building. I go over there to pick up my check, you know. Ran into her one day, said hello and right off I knew. She was eager. And I was right." Harry drew back, one eye pressed closed, nodding his bald head. Rogerson drained his glass and put Harry off with a sour smile and a philosophical shake of his head.

Walking to his car, he thought of Norah, who that same afternoon had helped him from Laplace's office, got his car, taken him home. He remembered standing with her in the hallway of her home. Had her attention been an effort to discover if he had recognized her? No, that couldn't be it. Not entirely. After all, she had copied his poems. But, my God, no wonder she had been so panicky when they had hidden in Harry's room the day of the election. That made twice that her effort to make love had come to disaster in that room. "I've never been in here before," she had said when they entered the Faculty Club. He could see her strolling through the rooms, her purse, held behind her, bouncing off her bottom. Returning to the scene of the crime. She must have a thing for older men, Rogerson thought, not liking the notion that he and Harry fell into the same category.

The air was scented with the smell of burning leaves; the waning light, the wisps of fragrant smoke, made the campus seem a magic place and, walking through it, thinking of Norah, Rogerson was glad for the first time that nothing had really happened between them. It might so easily have happened. Last spring he had been horny as an adolescent. Last spring. He wasn't now. Was he being deserted by that urgency at last? It had been months since he had slept with Marge. He tried to remember the last time, ticked off the months. Late October now, my God, it had been over five months and he had had to remind himself of it. In its way it was a relief. He couldn't remember if he had had an erection lately and, ludicrous as it seemed, he found himself trying to remember when he last had. He couldn't remember. Had he become seasonal? Must he wait for spring and the rising of the sap? The rising of the sap, Rogerson with an erection. Grinning, he quickened his pace. After he started his car he turned on the lights. Dark was falling.

"You'd better shave and change your shirt," Marge said. She had met him at the door; she was all dressed up. "I'm going to pick up Mrs. Snow."

"Mrs. Snow? What is it, Marge? Have I forgotten something?"

She smiled. Marge smiled. At him. She leaned toward him and lay her cheek on his. "The award, silly. We have to celebrate. Dinner out." She stepped back. "All right?"

"Fine. Fine." She went out. He heard the car start again, turned and went into the hall. From the living room the kids called hello. He looked in at them. They were in pajamas, looked freshly bathed. They were watching television. Rogerson went upstairs and, in the bathroom, lathered his face and found his thoughts confused. Norah, Marge, Harry, that goddam award. Of course that would please Marge. It didn't matter. Downstairs the doorbell rang and Rogerson stepped from the bathroom to see if the kids had heard it. Barbara's voice drifted up to him. "Hello, Mr. Dowlet. Daddy's upstairs. Mom went to get the baby-sitter. Want to watch TV with us?"

Dowlet? For Christ's sake, was he expected? Dowlet, of course, represented for Marge the vanguard of the new order on campus and this award might seem to put them in the same class. Had she asked him to celebrate with them? What a rare trio they would make, a never-never *ménage à trois*, for the love of God. But if Dowlet had been invited, why hadn't he mentioned it at the club? Rogerson brought the razor through the Santa Claus mask of lather, pulling his cheek down.

"Matt?"

"Come on up. I'm shaving."

Dowlet in the doorway of the bathroom, his manner almost awkward. "Marge called when I got home. I'm afraid it was too short notice to get a date. But I didn't want to miss the celebration. She's really proud of you, Matt."

"If students knew what power they possess."

"It isn't just the students. Grace tells me Wooley is happy as hell about it. To hear her tell it, you'd think he instructed the kids how to vote."

Rogerson brought a washcloth to his face, leaned toward the mirror and examined his eyes, widening them. Bloodshot. The poor light in his office, in his study, or just the beer? Dowlet remained in the doorway, one shoulder leaning against the frame. "Are you pissed off about something, Matt?"

"Why do you ask?"

Dowlet examined his thumbnail, buttoned his suit jacket, raised his eyes to Rogerson. "You acted strangely at the club."

"I've wondered why Harry is still working over there."

"Harry? Why not?"

"Isn't he robbing us?"

Dowlet seemed to find this an extraordinary suggestion. "Are you kidding? If he did something like that he'd be back in prison. Harry's no fool, Matt."

He dried his face and went by Dowlet into the bedroom. Rogerson slipped a shirt from its plastic envelope, discarded the pasteboard priesty insert from under the collar and began to unbutton it. The shirt on, slipping a tie under the collar, he looked into the mirror and said, "Why did you become a teacher?"

"It's better than working." Dowlet laughed. "Unquote. You see, your classroom remarks make the rounds."

"That's my reason. What's yours?"

"You're not serious."

Marge's voice became audible downstairs, the door slammed and Dowlet left him. Had he been serious? That

kind of fundamental Why had to be taken as a jest, didn't
it? To step back from one's predicament to ask how he had
gotten into it, what it is all about—what was the point of
that? No, Dowlet could be right. Rogerson could not claim
that he had gained anything by digging away at the foundations of his life. Except the Student Senate award, of
course, and that was a question, not an answer.

So he went down the stairs to Marge, who was radiant
and beautiful, again a stranger, and to Dowlet, the young
buck. They drove to the restaurant where Rogerson felt
like an aged chaperon. He insisted that they have another
and then another drink before ordering and met no resist-
ance; he liked the firm feel of the chair against his back as
he looked up to see the Johnsonian slogans lettered on the
beams above them. Marriage has its pains but celibacy
has no pleasures. Perhaps. Perhaps. Sailing through life,
the stern lexicographer, boyishly delighted by the title of
Doctor, an ass like the rest of us, finally, Sam. By what
right do you assume a vantage point above us, beaming
from that beam, commenting on the fray? You're down
here with us, you old bastard, one of the Old Bastards
really, wanting what you snidely dismiss. They ordered,
finally, why not, and Dowlet insisted they have wine, his
treat, and the warmth increased until, with brandy, Rogerson began to believe he was actually elated by the prod
he had received from fortune's dubious digit. Celibacy has
no pleasures, he quoted to Dowlet, and received the first
half as reply. Dowlet apologized to Marge, present company excepted of course. Look at him, Rogerson thought,
five minutes older than thirty and what does he see when
he looks at Marge, what does he see when he looks at
me? Thank God for this disguise of skin; the pain of marriage comes down to the fact that the layers of deception
are peeled away, one by one, and one is known even as
he is unknown to himself, and isn't it mercy we need rather
than justice? Dowlet was anecdotal as hell now, in class
today, blah blah, and Rogerson turned them off, delivered

himself over to the multiple caresses of the drinks he had
had, hating the thought of having to get up from this
table, drive home, dropping Dowlet—no, his car was at the
house—and returning Mrs. Snow. Perhaps he could prevail
on Dowlet. Which is what he did when the journey through
a forest of headlights was done, the three of them ass to
ass on the front seat of the godforsaken Plymouth, asked
Dowlet if he would mind dropping the baby-sitter and
what could he be but delighted to hand the ebony Mrs.
Snow into his Chevy convertible and whisk down the driveway and into the night with her.

"Well, that was fun," Marge sighed, stretched, her breasts
swelling in her dress, looking at him with bright tired eyes.
"He's fun, isn't he?"

"Boswell thought so."

"Boswell?"

"He pitches for the Twins."

He went into his study and she followed him. He turned
on his desk lamp and looked over the chaos as if he were
seeking something. Marge yawned. "I *am* exhausted," she
announced. "In a lovely way."

Without looking up, he said, "Do you want me to come
up?"

She yawned again. "I don't care."

What did he expect, the dance of the seven veils? But
it stung him to be suffered rather than wanted. He brought
his heels together, became aware of his soft genitals, and
the incipient anger left him. He didn't really want her.
Realizing that, he wanted to want her, but she had started
from the room. "I think I may work for a while," he called
after her. "Okay?"

"I'm going to sleep."

"That's all right."

"Good night."

Good night, good night. The greeting addressed to his
wife and children, to his dusty father, that reasonable
facsimile in the urn before him, yes, and to his mother too,

wishing to the living the little death of sleep and to the
dead the peace of their permanent one. The little death?
Not sleep but sex, and his desire was certainly dormant
now; he could not pretend that he was sitting here out of
pique at Marge's inadequate eagerness. Almost, he had
been reluctant to put himself to the test. Better to say no
here, in the safety of his study, than to fail to conclude
what had been started. Aphrodisiacs? Not even the faint
jealousy he felt of Dowlet, the young man able to recall
youth to Marge, not even that was sufficient stimulus. To
think of sex as solace was easy enough, but Rogerson's
marriage had been lived under the sign of his wife's religion, the act was teleological, its purpose procreation
however infrequently that might be achieved. Great oaks
from little acorns, however many acorns are doomed to
rot upon the lawn. Was that it? Did sex so seen require
faith in the point of going on? A stage of life, try that as
explanation. Whereas when younger, prodded by hope, the
line of life possessed a destination and meaning, now it
seemed merely a suite of events bearing at best an indirect
relation to what he had set out to do. Success or failure,
both seemed functions of luck rather than choice, even if
luck required the fact of choice to work its arbitrary will.
Had he been blind before or was he blind now? How odd
if the meaning of life could be grasped only at certain
times of life; if it had meaning it should be accessible
always. His package of cigarettes came toward him on the
desk as he tried to pull a cigarette from it; freed finally
and in his mouth, Rogerson struck a match, watched the
blue center of the flame, its yellow edge, inhaled and
with expelled smoke snuffed out the fire. Where does fire
go when it goes out? Barbara had asked once where pounds
go when we lose them and Rogerson, standing on the
bathroom scales, laughed, but when his daughter left, wondered who the joke was on. *Ex ore infantium.* Where is the
abode of the dead? Do they lodge only in the memories
of those they leave behind? A faint immortality that, a

persistence doomed with the memories of those who grant
it, once removed when they who remembered are only remembered. His children, what he had written on the slips
of paper stashed in his study, boxed in the attic, jammed
in his office at school, all that seemed equally a protest
against his ultimate going. Matthew Rogerson, unlisted poet,
the lost works thereof.

A week later, a little week or ere those shoes were scuffed with which she had accompanied Rogerson and Dowlet on a festive evening, Marge was strangely insistent one morning when she sat in the study where Rogerson, sipping a third cup of coffee, was trying not to think of the Thursday run of classes he faced. "Fine," he said, and centered the cup in the saucer where tan rings told of a series of such returns. "I feel fine. Considering that it is nine in the morning, that this is Thursday and I have three classes and a slight headache."

"Were you drinking last night?" But there was no nagging edge in her voice; it was a simple inquiry, if anything indulgent.

"I had a drink, yes. I don't have a hangover, if that's what you mean."

He realized that she was crying. She sat upright in the chair, staring at him, her mouth distorted, tears running down her cheeks. At his startled look she sprang to her feet and came next to his chair, stooping to put her arms about him. He felt her wet cheek against his, the odd intensity of her clinging to him. When he tried to turn his face, thinking she wanted his kiss, she pressed her cheek harder against his, preventing the move. He sat there with Marge clinging to him until she stood and wiped her eyes and smiled. Bravely. He did not ask her what was wrong. But something was wrong, something was very wrong. This was an entirely different Marge and he could think of nothing as preparation for this epiphany of her as weeping, possessive wife who stood now looking at him with tenderness, with contrition, with some nameless fear swimming in her eyes. He was glad to go to school.

Until he ran into Dowlet. Dowlet hailed him as he was disappearing through the door under the library steps. Rogerson turned and came out again into the bright autumn sunlight that failed to warm, saw his younger colleague approach as a silhouette limned by a corona of light. Dowlet took his arm, of course, but the familiar gesture seemed less condescending today and Rogerson did not shake off Dowlet's hand.

"How are you, Matt?" Dowlet said the question, not as a substitute for hello, but attending to its meaning.

"Do I look ill?"

Dowlet studied him, his hand actually turning Rogerson so he could get a better look. "You look fine."

"You sound surprised."

"Here, let me get that." They had gone beneath the steps and Dowlet lunged for the door, stepping aside with some ceremony to let Rogerson pass. Inside, he skipped to catch up and when Dowlet stopped at his own office Rogerson felt his eyes following him. At his own door he put the key in the lock, turned it and went inside. Before closing the door he looked out. Dowlet was still standing in the hall, and when their eyes met he looked away as though embarrassed. Shrugging, Rogerson slammed his door, flicked on lights, unnecessarily—he had left the blinds open and sun lay across the room in pale bars.

A half an hour later, on his way to class, Rogerson had just closed his office door when he heard his phone begin to ring. He stood in the hallway, hesitating, then went off to class. Having taught his class, having had lunch, he returned to his office and, as he unlocked the door, became aware of his phone ringing. With the door opened, he went across the darkened room, groped for and found the phone.

"Professor Rogerson?"

"Yes. Maureen?"

"Mr. Rogerson, your wife phoned here yesterday afternoon. She asked all kinds of odd questions. Do you know anything about it?"

He told her to hold on. He closed the door, turned on the light, returned to the phone and asked Maureen to say it again. It had been Wednesday, Maureen was in the office alone, Marge had called and demanded to speak with Dr. McNaughton. The doctor was not in, of course, and he was unavailable. Then Marge had asked Maureen if her husband had ever been there. She was not satisfied when Maureen told her that she was not able to give out that kind of information. Maureen, flustered by her insistence, had ended by telling Marge that Mr. Rogerson had indeed been to the office.

"Everytime the phone has rung today, I've jumped nearly out of my skin. What is going on, Mr. Rogerson?"

He didn't know. He calmed Maureen, told her not to worry about it, but if Mrs. Rogerson called again she was to let him know immediately. Afterward he sat there wondering what the hell Marge was up to. McNaughton was no one she should know and, even if she did, there was no way she could have learned that he had been there to see Maureen. Jealousy? Rogerson tried the possibility but it made no sense, not after Marge's behavior that morning. Should he call her? What prevented his doing that, phoning and asking her why she had called a doctor in Morton, was the memory of her tear-filled eyes when she came across the study to him that morning. She was terribly upset about something and it seemed to connect with this crazy phone call to McNaughton's office. No, he had to go home and face her when he asked. This entailed skipping at least one class, but that could scarcely faze the announced recipient of the Student Senate's faculty award.

"What are you doing home?" But Marge's surprise quickly gave way to something else. "Don't you feel well?"

"I feel wonderful," Rogerson roared. "Why are you so goddam solicitous of my health all of a sudden?"

"I'm not, Matt. I'm not. Don't you have class this afternoon? It's Thursday."

"I'm surprised you know my schedule." And he was. He

went into the kitchen and she followed him. The coffeepot stood on the stove but when he picked it up it was empty.

"Do you want me to make some?"

He shook his head. "Why did you call Dr. McNaughton's office, Marge?"

Her eyes, when he turned to her, were rounded in horror. "How did you know?"

"Why did you call?"

Her eyes moved around the room as if the answer were lurking there. She drew a deep breath and her mouth trembled. She sat at the kitchen table, handling the empty wooden fruit bowl as if she were inspecting it for flaws. "Matt, why didn't you tell me?" She began to cry, great heaving sobs, gripping the wooden bowl with both her hands, her eyes pressed shut.

For Christ's sake, it's about Maureen. She must think . . . God, God. "Tell you what?"

"Oh, please! You know why I called that doctor."

"Marge," he said, his legs weak. "I haven't the faintest idea."

She looked up with tearful, angry eyes. "Stop it! Just stop it! I found his letter!"

His letter? Rogerson stared at his wife and then he remembered the letter he had typed in McNaughton's office. For the love of God, was that it? He smiled but Marge's look when he did so chilled him into sobriety.

"I was sending things out to be cleaned. What did he say when you went back?"

"When I went back?"

"Why couldn't you have spoken to me about it? This is such a dreadful way to learn."

"Marge, forget about that letter."

"Forget about it?"

"That's right. Forget about it."

Marge's eyes were disturbed fleetingly by hope. "Did he say you're all right? When you went back?" Even as she

asked she seemed to be telling herself that her hope was
foolish.

"Marge, I wrote that letter."

"*You* wrote it." She studied him, hope trying again to
take possession of her, but then once more it was gone.
Some of the familiar contempt came back into her manner.
"Matt, please don't joke about it. Please."

"I mean it."

She made an exasperated noise, she got up from the
table and left the room. He followed her, wanting to expand
on his admission and then stopped short. He would have
to explain how he got hold of the stationery and that could
become complicated. Marge had turned to hear him, incredulous, still angry, but trying, it seemed, to be patient
with him and when the explanation did not come she
looked at him, shaking her head, anger, concern, pity and
dread making a curious mix in her still-wet eyes. She thinks
I am going to die, Rogerson thought; she has already cast
herself in the role of the distraught widow. His role, the
one that had briefly teased his imagination that afternoon
in McNaughton's office, was that of the dying man. Standing in the hallway, facing Marge, he felt himself assume the
role, inhabit it, acquiesce in her misunderstanding. He
wanted to experience the proximity of his own death, not
only in his imagination, but in Marge's belief as well, an
outside observer to grant it inner conviction. Something in
his manner must have signaled to her; she looked at him,
knowing the worst, and then she ran to him, took him in
her arms and shook with inconsolable sobs. Rogerson, his
arms pinned to his sides, managed to raise a hand with
which he stroked her back as he murmured into her ear,
There, there. I am a dying man, he thought. The doctor
has given me the dread news, my wife knows and here we
stand on the brink of the grave, my grave, bidding one
another a surprisingly fond adieu. When they stepped back
from one another he said he wanted to be alone. She
nodded, watched him to the door of his study and then

he could hear her in the kitchen. When she brought in the
coffee he sat at the desk, smoking a cigarette; he smiled
his thanks and saw that she found his nonchalance ghoulish.
She seemed to hurry as she left the room.

The coffee was sweetly hot on his tongue, the weight of
the cup exerted its slight downward influence on his hand,
down, down, *in pulverem reverteris,* a hoax like the urn of
cigarette ashes, his father, oh fabulous artificer. Rogerson's
smile became macabre. All men are mortal. His eyes lifted
to the smiling Rembrandt woman, his collaborator in this
as in all else; she understood. Caught in what time-defying
medium, her cap and brow and eyes and pudgy nose above
her smile escape the munch of time, forever he pursues
and she pursued, ode on a question earned: What has
really changed? I shall die. Quit smoking and be eternal.
Rogerson is mortal. The tautology was dread news to Marge
but the wrist's inner watch pulsed as before, unwinding one
only mainspring to the moment where the hands are destined to stop. I am a dying man, Rogerson mused, the
gray accumulation, his father's lieutenant, saluted with a
dash of added ash. This lie was the simple truth, a truth
to set him free from the cooky cutters of failure and success.
Yes, yes. He sipped more coffee, crushed his cigarette.
Where does light go when it goes out? I am a dying man
and this no act.

Dowlet. Marge must have told him, for the love of God,
of course. All right. The secret out. Poor Rogerson. Have
you heard? Terrible, terrible. As if he nursed some malady
the rest had not contracted, a dusty intruder, casting a
shadow over the unalleviated sun of their interminable day.
Jolly Rogerson, a bony skeletal grin aloft, a threat to every
living treasure on the high seas of hope, his handshake a
grappling hook, then over the side, your money and your
life, destructive moth, erosive rust, the thief of your to-
morrows grins skinless on the claimed deck. For flesh must
go and the marrow in drying bones take on a porous
desiccation, flaky and yellow, dead. *Memento mori* indeed.

Another cigarette, more coffee; less hot now, a khaki taste, the drift of bluish smoke, going, evanescent, lifted in a line whose moments hold for memory until memory too rises in the wisp of time, then silence, rest. Why not? Jolly Rogerson. Yes. The role was written for him and in him; the play's the thing and his caught conscience gave assent.

Two days later, before a bulletin board on the main floor of the Arts Building, Rogerson studied the pinned notices of dances and meetings, the announcements from a hundred graduate schools as promissory as enlistment posters, and fittingly so, when the rasping breath beside him took on olfactory identity and Rogerson helloed Schmidt without turning. "I am thinking of continuing my studies, Reinhardt."

"Where?" Schmidt shuffled the violet, the yellow, the red sheets pinned one over another on the board.

"Munich wants me, but I'm turning them down. My obligation is here, Reinhardt. Our research project. You understand."

"We must get started." Schmidt's voice was hollow, edged with a vague preoccupation. Face to face now, Schmidt looked sheepishly away. He had heard. Good. Trust Dowlet.

"Oh, there's plenty of time, Reinhardt. No hurry."

No hurry, Schmidt repeated uncomfortably, darting a glance at Rogerson, seeking what? Some infallible index that the rumor is true? Rogerson moved slowly down the hall, not quite a limp, inching toward the stairway; Schmidt fell in beside him, Schmidt offered to take the main burden off his hands, get started on the project; perhaps Rogerson was busy now but he, Reinhardt, had cleared the decks as he had said he would, could give it his undivided attention. The bastard only wants to inherit, Rogerson thought.

"Do you really think we have the facilities?"

Schmidt was sure they did. What they didn't have, they could get with the grant money, could they not? Wasn't that the idea?

"It bothers me that we may have misrepresented ourselves."

In what way? One of course spoke only of the bright side of things in an application. That is understood.

"The library is a disaster, Schmidt, as you have often pointed out."

A corrigible situation, Schmidt opined. Is something wrong? For Rogerson had slowed his already slow pace, brought a probing hand to his chest, now smiled through a grimace of pretended pain. Schmidt's eyes were bright with fear.

"Couldn't I have a copy of the application, Matthew? If you should lose it . . ."

Or it me. Unnecessary, Reinhardt. It's perfectly safe. Leaving a crestfallen Schmidt, Rogerson started up the stairs.

Now Rogerson *moribundus* moved across an altering scenery, his role identified. His relations with others shifted. Schmidt was first and predictable, then the others and Rogerson watched his skull-like presence work its tricks. The auditorium, some days later, was not noticeably less full as it subsequently became, but when he walked down the aisle to mount the steps to the stage he was conscious of the silence in his wake and, at the podium, turning, he felt the eyes graze him morbidly. Lofting at the creamy ceiling a parody of a lecture, bright thoughts on Kierkegaard's aesthetic sphere, opining that love is not love which alters when it altarward inclines, he felt his hold on his audience loosen, the hold he had not sought, but feeling it go, he reached for puns to detain them and knew he could not, knew already that in the days to follow, having seen him in this new light, he an impermanent arrangement of dust motelike in it, they would want a less metaphysical sun in which to bask. Within two weeks there was no more need of the auditorium and he told Laplace he was moving his class back to the Arts Building. My auditors who take it in the ear have left me.

Laplace with a hand on Rogerson's arm guided him past the new secretary, who would have been safe in the Navy, and into his office. "How do you feel, Matt?" The question was sober and intimate; Laplace's averted eyes squinted with embarrassed pain.

"Wonderful."

"Cigarette?"

"No thanks." Rogerson sat and watched Laplace fuss over the lighting of his cigarette, dip toward the match cupped in his hand, draw the smoke into himself. "As a matter of fact, I quit."

Laplace looked at him in surprise and then, as if understanding, shook his head. "It's a stupid goddam habit." He ground out the cigarette and expelled smoke as if he were throwing up, his mouth popped open like a caught fish's. He turned in his chair, elbows on his desk, looking at Rogerson. "Is that what it was, the smoking?"

"That and breathing, Herb. It's a tossup between the two."

Herb smiled as if he had just heard a humorous remembrance at a wake. "God, it makes a man think, Matt. What the hell's the point of anything anyway?" Laplace's hands went out and he stared at Rogerson as if expecting an answer to his improbable question.

"Of quitting smoking? I think it makes me feel better, I guess. No major reason really." He smiled sweetly. "It's a little late for good reasons."

Laplace went back to grinding his extinguished cigarette in the tray; it might have been a snake he was unsure of. "You want to move out of the auditorium?"

"There's not much point in meeting there now."

"Kids," Laplace said, looking tragic.

"I seem to make them uncomfortable now."

"What do they know, Matt? They don't understand."

"I don't understand it myself, Herb."

"I know. It doesn't make any sense. It just doesn't make any sense."

"Well, we have to carry on. That is, you do."

"You're right," Laplace said tonelessly. He looked as if he were going to cry.

Rogerson did stop smoking. To his own surprise. Thinking of himself as a dying man made it remarkably easy; he imagined the countless cigarettes that had brought him to his present imagined plight and it was like taking revenge on them not to have another. His head was light at first and at night, when he sat in his study, he was overcome by weariness and found himself going upstairs to bed hours before his usual time.

"Matt?" Marge said one night, speaking to him out of the dark. As usual he had not turned on the light in their room when he came up, not wishing to disturb her. Rogerson sitting on a chair, removing his shoes, peered into the dark and asked her what she wanted. "Matt, aren't there any treatments? Isn't there something they can do?"

"Don't worry about it, Marge."

He heard her stifle an angry noise. "I called that doctor again today. He has to talk to me. He's gone to Bermuda. Can you imagine! Or did you already know?"

"I don't care where he goes."

"Isn't he doing anything for you? That doesn't make sense. Matt, I want you to see another doctor. One in town."

"That wouldn't help." He added, "I've quit smoking."

"What difference does that make?"

"My appetite has increased, for one thing." It had. In midafternoon now he was in the habit of going to the cafeteria for a hamburger and a glass of milk. His coffeepot had been deposed from its customary place on his desk. Coffee no longer appealed to him now that he had quit smoking. He could sit for hours in his office now, doing nothing, his mind a blank, rocking slowly in his chair, letting his eyes travel slowly along the edges of the ceiling, counting the acoustical tiles. He thought when he thought at all of Henry Suso, thought of conquering his appetites, suppressing his desires, gaining control over his body in order to release his soul. He had never been able to stop smoking before; he had tried many times. Now by luck or accident he had managed to stop and it didn't seem an accomplishment. Next the incessant drinking of coffee was stopped and that too had seemed small, not really a sacrifice. He would stop going for that afternoon snack; he could sit, wracked by hunger, his arms folded as he rocked in his chair. That would be something. In the darkened bedroom Rogerson promised himself to get out of the habit of that afternoon hamburger. "I'll have to watch the eating, though, Marge."

On the bed Marge was crying. Why does she weep? Does she imagine now that she has always loved me, that ours was an idyllic marriage, that she is about to lose something she cannot live without? "What's the matter, Marge?"

"Oh, Matt, stop it. Please."

"I'm sorry, Marge." He stood. He could make out the bed now, the lump she made under the covers. He *was* sorry. He had caused her much grief for many years. It had been reciprocal, true. Still. "Would you rather I slept downstairs?"

"Downstairs?"

"On the couch. Say, isn't that canvas cot still in the garage?"

"Matt, are you crazy?"

Crazy or not, he was gripped by the idea. He would put the cot in his study and sleep there; it would be like a cell. "I'm going out to get it."

"Matt, come to bed. You can't be serious."

He stopped by the bed. "It will be easier for you," he said. "Later."

With that ominous addendum, he left her, creeping through the darkened house. On his way to the garage, barefoot, shirtless, in trousers only, he heard a dog baying several streets away. There was no moon and it was very dark but he felt his way to the garage and fumbled for fifteen minutes before he found the cot. It felt dusty but he didn't mind. Carrying it back to the house, he saw that the light was on in their bedroom. Marge stood in the window looking down at him but she was in shadows and he couldn't see the expression on her face.

He set the cot up in his study, moving his easy chair to make room for it. He had turned on the desk lamp and was sitting on the edge of the cot when Marge turned on the hall light; she came in carrying a blanket and sheets and his pillow from their bed. "Let me make that up," she said calmly. Obviously she had decided to accept his behavior as perfectly understandable.

"I'll do it, Marge. Just put that stuff down. Here." He stood and took the burden from her. "You'd better get some sleep."

She looked at him; she had stepped back when he took the bedclothes from her but now she stepped toward him. She seemed to want to say more, do more, and didn't know how. "That cot is filthy, Matt."

"It doesn't matter."

"There's no point in putting clean bedclothes on *that*. I'll wash it up."

"I'll do it."

She stood in the doorway and looked pleadingly at him. "Matt, come upstairs. This is silly."

He took her arm and led her gently into the hall. "I'll clean it up," he promised. He went on into the kitchen to get a cloth. While he rummaged through drawers he could feel her presence in the hallway, not wanting to leave him. This first night will be difficult, he told himself. After this she will accept it. When he went back to his study Marge had gone upstairs.

Brother Rogerson sat monkish on the cot over which he had thrown the blanket, sat in his underwear, his pants draped over the easy chair, wishing he wanted a cigarette so that he could feel the point of not smoking. But his desire had died, for smoking, for coffee, for liquor. For sex too, it occurred to him; his imagination no longer carried him on flights of carnal conquest. This was where the battle has always been, he thought, staring at the gray rectangle of the window. The microcosm. To hell with success and failure in the macrocosm. Retreat within thyself. Augustine. Failure and success took on a different meaning here, safe from chance, the uncontrollable event. Rogerson master of his soul and leaving the captaincy of fate to other forces. He sat there waiting, listening to the silence within; the dim light of the window was hypnotic, it might have been a mirror of his essence, his soul, a screen across which nothing passed. The dark night of the soul, the dim light of a nocturnal window this moonless night. That dog still moaned in the distance, a mindless protest against the absence of day. In the morning he would have to look into Suso again; read it this time. Maureen. Is this where her peace came from? In the world but not of it. My God, I am becoming religious. An odd religiosity. It had nothing to do with asses like Martin Luther Hoag. Or did it? Could that babbling dunce know something, carry disguised a knowledge Rogerson needed? Unlikely, extremely unlikely.

Monk. Monad. Alone. The best way, after all. Lying back on his cot now in the quiet house. Ataraxy. Away with desire, away with dependence on the outer, the other, the conferred or happenstance. Mind as master. Rogerson, smiling, suddenly wanted a cigarette, wanted to write in the tracery of expelled smoke the beauty of that thought, the simplicity of the ideal. He rolled on his side, one arm hanging over the side of the cot, feeling along the floor for the pillow he had dropped there. He jammed it between his shoulder and head, facing away from the window toward the wall, enjoying the repressed desire for a cigarette. The demand of the body vetoed by his stern mind. No. Never again. The bleak vista of years without pleasure pleased him. Years. But he was a dying man. No smile now; the

role possessed him. How long did he have? Breathing
deeply, conscious of the lack of rasping in his chest now,
he became aware of the press of flesh on ribs, knew the
fragility of his hold on life. At his age the heart could get
him. A seizure. A minute of silent throes and then slipping
into the dark. Rogerson frightened. I could die. His father
saying once, when they were returning from a wake he
had found emotional and maudlin, If I ever die . . . And
stopping. His mother repeating If and laughing but Matthew in the back seat had been momentarily gripped by the
certitude that they would die. He knew *they* must die;
how odd that the realization had escaped them. Death had
not.

He tried to remember his father at his own age, forty-
four, and couldn't. The sound of his heart beating came
to him muffled; he lay there with his ear pressed into the
pillow and the rhythm of his heart seemed syncopated,
grew louder. He felt his dependence on that mindless pump-
ing in his chest and his self seemed curled like a foetus
about that squeeze and pulse and flush, the round-and-
round of blood. The sound seemed deafening and he
couldn't bear it, couldn't begin to think of sleep. He sat
on the edge of the cot, his forehead moist; the window
seemed brighter now and he could make out the lattice of
panes behind the shade. He breathed deeply, relieved that
he could no longer hear his heart beating. He wanted a cigarette. Just one. What the hell. No. Never. Goddam it,
never could start again tomorrow. How long had it been,
a week, didn't that prove it had lost its hold on him? He
got up, turned on the desk lamp, pulled open a drawer
and shuffled through the mess within. Nothing. In the
kitchen, the light on, he went through all the drawers.

"Matt? Is that you?"

"Where the hell are some cigarettes?"

There was a moment of silence. When she spoke again,
in a carrying whisper, it was from the landing. "I thought
you quit."

"Are there any cigarettes?"

"No."

For Christ's sake, Marge smoked. There had to be cigarettes. "Don't you have any?"

"I stopped when I noticed you had. I thought it would make it easier for you."

He turned out the kitchen light with an angry swipe of his hand, his nails scraping against the wall, sending a chill through him. "All right!" he shouted.

"You could look through your clothes. Maybe there's a pack you forgot."

"It doesn't matter." When he realized he had quit, he had gone through coats and sweaters and drawers, getting rid of all half-empty packs he found.

Back on the cot, the light out again, he dreaded lying down, could not bear the thought of listening to the constant throb of his life. I am going to die. I don't know when. But I shall die. He was suddenly sure of that fact, felt it, was frightened by it. His fear seemed a punishment for the hoax he had perpetrated. Have you heard about Rogerson? His body no longer seemed an enemy to conquer; he was one with its surface, wholly within it, indistinguishable from its fate and that would be settled by factors he could not control. He wanted to go upstairs, to slip in beside Marge, not to touch her. How she would shudder now if he laid a hand on her. Good God how ghoulish. She could see him lifeless in a coffin and would surely cry out if like Jerome he betrayed a deathbed futile rise of lickerish desire. No, not to touch her, just to feel her living warmth beside him. But he remained in his study, sat for an hour on the edge of the cot and, when he lay down, lay on his back, his heartbeat out of hearing, and sometime he must have fallen asleep though he dreamed he lay awake and in the morning when he opened his eyes to see Barbara looking curiously in at him he could have cried with delight that it was morning, that the sun shone at the window.

"Professor Schmidt said you would know about these."
Emily Pruitt fanned a pile of requisition slips and studied
them as if they were a losing hand. Rogerson, who had
wondered if she had heard the rumor, had been avoiding
the main floor of the library lest she descend upon him
with proprietary concern.

"What are they?"

Emily handed the slips over the high table between them,
over the drawer from the card catalog through which
Rogerson had been desultorily fingering, the cards repre-
senting mountains of unread matter, the pull of the future
as if he bore an obligation to peruse it all. Books spilled
incessantly from the presses, efforts to keep mortality at
bay, mimicking the pointless flood of humans, each gen-
eration pushed onward by the growing masses behind.
Schmidt's order slips were part of the insane effort. Rogerson looked at them, at Schmidt's odd curlicued Continental
hand, nodding soberly, posing, but Emily's eyes were not
on him.

"How have you been?" he asked her.

"Can't complain . . ." A catch, a caesura, not going on to
return the question. She knew. Her old eyes would not
meet his, would not look to see what might be there.
Rogerson was disappointed. Was she jealous? Did she feel
he had elbowed ahead and got position on her?

"What's the problem with these, Emily?"

"They won't fit into your departmental budget."

"File them. I think Schmidt expects to come into a fund."

She took the slips, held them in both hands, brought
them down with a slap on the tabletop. Revealing her

denture in a smile, she let her eyes settle on his forehead. "Haven't seen much of you lately."

"No." Rogerson picked up the drawer of cards. Emily made as if to go and he wanted to detain her. "Don't believe everything you hear, Emily."

"Oh, I never do," she said gaily and then looked him in the eyes. "What do you hear from Norah?"

"Norah?" The question rattled him. "Why do you ask?"

"Just wondered. Her mother and I were good friends, you know. A dear woman. I miss her very much."

Rogerson looked solemn, felt Emily's eyes studying him and wanted to get away from the crone. For the love of God, had Norah's mother mentioned his being in the house that night? Emily's denture, more exposed now, fitted in with the fluorescent lights, the pastel décor of the room, the hush and whisper and endless passing to and fro. "If you hear from her, give her my love." And, hugging the little bundle of slips, Emily went off, one shoulder hunched almost to her ear, her high hips, thin legs and sensible shoes giving her walk a faintly acrobatic air. Rogerson's mouth was salty with the need of a cigarette and he slipped the drawer into its waiting cavity, feeling it catch the runners and ride of its own accord within until its knobby front was flush with the others. His gait as he left was measured but swift. He had gone back to cigarettes. What did a negation prove against the insistent affirmations of everything else? And he wanted a drink. His arm lifted, a shake of wrist and emergence of watch. Two-thirty.

"Where you off to, Matt?" Dowlet. His younger colleague, in coat and rubbers, briefcase in hand, looked surprised to see Rogerson coatless on the outside steps.

"Just getting a breath of air."

Dowlet came up the steps to him. "You'll catch cold."

Rogerson smiled, striving for the enigmatic look of the past two weeks. He drew forth his cigarettes and extracted one.

"I thought you'd quit smoking, Matt."

"Who told you that?" Rogerson lit the cigarette, inhaled, felt once more the disappointment smoking had become since his week of abstinence. Dowlet shifted his briefcase and looked out over the campus as if he had not heard the question. That news like the other had traveled. No doubt Laplace had told him.

"Well," Dowlet said. "I must get busy."

A drink, Rogerson thought, a talk with Harry. If smoking, then drinking too. Why not? He still slept on the cot in his study though it was no longer an element in a monkish picture of his life. He simply preferred it now. At his desk, he wrote into the night, addressing an endless letter to himself, trying desperately now to find the form of these past months; it had to be there. The rise and fall of his fortunes, this latest misunderstanding that had turned him into a ghost at this meager academic banquet, a grim reminder to everyone but, it would appear, Emily Pruitt. His classes were back to normal, the lectures no longer deliberately dull, just predictably so, his students disinterested at best, their faces registering only modifications of a constant boredom. The December convocation was two weeks off and Wooley had already offered him a way out of that fiasco.

"A private presentation could be arranged, Matt." Wooley moved the fingertips of one hand along the inner fingers of the other and wet his lower lip until it gleamed. "If you would find that more, say, comfortable. But whichever you wish, of course."

It assumed the air of a talk with the warden before the long walk to the chair. Wooley had assured him he needn't decide now and Rogerson said nothing, sat there as if distracted by deeper thoughts. He had found that he was now permitted any eccentricity. He gazed woefully at the painting behind Wooley and asked quietly what, in Wooley's opinion, that goddam mess was all about. Wooley spun in his chair, as if glad to get off the subject. "It was a gift, you know."

"That tit I can make out but the rest, well, I don't know."

Wooley giggled at the word and Rogerson wondered if the president was still hearing from dirty-film purveyors. "I find it gives me a disarming advantage over visitors, having that peeking over my ear."

"See nipples and die," Rogerson said.

"That's Venice."

"De Milo? Well, I'll think about it. The only difficulty is that I've already begun collecting my thoughts for the occasion. My reception speech."

Wooley looked alarmed. "There's no need to give a speech."

"Nonsense. I couldn't let my fans down."

"What kind of talk did you have in mind?"

Rogerson up now, on his way to the door, lifted his shoulders. "Oh, you know. The usual sort of thing."

Now he was sure Wooley would push for a private presentation. Did he care? Did it matter? Rogerson was unsure that anything mattered as he went back to the library for his coat. In his office he called Harry to make sure he was there, told him he was thinking of coming over. Harry thought that was fine. By God, if it was going to be a wake, let it be an Irish wake.

"Have you seen her?" Harry pushed a glass toward Rogerson. The steward had met him at the door and admitted him as if the club were a speakeasy. He locked it when Rogerson was inside, helped him from his coat, shook his head when Rogerson mentioned beer and made him a stiff bourbon. He made one for himself as well. "We can chalk it up to seepage," he said when Rogerson brought out his wallet. Now Rogerson lifted his glass, answering Harry's toast. If the steward had heard the sad news about Professor Rogerson he was handling himself with remarkable indifference. Rogerson felt slightly peeved as he tasted his drink.

"Seen who?" he asked, fitting his glass into the wet circle
it had made on the bar.

"Norah Vlach." Harry's thin lips assumed a cute bowed
smile, his eyes squinted with shared knowledge. Rogerson
saw the flesh sagging from Harry's jawline, the spray of
hair emerging like antennae from his ear.

"Have you?"

"Not to talk to. But she's around. I thought I recognized
her on the campus and I asked the dean."

He meant Laplace. He nodded when Rogerson asked,
impatiently, as if it was an interruption, and it was; Rogerson wanted to hold him off, ask if he meant the girl who
had worked for Laplace, the girl whose mother had died,
now that was a strange case, wasn't it, overdose of pills
or something, God, there ought to be a law, and on and on,
to keep away from the girl Harry had had upstairs and
who had fled down the stairs and outside on another afternoon like this when Rogerson had come early, before the
crowd, in need of companionship and getting far more
than he had bargained for. Harry was a describer. He
wanted Rogerson to have the details; *hungry* was his sum-
marizing word, the pin with which he stuck Norah to
the wall behind the bar above the bottles with their different odd-shaped inserts, bulbous spouts, a valved ounce,
another drink, more vulvar explicitness from Harry and
Rogerson unable to stop his ear or Harry's mouth, listened
with a receptive smile while waves of nausea rippled over
him, the chill of shame and accusation and embarrassment,
for Norah, for himself, not for Harry. The steward still
could not believe his good fortune with Norah; she had
been no bauble on a many-beaded string; his normal fare
was the glossy airbrushed unreal mammalian of the girlie
magazines, not a hungry girl of thirty with the bewildering
network of underclothing and flushed wanting desperate
face, her eyes squeezed shut most of the time, opening
briefly and in horror to survey the everyman she was with
and then digging her fingers into his shoulders (she was

taller than Harry) and pulling him into her arms. Harry's
eyes grew soft at the recollection, a return to the maternal
breast after half a century's absence. Almost, he seemed
to regret telling Rogerson about it.

You never know, Harry opined, scooping the world into
the haven of the remark. A sweet sad smile on his face,
he turned and let his eyes lift and go to the window and
beyond where the trees stood leafless and inflexible against
the wind whose presence was made known by a newspaper
page full-bellied, dragging a corner, moving comically
across the street until it pasted itself flat against the window of a parked car. Custard pie. Pratfalls. Poor Harry,
Rogerson thought. Poor Norah.

"She looks like a million bucks." Erect now, occupying
this moment, Harry spoke matter-of-factly. "Hair different.
Different glasses too."

Rogerson bobbed his head, tipped his glass and looked
into the monocle of its thick distorting base. "You recognized her right off?"

"Are you kidding?"

"But you asked Laplace."

"What I really wanted to know was is she back to stay."

"Is she?"

"Looks like it. She's getting her old job back. I hear
things, you know. I know the dean hasn't been happy
with his new secretary."

Rogerson had not been in the habit of going to Laplace's
office lately but now not going there became deliberate
avoidance. No doubt he would see Norah sooner or later,
but he wanted to put it off. Sitting in his office or in
his study at home, at the desk or on the cot, with the
light out, he would imagine their first encounter. What she
would say, how she would act, how she would look. Had
she heard the rumor that he was ill? If she had, why didn't
she seek him out? But what would she say if she did? As
it happened, she phoned.

"Professor Rogerson?"

"Yes."

"This is Dean Laplace's office."

"That you, Norah?"

A moment during which she might have been hunting a reply, perhaps a rehearsed one, then she said yes. Just yes.

"Welcome back."

"To the scene of the crime?" Her voice was toneless.

Rogerson stared at the mouthpiece of his phone, his fingers slipped nervously along the phone's curled cord. What crime did she mean? "Disaster would be more like it. The place hasn't changed."

"Did you say Laplace?"

"You tell me."

"Your fortunes seem on the rise."

"The flight of the skeet."

"Herb has to know if you want the award presented privately or publicly."

"Have you guessed his preference?"

"Private."

"Why?"

In the pause she breathed through her nose; Rogerson closed his eyes, the sound of her breathing affecting him as his heartbeat had the first night he slept on his cot. Did she know? Had she heard?

"Why do you think, Matt?"

"I'm a dying man?"

"Aren't we all?"

His eyes popped open, a smile wreathed his face. Bless her, God bless dear undeceived Norah. "You're wonderful, Norah, do you know that?"

She laughed almost gaily. "It was just a guess. But I have an unfair advantage."

"Yes." Whatever that meant. "Tell him I want it in public."

"You're the doctor."

"In more ways than one."

"You have to tell me about it, Matt." Pause. Cooler now. "If you want to."

He said he would. Why not? At last a confidante. He had thought of telling Maureen when he called to verify Marge's statement that McNaughton was in Bermuda. He had been sure this was a lie Maureen had come up with to put Marge off, but it hadn't been, McNaughton was gone. "Will she call back when he returns?" Maureen had wanted to know.

"Don't worry about it."

"But I do. I wouldn't want her to think anything wrong."

"She won't."

"I'm not going to write you any more."

"I understand."

Farewell, farewell. It had been difficult to say. He needed someone to talk to. All he had had was Harry and that was a matter of listening rather than talking. Norah's return made him feel less isolated; he could share the madness with her, have someone to laugh with, plot with. Before he hung up he had arranged to meet her in the cafeteria.

The children, what about the children? Marge with broken voice questioned one night, sitting in his study. She looked at the cot, then looked away. The small room was crowded enough without that; with it, the easy chair was jammed into a corner, snug in its right angle. "How can I prepare them?"

"That I'm a dying man?"

Her jaw dropped, her eyes pleaded with him to employ some soft obliquity, a euphemism. But she nodded with dry desolate eyes.

"Marge, about that letter. I meant it when I said I wrote it. You inferred . . ."

She closed her eyes and shook her head violently from side to side. "Matt, please."

"No, Marge. You please. I wrote that letter myself. That is the truth. Now for God's sake, stop practicing to be a widow."

"But how could you?"

"The stationery? A former student of mine works in that doctor's office. I visited her . . ."

"Her?"

"She had written me. Maureen Nugent. The girl who was expelled."

"You drove to Morton to see her?"

"Yes. To *see* her. While we were talking I typed that letter."

"But why?"

"I had forgotten all about it until you found it."

"You mean it was a *joke?*"

"I didn't expect you to find it."

She watched him warily, looking for some sign that he

was lying now. If he had convinced her, all hell would break loose and he wanted it to. He was tired of the role. But Marge sighed. "Thank God," she said. "Thank God."

"I expected an angrier reaction."

"Oh, Matt, Matt." She came to him now, crying convulsively, and he stood, he did not want to be slobbered over, but she pressed tightly against him, her body a stranger's at first and then eliciting long-ago memories. Marge. For God's sake, listen to her cry. Rogerson was moved. He had never expected this, never.

When she had gained control of herself she made coffee, taking his hand and leading him into the kitchen to keep her company while she fussed at the sink. They drank it sitting at the kitchen table, side by side on a bench, not even a corner of the table separating them. "Why did you let me believe that, Matt? Why? And everyone else? Don't you realize that people have been sympathizing with me, treating me like, well, I don't know?"

"I told you the truth. At the beginning."

"You let me think it and you know it."

"Yes."

"Why?"

The ceiling lamp, reflected, swayed in the dark surface of his coffee. You are feeling very sleepy. And he was. He watched the hypnotic movement of the light. Why? The attraction of the ultimate loss, a satisfying finis to the dramatic disaster of his life? Good God, if he knew the answer to that essential Why, would he be what he was? Knowledge is virtue, finally, that kind of knowledge anyway, but what he had been after, if he had been after anything, was some light in which to see himself, some principle of interpretation. He shook his head. Lifting his cup, he made the drowned light dance crazily but when he tried to drink it, it slipped across the surface toward an artificial west.

"Matt, these past weeks have been terrible." She had put her arm through his and pressed against him on the bench.

"I'm sorry." He couldn't understand her reaction. She
had earned the anger he expected from her. For far less
than this she had chewed him out endlessly and now
she was limp and clinging, bringing dimly to mind happier
days when they had been man and wife, their life a shared
one, some days at least finding their excuse only in being
a necessary fanfare for night and the commingling in the
dark.

"More?"

"No." He pushed his cup away.

"Are you coming up?" she asked him from the sink with
the water running, her back turned. She was asking him.
He couldn't believe it. A corollary of her relief, perhaps,
but he still could not believe that she was relieved to find
their life must go on. The thought of climbing those stairs
with her suddenly frightened him. He had been sleeping
in the study for over a month. He had grown used to the
sags and crossbar of the cot. Marge turned and his eyes
moved over her body as over a land unknown. No. Not
tonight. Not yet. Their life could not turn this swiftly from
the sexual desert it had been. He just wasn't ready.

"I have some work to do."

"Will it take long?"

"I don't know." She came with him into the study. Good
God, did she intend to wait for him?

"Come up when you're through," she said. "And let's get
that damned cot out of here."

"It's not so bad. I've grown used to it."

"Matt, it doesn't make sense. What am I supposed to say
when someone sees it there?"

"Tell them to get the hell out of my study, I guess."

"Will you come up?"

"Not tonight, Marge. Okay?"

"Tomorrow, then?"

To get rid of her he said yes. He sat at his desk for an
hour to justify being there, filling an examination booklet
with a memorandum to himself. Why? Why? I am a role

in search of a drama. A series of actions in search of a playwright. The reluctant loser embraced his seeming role and
the plot shifted, he is a loser as a loser, and what did it
mean? The why was addressed to someone or something
other than himself. Addressee unknown. Return to sender.
Tragedy. Comedy. For the love of God, which was it? He
would settle for a mix of genres, no purist he, just give
me a clue to the meaning. How is it supposed to look,
what am I aimed toward? Death had seemed an end if not
a goal and absurdity the clue. Which made it less than
absurd. Camus. Snub. His nose broken on the rock of Sisy-
phus. It had been insufficient; death needs an explanation,
it wasn't itself the reason. Ascetics. Spiritual gymnastics
to a march by Suso and who kept score? Was the mind
meant to triumph over body?

He wrote on, writing nothing, no answer emerged from
his ballpoint pen and when he turned off the light and sat
on his cot he expelled the questions. Later, lying on his
back so as not to hear his heart beat, he stared at the
ceiling. Was Marge waiting for him up there? He hoped
she had gone to sleep. Not tonight. But soon. The warmth
of her receptive thighs, yes, yes. For all he knew, that could
be the meaning of life.

Her hair was shorter, helmetlike, and the new glasses had dark frames of oval shape that made her eyes seem wide and inquisitive. She had a more standard look now, she could be mistaken for many other girls, but Rogerson agreed that Norah was more attractive.

"You look different," he said when they had wended their way among the tables to a far corner of the faculty room in the cafeteria. "Nicer."

"Thank you. You haven't changed. In appearance."

"As opposed to what?"

"I've been hearing strange things."

"Lies. My enemies are legion."

"Some of it is good. Much of it, in fact." Norah turned her head slightly and regarded him askance, her brows raised, lips pursed. "Imagine, the Student Senate teacher award."

"I told them to stuff it."

"The ballot box?" Her hands in her lap, she leaned toward him. "You are different."

"Older." Sitting across from her, he felt older. It seemed years since his birthday, a lifetime ago that this girl had taken him drunk to her home, had invited him to dinner. And yet it was she who had altered, wasn't it? He thought of what Harry had told him and could not put the story of a desperate hungry woman together with this Norah across the table from him. And he thought of her mother. "Where are you living?"

"Home. I had the house up for sale but no one made a decent offer. That's the main reason I came back. If I have to keep the house I may as well live in it."

"Isn't it lonely?"

"Mother wasn't exactly companionship." Norah took a cigarette from her purse and Rogerson struck a match and held it toward her. When she had lit it she put an elbow on the table and blew smoke at the tip of the cigarette. "You acted rather strangely at the wake, Matt."

"Did I?"

"You know you did." She laughed and, looking across the room, said, "Did you think I did it, gave her an overdose?"

Rogerson too laughed, the noise a cushion between them, a fence of sound.

"You did think so. I saw it in your face. All right. I can understand why you would. If I had tried to put her to sleep once why wouldn't I go the whole way?"

"It's hardly the same thing." He concentrated on lighting a cigarette. Had he ever really doubted she had done it?

"You weren't the only suspicious one. I've been getting looks from Emily Pruitt. I'm surprised she hasn't gone to the police."

His coffee was cold. He put his cup down, picked up his cigarette and rolled ash from it into the aluminum tray that spun with the motion. The name of a brand of cigarettes was stamped in raised letters on the bottom of the tray, emergent from ashes.

"How is Mrs. Rogerson?"

"All right." How odd that she should ask. He couldn't remember Norah ever mentioning Marge before.

"I saw her the other day. Better keep an eye on her, Matt."

"You think she'll give me an overdose of sleeping pills?"

"Say, does she think you're ill?"

"No. Not any more."

"I wish you could have seen Laplace when he gave me the tragic news. It was practically the first thing he said. I think he expected me to commiserate with him. I can't imagine why."

"A death sentence is harder on the spectators."

"How did that rumor get started?"

He told her and the narrative seemed improbable. Perhaps because the hoax no longer interested him. It seemed a silly game. The last in a series of silly games. Last night, early that morning actually, nearly two o'clock, he had emerged from sleep as if someone were waking him; he lay staring at the ceiling waiting, for a thought, for some indication of what he was to do. He had felt he was nearing some important turn in his life and the expectation made the past several months distasteful to remember. Whatever revelation had teased the periphery of his mind had refused to come fully into view. But Rogerson was not anxious. It would come. He must be ready, that was all. When he least expected it. Until it came he would continue to sleep on the couch.

"Why did you let your wife believe you were ill?"

"I've told her I wrote the letter."

"But you didn't try to convince her at first. Why?"

"I don't know." No modulation of his voice, no plea for understanding nor rejection of it should she choose to give it. Facts first. He really didn't know why.

"And she spread the news?"

"Spread the news?" What a silly remark.

"Did you tell anybody else?"

"No."

"How did it get all over campus? According to Herb, it's common knowledge even among the students."

"I think she may have told Dowlet."

"Aha!"

"She couldn't be expected to keep it a secret, Norah."

"Oh, I know. But Dowlet?"

"What about Dowlet?"

"She was with him when I saw her."

"I'm not surprised."

"Well, that's nice. The campus Romeo and you're not surprised."

"Good God, don't be ridiculous. She's older than he is. And she isn't the least bit interested in that sort of thing."

Norah's brows lifted knowingly. That, together with the shape of her glasses, gave her the look of a naughty pixie. Where the hell had she been these past months? Surely she didn't think that Marge . . . Rogerson smiled. But how could Norah know what Marge was like? From that birthday note of his she'd read, but perhaps she hadn't caught the full implications of it. Or had forgotten. Marge having an affair. It wasn't even funny. She wasn't generous enough for married love; it was unlikely she could rise out of the nest of rules that governed her life and make love with another man.

"You'd be the last to know," Norah said.

"In this case Marge would be the last."

She patted his hand. "Such a trusting Matthew."

"Such a doubting Norah."

"You're not offended?"

"Certainly not. Nor flattered. But perhaps Marge would be." He smiled to change the subject. "It's good to have you back."

"I swore I'd never come back." She drew her upper lip between her teeth. "I'm not sure why I did. Really."

When they were leaving the cafeteria she said, "I'll be there for your hour of triumph."

He had not expected to feel triumphant, of course, but when he sat on the stage at the last convocation before the Christmas holidays looking out at the restless rows of students who struggled to survive the unctuous homily Wooley wafted toward the back of the auditorium, Rogerson recalled that brief period during which he had required this hall to handle the flow of auditors to his class. They had gone away with as little reason as they had come, but that brief ascendancy was the main reason for his being selected for this unwanted award, the explanation of his presence on this stage, elevated above his peers. He could see Marge in the front row, Harriet Wooley at her side. Marge looked at him in dubious pride and some apprehension. When she had asked about the ceremony he had given her an impromptu sample of the remarks he would make and she had been indignant. "You wouldn't," she said, but her expression said otherwise. As he looked out at the faces of the students, seeing the Old Bastards in a clutch near a door, it no longer seemed important that he say what he thought of the award. The Old Bastards hunched forward in expectation; he had given a preview to Freeman and James in the Arts lounge an hour before, and they had vowed they wouldn't miss it for the world. Wooley had turned at the podium and was looking back at him; the auditorium filled with applause, people were getting to their feet. Rogerson got to his and went toward Wooley, toward the presidential smile that gleamed like an undertaker's, and that, Rogerson realized, is probably what Wooley feels like, he hasn't heard otherwise. A framed citation was put into his hands; he looked down at it, looked over it to the still-applauding students, saw Marge

bright-eyed and happy. Embarrassed, his mouth dry, Rogerson leaned toward the microphone and said against the
din, "Thank you. Thank you." The applause faded as he
went to his chair, went on for a moment more while he
sat slumped looking at his reflection in the glass of the
framed award. Rogerson is a sonofabitch, he said half aloud.
Rogerson is a sonofabitch.

"You handled that very well," Marge said much later.

"It's over."

"Matt, I was proud."

He looked at her, checked the impulse to say something
sarcastic, smiled wanly. "I'll put this away."

After the convocation they had been invited to the
Wooleys' for cocktails and dinner. Marge took the occasion
to launch a bit of countering gossip: the diagnosis had been
incredibly wrong. Matthew wasn't sick at all.

"Only fungus in the lung," Rogerson interjected. "I shall
live forever."

"Good for you," Harriet Wooley said. "Good for you." As
if all it took were making up your mind to do it. Rogerson
had drunk deep, had made it through dinner without mis-
hap. Wooley was full of good news. A committee from the
state legislature would visit the campus in January, the
future looked bright. Very bright indeed. His puffy-eyed
smile described a ninety-degree sweep of the table with
the impartiality of a beacon, did not waver when Rogerson
came into view. He had heard. When the Rogersons were
saying good-by he had gripped Rogerson's arm and lisped,
"God, what good news, Matt. I'd sue that doctor if I were
you. Psychic attrition."

Perfect contrition. A phrase from the catechism he had
been asked to read before marrying Marge, Wooley's remark prodding it loose from memory, it drummed in his
head as he drove carefully home through the drunken
snow-covered streets. The first snow in weeks had fallen
that afternoon, drifting like grace to shroud a sinful world
in innocence. Perfect contrition. If one can't get to con-

fession. Sorrow prompted not by fear of punishment but
by . . .

"What is meant by perfect contrition?" he asked Marge.
She sat nervously on the edge of her seat, not trusting him
in his condition, calling out vague warnings like a river
pilot.

"Are you serious?"

"What is it?"

She tried to explain. She seemed embarrassed. Her explanation made no sense. It didn't matter. Only the sound
of the words interested him. "Do you take the children to
confession regularly?" He had promised they would be
raised Catholics but the task of course was Marge's, all
they had wanted was his acquiescence.

"What's got into you?"

"Do you?"

"Watch it," she cried. Rogerson, alarmed, let up on the
gas and peered ahead. Nothing.

"For Christ's sake, don't do that."

"Well, stop jabbering and look where you're going."

It was when they got home that she told him she had been
proud of him. He was hanging up his coat; she had waited
for him to return from taking the baby-sitter home. The only
light on was the hall light. As she stood almost directly
under it Marge's hair glowed. Rogerson, looking at her across
the table at Wooley's, had been reminded that she was
attractive. How long had it been since he had had her?
Months and months. Nearly half a year. No, more than
that. It angered him that such abstinence had come so
easily, felt mildly irritated remembering Norah's absurd
hint about Dowlet.

"Now don't tell me you intend to work tonight, Matt."

"I don't know."

She moved and her hair lost its luminescence; she stood
before him, tall in heels, perfumed. He put his hands on her
arms and she came against him, her body pliant, pressing,
soft, soft. She lay her forehead on his shoulder, her hands

moved under his arms, her fingers drummed on his rib cage. She exhaled in a sighing tone.

"Let's go up."

The award? Mingling with the Wooleys? A safe period in her menstrual cycle? Her fingers continued their tattoo on his ribs, rhythmic, like his heartbeat. He pressed his arms to his sides to still her fingers. She thought he was being playful and began to tickle him; he twisted away but she kept after him, her fingers digging at his sides, her face distorted with determined gaiety. He grabbed her arms and stared at her; her look was almost desperate. "Come on," she said. She took his hand and tugged him toward the stairs.

"No." He resisted her, caused them both to stop. "Marge, all those drinks. I'm bushed."

She was embarrassed now; this mad excursion out of character on her part embarrassed them both. An eager, available Marge was too different not to be surprising. And he was tired. Too tired to go to bed. "Maybe I will sit up a while."

She avoided his eyes. "Should I leave a light on upstairs?"

He shook his head. He felt as though he had just confessed his impotence. The hell with it. He went through the living room to his study, turned on the desk lamp, making his elongated shadow form upon the wall. Marge turned off the hall light but in the living room the Christmas tree sparkled with the caught light of the desk lamp. Rogerson groaned. There was Christmas to get through. But at least there would be no classes for a few weeks.

He continued to go to his office during the holidays, wanting to get away from the house. The children too were on vacation, excited by the approach of Christmas, and when it was past they lay indolently around the house, making it impossible for him to go through a room without having to step over someone. He kept repeating his promise to go with Barbara and Tommy to the rink so they could do their stuff for him on their new Christmas skates. The television seemed never off. Other children visited. Thank

God for his office. He was there when Maureen telephoned one afternoon the last week in December.

"What a wonderful Christmas present," she said after he had said hello, after he had expressed his surprise that she should call.

"Present?" Did the girl have the mistaken notion he had sent her something?

"When she came I thought it was about you and then I worried that it might be about me but when I found out what it was, well, I'll bet I'm as happy as you are."

He got her to slow down. Perhaps he had known from the moment she had begun to speak but he made her spell it out a step at a time. And she did. How surprising that Mrs. Rogerson would come that far to see a doctor but then, well, she might have had a lot of reasons and the tests were positive and she had been wanting to call but she had gone to her grandparents for Christmas, the whole family had gone, but now she was back, and didn't it fit into the season nicely, really couldn't he tell how excited she was, to think that after being so scared all it was was that Mrs. Rogerson was going to have a baby.

When he had hung up he turned off the lights in his office. He drew the blind, pulled the drapes and groped his way back to his chair where he sat in the dark, rocking slowly back and forth, back and forth. If you had asked him what he was doing Professor Rogerson would have replied that he was fishing. Ice fishing. Professor Rogerson had the reputation of being a kind of eccentric campus wit.

PART THREE

Winter

Old snow, dingy and porous, lay on the campus. The walks were wet avenues between gray diminishing mounds and a January sun hung pale and ineffectual in a light blue sky, creating nothing but faint shadows, blurred Doppelgängers of trees flat at their feet on the pocked snow. It was a wet, cold and now unreal world through which Rogerson walked having emerged stunned from his office in the library, his unrubbered feet raising as he walked a fine spray, a phenomenon on which he concentrated as if seeking his bearings in this wintry landscape, as much a condition of his heart as of the campus setting. When he moved past the Arts Building he saw lettered in scuffed and fading paint the legend he had brushed one evening last fall. Rogerson is a sex maniac. Rogerson cuckold, echoed in his mind, his pace slowed, his direction unaltered. His destination was the Faculty Club, Harry and a series of alcoholic inoculations against the incredible news Maureen has just given him on the phone but his mind was still so numb he felt no compulsion to hurry, a half dozen drinks could only insure there would be no abrupt awakening from this first protective stupor. Marge, my God, it made no sense and yet in the dread world to which he had been suddenly introduced it made perfect sense, another self as capable as one's own of the improbable deed, the move outside the public character that clashed with the role assigned by the interested onlooker. But Rogerson refused to think of her partner in this perfidy, having no doubt who it was, unable to cope with his image before his mind or with the sad sentence expressing the simple truth.

He arrived at the Faculty Club, found himself at the door with little memory of the walk there, lifted his hand and knocked, then rang the bell and, as he waited, once more knocked, repeating the sequence for several minutes until it became clear that Harry could not be there, no reason why he should be, the club closed during the holidays. Rogerson went around the house to the back door, found the key on the ledge and let himself in. With the door closed behind him, he stood in the little hallway and brought his hands to his face in a quick toweling gesture, raised his eyes and saw the closed cupboards behind the bar. Their handles did not respond to his pulling; he jiggled and shook and knew that they were locked. In a drawer beneath the bar he found a bottle opener, jammed it between the doors of the cabinet and pushed until the veneered wood split. Digging with the opener, urged on by the clink of glass against his metal wedge, Rogerson removed enough of the surrounding door to render the lock ineffectual. He opened the damaged door, the first bottle he drew forth was scotch and scotch he drank, splashing it into a glass, no ice or water, took it into the living room and sat before the dead fireplace and brought the glass to his mouth. He was sitting there several hours later when Harry came in.

"I'm relieved you're alone," he said to the startled steward. "Why don't you join me?"

"How did you get in, Professor?"

"I broke in, Harry. Get yourself a drink. I'm afraid I smashed a door or two in the kitchen. Think nothing of it. We live in a world where thief breaks in and steals, where moth and rust consume. Nothing safe from the invader, Harry, nothing. Have a drink."

Harry had a drink. And another. The sun was less insistent at the windows of the club and they sat, refilling their glasses, while Rogerson talked, filling the room with remnants of old lectures, random thoughts, a screen from his scuttling quiddity to keep his mind from the sad fact that had brought him here.

"You never autographed your picture," Harry said plaintively, during a lull in Rogerson's monologue, and went for the book when Rogerson indicated his willingness to do so now. Harry thrust the much-thumbed book into Rogerson's hands.

"This is last year's," Rogerson said, flicking through the pamphlet from which the faces of colleagues looked out at him in various expressions assumed for the sitting. For a week they had gone in clots and crowds or singles to the reception room in the Administration Building, where a student photographer had settled them before his glaring lamps and snapped their embarrassed faces. Wooley's idea to insinuate *esprit de corps* into the school, a faculty roster with picture, degrees and rank, useful for students too, for weeks they had matched passing professors with their photographs in the booklet. Harry's copy contained the autographs of all who would give them.

"They didn't put out a new one this year."

Rogerson looked at his own mournful face regarding him from the page. He lay the booklet on the coffee table in front of him, uncapped his pen and signed his name with great concentration. "I don't want you using this on any checks, Harry."

"Don't worry. One more offense and I'm gone for good."

Rogerson was not listening; the plan had appeared full formed in his mind. He looked at Harry, knew he was drunk, felt in the turn of his head the basic instability of the room's dimensions, the odd canting of its floor, thank God he was seated, but the idea stood out in sober clarity in the fuzz of his mind. *Après moi le déluge* and one cannot in a time of crisis be too fastidious in the choice of allies; he needed Harry in his ultimate assault on his soured circumstances. But no word of it now, now was the time of drinking. He raised his glass. "In boozo veritas, Harry."

"Same to you," the steward replied.

It was the first thing Rogerson remembered the following morning, waking with thundering head on his cot in the study, and the plan seemed to compensate for the

leaden unwillingness of his body to rise and pull the shade
and shut out the sun of this new day. He could not remember coming home, could not remember undressing and
lying on the cot, but here he was, his clothes were thrown
about the room. He lay listening to the sounds of the
house: from the kitchen the guttural purr of the radio, from
upstairs the voices of the children. Marge. He did not want
to see her let alone speak to her. Not yet, not yet. But no
amount of time could be enough. When he tiptoed through
the living room and upstairs he did not encounter her; in
the bathroom he shaved, trying not to look himself in the
eye. Guilt lay on his soul heavier than the lather on his face,
but lightly too, covering the undergrowth of indignation
and anger and sorrow, the wild desire to destroy, to ravage,
to pull down about his ears his home and job, friends and
enemies, all of it, everything, no stone upon a stone, so that
in the rubbish and ruins he might say *si monumentum
requieris circumspice,* a personal Hiroshima with an ending
as definitive as death and no more meaningful.

In the kitchen coffee and the pungent smell of bleach
conflicted, the washer whirred and throbbed and Marge
looked at him with reproach. Reproach! Drunk last night
was the accusation in her eyes, but the roar of the machine
prevented any exchange on that subject; Rogerson put
bread in the toaster, coffee in a cup and stood at the door
looking out at his brief backyard where the children had
played cut-the-pie, their footprints making an irregular
spoked wheel in the snow. The cycle of the washer reached
a period of subdued noise and Marge asked what he intended to do that day. It might have been any morning.
God, the treachery of her everyday voice.

"I'm going to my office. I have letters to write."

"You promised the kids you'd take them skating."

"Tonight." A minute later, when he turned, she was gone.
He finished his breakfast, went out to his car and drove to
his office.

What signatures Harry did not have already could be

gotten easily by Rogerson, signatures for the letters he must write, a barrage of epistles crossing the campus bringing into abrasive confrontation his supporting cast that each might be the instrument of justice for the other. Rogerson was enthralled, busy, excited, thumping at his typewriter. Wooley to Dowlet, first, the president pained but prompted by the exigencies of his office wished to bring to Dowlet's attention the numerous reports made to the president of the moral behavior of Peter Dowlet, reports which if less frequent might have been overlooked as the letters of cranks, which if they did not concern affairs with students might be thought to fall outside the school's concern. Professor Dowlet must realize that, quite apart from state and federal statutes, the code of his profession and the terms of his contract were such that this sort of thing could not be countenanced. He would be so kind as to consider this presidential letter as a most solemn penultimate warning, disappointedly yours, signed Francis Wooley—or would be signed when Harry had been approached. For balance, a letter from Dowlet to Wooley. Dear sir, as president of the local chapter of the AAUP it is my duty to register the widespread feeling among the faculty that the tragic Maureen Nugent case should be reopened. The president's failure to confront the girl with her accuser, the swift and kangaroo courtlike dismissal of the alleged offender could not fail to anger right-thinking individuals and to suggest that the president (or his wife!) had some ulterior motive in so summarily sending on her way a student whose record left little to be desired. An answer would be appreciated at President Wooley's earliest convenience, meanwhile, sincerely yours, Peter Dowlet. Dowlet's signature in Harry's booklet, as if boldly pledging his life, his fortune and his sacred honor. Indeed, indeed. Rogerson typing clean copies on college stationery, laboring over the machine.

He went down the hall with his coffeepot and, back again, lit a cigarette and listened to the rhythmic splut from the plugged-in pot. He had a feeling of accomplishment but there was so much yet to do. He phoned the Faculty Club and Harry sounded as if he had scrambled out of bed to answer it; he told the steward he would be over later, about four o'clock, don't admit anyone else if they should show up, a confidential matter the two of them must discuss. Harry was wary but acquiescent, Rogerson's own head throbbed with pain, knowing how the steward must feel, but what he had now begun took precedence over any momentary discomfort he and Harry might feel. To work once more, another sheet into the machine, a meditative puffing at his cigarette, the wet bubbling of the coffeepot contributing its background murmur.

To Miss Norah Vlach from Mrs. Eugene Pruitt, this typed on plain paper and brief, the simple accusation. Now that you appear to have gotten away with it, how does it feel to know that you were the cause of your mother's death? The next move *could* be yours, signed, or would be, Harry could simply invent an aged wavering hand. No silent sufferer Norah, she must write to Laplace, tendering her resignation, or threatening to resign, a letter to cross with Laplace's cool suggestion that perhaps it had been unwise for Norah to return to her old job, he would be glad to help her secure employment elsewhere. But Wooley was busiest of all, writing to Schmidt (corroboration of the charge of plagiarism has recently reached me from Munich), to the local state senator, O'Connell, his name dug from a back issue of the student paper, the man who had been Wooley's chief advocate with the legislature, now chairman of the committee which would visit the campus later in the month (your foot dragging and ineptitude have all but doomed my hopes that this college will be incorporated within the state system; I trust you will understand why your opponent, whoever he might be, will receive my wholehearted support in next fall's elections), to Laplace (Professor Schmidt has brought to my attention your failure to support his recent request, in conjunction with Professor Rogerson, for foundation support of a research project . . .). The concatenation of letters grew, Rogerson began to see he had days of work ahead of him. Felix must formally request that Dowlet call a meeting to discuss irregularities at the Faculty Club, Schmidt must send to Wooley a carbon of a letter written to the legislative committee warning them of the fiasco awaiting them when they visited the campus, Laplace must write Wooley protesting the latter's unwarranted tampering with the registration process in the Rogerson episode. The possibilities multiplied as Rogerson hammered at his typewriter, a massive crisscross of letters, insulting, accusing, groundless or the simple truth, bringing rancor and chaos to the campus, an explosion just before the legislative committee arrived.

When he hurried across the campus to the Faculty Club at four, clutching a manila folder filled with letters, his head singing with plans for more, Rogerson's eyes grazed the college buildings with disgust, each brick obtrusion coming into the hairline of his bombsight, stand-ins for the cast of characters who would soon be at one another's throats.

"Just a joke," he explained to Harry when the steward looked at the letters and considered the plan Rogerson had just outlined for him. "Mix us a drink, would you?"

"It's been a long time, Professor," Harry said from the other side of the bar. "I don't know how good they'll be."

"They'll be perfect, Harry. I'm sure it's not a gift easily lost."

"There's no money involved now? It's just a joke?"

"Not a cent, Harry. Not a check in the bunch."

Rogerson watched while Harry practiced each signature before affixing it with a flourish to the typed letter. He might have been a busy executive clearing his desk. When they were once more in the manila folder Harry suggested another drink.

"Just one more," Rogerson said. "Tonight I'm going skating."

The skating rink, a flooded tennis court, was rimmed by ridges of snow shoveled from the surface. Round and round it counterclockwise Rogerson went with Barbara and Tommy, he in rented skates, they in their new Christmas ones, the loudspeakers blaring rock 'n' roll music. Under the arc lights and into the shadows then again into a pale puddle of lighted ice, round and round. On the ice as in the building where they had put on their skates there was a press of people, mostly teen-agers, noisy and sullen, not giving way when Rogerson went unsteadily with the wire basket containing their shoes to the checking window, Barbara and Tommy waiting by the door, and then onto the ice and into the swirl of skaters, their blades finding the ruts made by earlier blades, but the night air was fresh in his lungs, his cheeks stung pleasantly with cold and his children, one on either side, happy, happy. It had seemed only an excuse not to be in the house but now he was glad he had offered to bring them to the rink. His children. He was tired of making feeble excuses to flee the house for his campus office, staying there until Marge must be asleep, and then coming almost furtively into the house, turning on no lights, collapsing on his cot, praying that sleep at least would be given him. For he refused to think. He did not want to think. He had concentrated all his effort on keeping his mind as blank as he could, repressed the hot rise of anger and shame, Rogerson cuckold. Now he had his plan, something to do, and his circuit of the rink seemed a satisfyingly purposeful motion.

At the end of the rink farthest from the warming house a boy and girl sat in a bank of snow in the sallow glow of an overhead light, arms around one another, bundled to the neck, skates on their feet, kissing dispassionately. The girl's hair fell to her shoulders, the boy's face was ripe with pimples, she half lay in the snow as he jammed his face to hers and her eyes, open, watched the skaters going by, neither defiance nor fear in her expression. Boredom. Rogerson wanted to avoid the scene and he wanted to speed up to hasten their return to it. Did they never break? He didn't want Barbara and Tommy to see the couple but he had to see them again and again. He felt as if he had come upon some new species whose habits being unfamiliar were distasteful and repellent: the fit of bodies, the grind of face. His grip of Barbara's mittened hand tightened and when they neared the building once more he said, "Let's go in. My ankles are killing me."

"You go in, Daddy. Tommy and I will be all right." They had come to a stop, Rogerson less than gracefully, which irked him: as a boy he had been a good and tireless skater.

"No. Come on. We'll come out again."

The din inside was deafening though the awful music was muted; that was piped only to the four winds. Within the room the shouting, giggling and horseplay made up for it, keeping peace at bay. Rogerson slumped on the edge of a bench; there was only room for one. He crossed his legs and unlaced a skate, with thumb and forefinger removed from the skate's blade the shaved clinging ice. Barbara and Tommy stood before him, their faces glowing, their manner impatient. The other occupants of the bench looked at Rogerson, then looked away.

"We can take turns sitting," Rogerson said.

Tommy balanced on the tips of his skates. "I'm not tired."

"Neither am I," Barbara said. "You rest, Dad."

"Would you like something to eat?"

"Not now." Barbara looked longingly at the door leading to the rink.

"Okay. Go on out and skate. I'll join you in a minute." They went toward the door and Rogerson called after them, "Keep to this end of the ice!" But other kids had come be-

tween him and Barbara and Tommy and he didn't know if
they had heard him. Rogerson started to lace up his skate
and then stopped. Not yet. A few minutes more. All around
him teen-agers were necking brazenly. Necking. Had he
thought of that word in years? Why in front of everyone?
He dropped his eyes, laced his skate and stood. Wobbily he
went to the door and outside, keeping his hand on the railing as he went down the board walk to the ice. There was
a bench on the ice, half unoccupied, and Rogerson pushed
off and glided to it and sat once more. Barbara and Tommy
went by at intervals, shouting to him, and he waved and
smiled and wished they would turn down the volume on
that loudspeaker. He would stick it out. He wanted Barbara
and Tommy to have a nice evening because it occurred to
him that he had never done anything like this with them
before. Of course they had been young. But there were
things to do with younger children too, weren't there? What
would their memories of him be? He chipped at the ice
with the tip of a blade, sending slivers of ice skittering about,
chipped as if below the ice were water and in the water
fish and he might coax them into the lethal air. Had his
father worried about him? It didn't matter. What binds
parents and children is not established by consciousness of
it; it is prior to that, of the blood, darker and deeper, yet
affecting consciousness. Sometimes during these past dreadful days he had wondered if his children were not the
purpose of his life, but if he was bound to them they bound
him in turn to Marge and that brought him to a point he
could not think beyond, not yet. Perhaps not ever. Now
there were the letters to finish and mail. His chipping had
become savage and a passing skater, made unsteady by the
mess he had created, shouted Hey and Rogerson stopped
and sought his children in the crowd.

When he had found them they went inside again, this
time to change from the skates. In shoes, leaving, Rogerson
felt stunted, his feet numb and unreal, the floor hard on the
soles of his feet. "You kids hungry?" he asked in the car.

They were. He would get them something. They would stop. A memorable evening. Would it lodge in their heads to be summoned forth decades hence, an image defining their father? Not likely. What images had he given them already, not meaning to? The recluse in the study, the voice telling them to turn down the damned television, the phony look of interest when they asked him something, his manner betraying his hope he could expedite this, send them on their way.

The restaurant was a thing of counters and booths around the walls. In a booth, Rogerson on one side, Tommy and Barbara on the other, they drank hot chocolate, Rogerson smoked, the children looked about the place, they said little but it was a comfortable silence. The modes of silence. The final test of human relations. A strained silence echoing with the noise of accusations; a preparatory silence; the silence of lovers; a silence after shared pleasure; the non-speaking parent and child. The last the sweetest of all, Rogerson assured himself. But he was glad when the children had finished their drinks, refused more and they went out to the car.

The children were his buffer at the house, filling the intervening air with the chatter of their report to their mother. Rogerson went into his study, listening from his desk, shoes off, his ankles deliciously aching, righteous Rogerson the ideal father though grievously wronged.

"Would you like coffee?" Marge from the doorway of the study. Rogerson had heard her come down from overseeing the children's going to bed, had begun to write more furiously in the examination booklet open before him on the desk.

"We stopped for something on the way home."

"Are you going to work late?"

He nodded and frowned at the scribbling before him. Marge receded into the living room, the scrawl of his writing seemed to hover an inch above the page. Abraham and Sarah, Rogerson unwittingly lending his wife to his adversary but to what advantage? To what advantage? Oh, God, the stupidity of thinking that there was no spark of desire for strange loins left in Marge. What would Father Abraham have done if Sarah conceived, if the lines of favored blood had become entangled by alien ardors? Marge was now eager to get him into bed, their bodies fused to confuse the issue, deceive him further into thinking the life housed by her reluctant womb had something to do with him. Why couldn't he keep his rage pure, directed at Marge and Dowlet? Why did this seem a judgment on him, a deserved punishment for all his sins? The first stone burned in his hand, but if he threw it he wanted a boomerang effect, he wanted a general desolation from which his individual ruin would not emerge as special or unique. When Felix drinks, everybody drinks. Freeman at the club, magnanimous at the bar. When Rogerson goes down in ruin, everyone must come along for the ride. His life had gone beyond logic now, reasons were unnecessary when the holocaust beckons. And the letters were his weapons. He pulled the manila folder from his briefcase, examined the day's work, began to sketch plans for the morrow's. The pen is mightier than the penis mightier than the mind and Rogerson crouched over his desk, the recording angel, scribbling in the book of judgment.

The letters, appropriately dated, went into the mailbox in front of the library the day after school reconvened and Rogerson lived an airless day as they went their appointed rounds and then entered the lounge in the Arts Building. The room was empty and, as he sat solitary under the winter panel of the four-seasons mural, Schmidt's furtive face appeared at the door, withdrew, once more looked in and Rogerson's colleague came swiftly across the room, eyes burning beneath the thatch of his brows.

"Have some coffee, Reinhardt. The brew is potable today."

Schmidt shook his head fiercely and slumped into a chair opposite Rogerson. "I have been betrayed, Matthew. Betrayed. Hounded across the world because of a youthful indiscretion." Schmidt rubbed his face with his hands, looked with hunted eyes at Rogerson.

"Reinhardt, where can we hide from our indiscretions?"

"You don't understand . . ."

"Indeed, I do not, Reinhardt. Come in, Herb." Laplace stood in the doorway; Reinhardt jumped from his chair as Rogerson spoke, now faced Laplace. The dean's face contorted and he stepped back.

"Come to my office, Matt. I have to run."

"Yes, you bastard, run," Schmidt cried, a minute after Laplace had disappeared. "There is a bastard, Matthew, an awful, awful bastard."

"He seemed unhappy to find you here. Have you been going over his head to Wooley again?"

"That goddam Wooley," Schmidt breathed, sinking into his chair.

"Duty calls, Reinhardt. It's been pleasant speaking with you."

"Matthew, don't go. I have to talk to you. You're the only one. You're . . ."

"Your only friend? Of course I am. Perhaps later, Reinhardt. I really must go."

And go he did, out of the lounge and down the stairs to the first-floor hall where half the building away he saw Felix approach. But when Felix saw him he turned and hurried back in the direction from which he had come. To his office, the reports would reach him there, the explosion was coming, there was nowhere one could fail to hear the detonation. It was there with his coffepot hissing companionably that Rogerson learned the first effects of his campaign. Laplace phoned, speaking in a strangled voice of his intention to have it out with Wooley, the sonofabitch; Wooley himself inquired through Grace if Professor Rogerson knew anything of an AAUP plan to protest the Maureen Nugent dismissal; half an hour later the president himself was on the phone.

"My God, Matt, I have never received a batch of mail like this morning's in my life. Overnight the whole world seems to be coming apart at the seams."

"I've noticed unrest on the campus. Nothing serious, I'm sure."

"Serious! God!" The president moaned and Rogerson thought he heard the click of ice cubes. He glanced at his watch. Ten A.M. "Complaints, incredible threats and accusations." An unmistakable sound of drinking as Wooley paused. "To top it all, I received, quite unsolicited, samples of Scandinavian pornography that is simply filthy. Let me tell you, it's pretty goddam embarrassing when Grace opens my mail and photographs of nudes drop all over her desk."

They came to the office too. Felix, sheepish at having avoided Rogerson earlier, the one Old Bastard he could still trust, almost forgetful of his own concerns because of the rumors he had picked up. Dowlet called on the carpet,

Herb chewing everyone out but Norah insists the dean is in more trouble than anyone. Norah herself was jumpy as hell. "The whole place is unhinged, Matt. In thirty years there has been nothing like it." Felix mustered a small smile. "What a reception that legislative committee would get if they showed up today."

"You think everything will be back to normal in a week?"

"What's normal here any more, Matthew? Would you tell me that?"

"If I knew, I'd be glad to, Felix."

Harry called from the club to whisper that he had opened at noon there had been so many requests to be let in early. "Boy, those letters really hit home, Professor. Lots of long faces. I thought you said it was a joke."

"People have lost the gift of laughter, Harry."

"I did a pretty good job, I guess."

"A brilliant job, Harry. So don't tip your hand now and spoil it."

"My lips are sealed, Professor. Nobody here is in the mood to talk anyway."

"Is Dowlet there?"

"He was the first one through the door."

He was still there when Rogerson went over at three o'clock, humming as he crossed the campus. A light snow was falling, a cottony layer covered the walks and clung to the soles of his rubbers briefly and then fell away, his passage recorded both by footprints and clotted half soles of snow. But it was no sullen group of solitary drinkers that awaited him at the club. As he removed his rubbers and got out of his coat he could hear the strident voice of Laplace vying with Dowlet's; when he came into the hallway Felix was shouting shrilly at James and Schmidt slobbered away unintelligibly at the universe in general. Rogerson called a cheery greeting and was ignored and when he came into the kitchen Harry looked frightened behind the bar. "They're getting rough," he said.

"I'll have a beer, Harry."

"I've never seen them like this. What do I do if there's a brawl?"

Watch, Rogerson advised, and that is what they both did when it started. Laplace pushed Dowlet from him, was pushed in return, the attention of the others was drawn to them, they were ringed by bloodthirsty spectators aching to be participants, a shoving, shouting group which became increasingly belligerent. The shouts seemed almost relieved when blows were struck and then bedlam ensued. The old and young mingled, forming momentary alliances, becoming once more adversaries. The clubhouse was a shambles when the campus police arrived. Harry would not call the city police, so Rogerson agreed to bringing in the campus constabulary; they were ineffectual enough to insure that the squabble would merely be postponed. A drunken Dowlet came into the bar when peace was restored, ordered a drink and looked tragically at Rogerson. Using the bar as guide and his forearm as runner, he moved toward Rogerson and faced him. "I have to talk with you, Matt. I have to talk."

"There isn't one goddam thing I want to hear from you."

"Matt," Dowlet pleaded, putting his hand on Rogerson's arm for emphasis and leaving it there for support. Harry looked on, alarmed, amused, eager for Dowlet to continue. Rogerson took Dowlet's elbow, easing the young man's hand from his shoulder, and led him into the hallway. Someone had removed the phone from the cradle and left it off. Rogerson picked it up with his free hand, held it to his ear and, hearing the dial tone, replaced it. Dowlet had been jabbering in a stage whisper as they walked from the bar and now Rogerson eased him into a chair and lit a cigarette, not wanting to listen, unable not to. Exhaling smoke, following the climb and curl of it, Dowlet's voice whining drunkenly on, Rogerson felt he had every right to smash Dowlet in the mouth, so why the hell didn't he, the sonofabitch deserved it. Dowlet was now whimpering that in his own defense he had to say he hadn't intended anything to happen, not really, and when it had she wouldn't use anything, wouldn't let him use anything either.

"It's against her religion," Rogerson said.

"That's what she said," Dowlet cried, attempting to rise, then falling back in his chair. "Goddam it, Matt, hit me. Do something. Don't stand there as if nothing has happened. I don't care what happens to me. All hell is breaking loose anyway. That goddam Wooley and Laplace, everybody, the whole place is insane." And Dowlet just didn't give a damn any more; he had to tell Rogerson he was sorry. But it really wasn't his fault, Rogerson had to see that.

Rogerson looked into Dowlet's abject face, wanting to strike out and punish this mattress acrobat who glided from bed to bed chalking up his pitiful triumphs. Who now in his drunken fear imagined he was ashamed of himself. He had to deprive Dowlet of the simpering, weeping satisfaction he was deriving from this public confession.

"What in the world are you talking about, Peter?"

Dowlet tried to focus his eyes, tried to register his surprise that he must be confessing something of which Rogerson was unaware. His glazed eyes stirred with hope and a different kind of fear; he pulled at his mouth, studying the floor.

"I hope you aren't under the impression Marge is pregnant," Rogerson said, assuming a sardonic smile. "Not at her age."

"Isn't she?" Dowlet did stand now, his eyes searching Rogerson's face.

"Did she tell you that?"

Dowlet seemed to be trying to recall Marge's words.

"An old hand like you should have been prepared for that kind of hokum, Peter."

"But she won't see me now; she . . ."

"Her way of saying good-by, Peter. Nothing more." He put his hands on Dowlet's shoulders and pushed lightly, causing him to collapse once more in his chair. "So if you feel like crying, cry for yourself."

He left him. In the areaway, with his coat on, leaning against the wall as he pulled on his rubbers, Rogerson looked through the curtained inner door at Dowlet. His hatred of the man was almost impersonal; Dowlet was little more than an instrument of the grief that ate at Rogerson, that went with him out the door and brought the sting of tears to his eyes as he hurried across the campus to his car. His shame had to be returned home, taken from Dowlet, his alone. Now the bastard will never know, will only be able to guess, and if the place comes down about our ears and he is dispersed with the rest, he will have forgotten all about it in months. Then only Marge and Rogerson need live with the result of Dowlet's pricky passage through the world of this campus.

"I put it back in the garage." Marge spoke from the doorway of the study.

"What?" But he knew before he looked. The cot was gone. That side of the room was in shadow with just the desk lamp on. "Why did you do that? I like sleeping on that cot."

"You can sleep upstairs, Matt." Her face when he looked up seemed drawn; she avoided his eyes. "It's embarrassing to have you sleeping down here like an intruder."

"Well, we don't want intruders sleeping in the house." Careful, careful. He didn't want to think about, didn't want to talk about it. The confrontation with Dowlet, cushioned by the bastard's drunkenness, had been bad enough, but he could not endure discussing it with a sober Marge.

"Do you want something to eat now?"

"No. I'm not hungry." That is what he had said when he came home from the club after leaving Dowlet.

"Not even coffee?"

He shook his head.

"Do you have to work tonight?" Oh God, Marge, don't beg, please don't beg. Things are bad enough without this pathetic effort to deceive me twice. He wrote a line, feeling her eyes on him. *Et sic sic sine fine feriati.* One of the few lines of Latin he remembered. Sextus Propertius. And thus endlessly we make holiday. Marge moved into the darkened living room but she did not go away. The removal of the cot had been predictable, her strategy embarrassingly obvious. When he had told her he was not hungry she had pressed against him, put her arms about him, sighed into his ear, the move so uncharacteristic Rogerson had felt an impulse to cry. Later he did, while she and the children had dinner, his head on the desk while pity for her, shame, self-pity, all or none, he didn't know, knew only he needed that release and reveled in it. Afterward he stood and felt the walls of the house surround him, its roof over him, and it seemed accursed. Once more he had felt the guilt was his though he was the one wronged. He the horny partner in this godforsaken marriage had, out of timidity or virtue, avoided adultery if not like sin at least as messy and dangerous. Even now, when the thought of a spiteful counter-affair crossed his mind, he rejected it instantly, though who would blame him now? Surely not Marge. The thought held no more attraction now when he sat at his desk staring at the line of Propertius as if it were part of a text he must construe.

"Matt?" Marge was still in the living room, watching him from the shadows. When he turned, squinting at her, she said, "Is it so terribly important?"

What? What? He shook his head. "No."

"Why don't you come up?"

"All right. I will."

"I'll wait for you."

"I won't be long."

Because he had it now, finally, what he would do. He would go to bed with his wife, be her ally in the deception, say nothing. Of course. Magnanimous Rogerson, settling for seconds. He lit a cigarette, listened to Marge go up the stairs. No, no. Not irony. Nor revenge. The thing to do. A secret into the grave with both of them. Did it make any less sense than anything else? Not using anything was against her religion and by God it wasn't funny, a child involved here somewhere. A dizzying thought that his father had not been his father and what certitude did he have? Our lives are lived on assumptions we cannot prove. He began to write. Marge would wait. He wanted to put on this ruled page in his jumpy script the truth that life without some lies would not be livable, that that thing forming in Marge's womb was more important than any

anger he could dredge up from his ruined soul, that whatever guilt there was enveloped him, tainted him, would
not pass him by and leave him simply wronged. What he
lusted for now was not Marge but the feeling of atonement
going up to her could give, the act taking the scattered
corners of his life and bringing them together in an intelligible package labeled Rogerson. Yes. He would. Writing
on, he anticipated the deed, the feeling, the profound logic
of it.

Upstairs a groan. His pen poised over the page, Rogerson
listened. One of the children? Again. No. Marge. He got
up and went through the living room to the foot of the
stairs. The bathroom light cast shadows on the high wall
rising from the landing to the upstairs ceiling.

"Marge?"

Again the groan and Rogerson ran up the stairs and,
rounding the landing, saw Marge in the bathroom on the
floor. He ran to her and saw blood, my God, blood, she
had pressed a towel to her and it was bright with blood
and she looked up at him with the eyes of the hunted,
the cornered, the victim.

"What's the matter?" Kneeling beside her, he felt a wave
of nausea at the sight of the blood. Marge was trying to
look calm but her eyes roved in search of a plausible
lie.

"I can't stop it, Matt."

"But what happened?"

"It just started." Perspiration stood out on her pale forehead, her hand gripping the washbasin slipped and Rogerson
caught her, her eyes looked glazed and her mouth hung
open. The towel fell free and Rogerson pressed his eyes
closed, unable to look. A doctor; he had to get a doctor.
He lay Marge gently back on the floor and thundered
down the stairs to the phone, dialed the operator, demanded
an ambulance, slammed down the phone and picked up
the phone book, flipped and found Dr. Earl's number under-
lined in pencil. Having told the doctor he was taking Marge

to the hospital and why, Rogerson unceremoniously hung
up and ran back upstairs. The children stood in the doors
of their rooms, eyes wide with fright, and Rogerson waved
them back. "Everything will be all right. Get back to bed.
Go on. Daddy will take care of everything."

"What's wrong with Mom?"

"She's sick. She'll be all right. Go back to bed."

They retreated but as he went on to the bathroom he
knew they were still there. Marge was unconscious. Shock.
Loss of blood. Oh God, God, don't let her die. How long
had she been here before he heard her groan? He should
have gone up with her, should have . . . "Shit!" he said
aloud, angry tears in his eyes. He lifted Marge's head to
his knee, sponged at her face with a washcloth, trying to
conceal the mess from the children's eyes. A siren? He
lay Marge back, stood, yelled at the kids to get the hell
to bed and went again downstairs. He flung open the doors,
turned on the outside light, ran back to the phone. He
found Mrs. Snow's number in the book and called her.
Could she come? An emergency. Yes, right now. He had
to take Mrs. Rogerson to the hospital. Eyes shut, he waited
for this to register with the woman. Yes, she could come.
He would wait until she came. The ambulance in the driveway now. He had to hang up. Hurry.

They came swiftly up the steps, an intern, the driver,
and Rogerson ran before them, pointing at Marge. The
intern examined her briefly and called for the stretcher and
Rogerson helped the driver and then followed the two of
them out to the ambulance as they carried the still body
of his wife. He couldn't forget the horrified looks on the
faces of the children when the men took their mother
away.

"I'll come down as soon as the baby-sitter arrives. I called
our doctor. Earl."

The intern nodded, pulling the door of the ambulance
closed behind him. As the driver backed out, Rogerson
saw Marge in profile, eyes shut, skin so terribly pale, and

then the beams of the headlights were bright upon him and he turned to go back to his children.

He gathered them into his arms in the upstairs hallway. "Mrs. Snow is coming. Daddy is going down to the hospital to see that everything is all right. Don't worry." Don't worry! Pressing their faces against him, feeling his throat tighten with fear, his eyes unseeing as he looked around the hallway as if he were lost in unfamiliar surroundings. He took them downstairs. They were there, Rogerson seated at the telephone table, his children clustered about him, crying openly now, both doors still wide to the January night, when Mrs. Snow looked in in wonder. The children seemed consoled to see her and Rogerson left.

He drove with great concentration, staring at the pointing lights of his own car, alive with a mist of falling snow, until he drew near downtown and seemed to be in a pocket of darkness moving through myriad multicolored lights and then a right turn and the hospital. At the emergency entrance he parked. Running to the door, he realized he had not put on a coat, that the night was cold. The pavement was slippery and he felt his feet go out from under him but seemingly in midair he regained his balance and brought both feet stamping painfully down. He was walking when he reached the door and pulled it open and stepped inside where memories of the anger and fear he had felt the night he brought Tommy here assailed him like the sudden warmth and he had to stop once more to gain his balance.

Marge was in none of the emergency treatment rooms. Rogerson ignored the desk and went directly down the hall, putting his head into each room, not finding Marge, and then back to the reception desk. A woman looked up, not the bitch he remembered, and the expression on his face held her attention. He asked where his wife was, she had just been brought in, a miscarriage, and the woman rose, came out of the enclosure and took him by the arm. "The elevator," she said, leading him back down the hall-

way. "You'll have to go up to eight. She'll be in maternity,
I guess. At least you can wait there. They'll know what's
going on." She waited with him until the elevator came
and when he stepped inside and turned he saw the woman's
face, in the exact center of the door, erased as if by a
guillotine when the door closed and then he was lifting
through the smells of the hospital, inching upward, the
numbers above the door lighting up one by one until 8
glowed red, the car lurched slightly and the door slid open.
Right or left? He could not tell; he had emerged facing
a wall and in either direction was an open door beyond
which was another wall. Left. He went through the door
and then to his right where at a nurses' station an elderly
nurse sat frowning over a paperback book.

"Rogerson," he said to her. "My wife was just brought
in."

"Who is your doctor?"

"Earl."

"Is she expecting?"

"She was. I think it was a miscarriage. She fainted."

The nurse's hair, once black, was streaked with gray.
She picked up a phone, looking at him expressionlessly.
Her eyes drifted away and she looked thoughtful listening
to the ringing in her ear. She spoke, a coded communica-
tion, a nod and, phone hung up, stood. "You can wait
in here, Mr. Rogerson. She's in the operating room." She
went ahead of him to what once must have been a patient's
room, now fitted out for waiting. Chunky furniture, television, newspapers and magazines. A man slept fitfully on the
couch, his clothes rumpled. On the screen of the television
set a woman's mouth moved but the sound was down
and whatever she said could not be heard. "As soon as
I hear anything I'll let you know."

Rogerson thanked her, stood looking around the room.
The sleeping man, grunted, tossed, settled down again.
Rogerson did not want to sit. He lit a cigarette and stared
at the television. Now there was a mob scene, pitch torches,

occasionally a face, mouth open in a soundless shout. Rogerson drew on his cigarette, went to the door and looked back at the nurses' station. No one was at the desk now. He went back inside and sat, closed his eyes but saw only that awful amount of blood in the bathroom. A commercial flickered on the screen, blessedly silent. He crushed his cigarette and sat staring at the ashtray. The sound of the sleeping man annoyed him, a sibilant whining less-than-snore, lying on his back. Why is he here? Is his wife having a baby? Rogerson tried to remember the births of his own children but the occasions blurred into one. By God, he had never slept; he had waited as nervous as a cartoon father until it was all over, Marge drugged and mumbling in her bed. So goddam long ago. Not in years. Tommy seven, no eight. Eight years during which so much had ceased to be. He tried to remember the special joy of becoming a father. It implied a hope he could not summon now. The sound of the sleeping man was unbearable and he got to his feet and went into the hall. The nurse sat at her desk once more.

"She won't be coming back to this floor, Mr. Rogerson. She'll be on seven. But you can continue to wait here if you'd like. I'll be called when she's brought down."

"Could I wait in her room?"

"It won't be a private room."

Rogerson looked toward the waiting room and then back to the nurse. "Have you any idea how long it will be?"

She tried to smile. "You could have a cup of coffee, if that's what you mean. The restaurant downstairs is closed, but there's a place across the street."

She showed him to another elevator and he dropped through the building, came into the lobby and went out the door into the night. He turned the collar of his suit jacket up against the cold and looked across the street. The window of a restaurant was bright behind a frieze of snow but Rogerson felt no desire to go there; he did not want coffee, wanted even less to be where people were.

He walked back and forth in front of the hospital, hands in his pockets, the passing cars sending sometimes several versions of his shadow racing toward him over the snowy walk, each shadow looming larger as it shortened and then slipped away beneath his pacing feet; in the other direction, elongated, his shadows flattened and stretched away. He went back inside. He sat in the lobby and looked longingly outside where carfuls of untroubled people went by in the night, free of the ominous atmosphere of the hospital.

When he went upstairs again half an hour later he got off at the eighth floor. No news. The man no longer slept on the couch in the waiting room. "He had a boy," the nurse explained. "He's gone home now."

"To get some sleep?"

"He's been here all day. First child."

The phone rang at her desk and she hurried to answer it. Rogerson followed and she looked at him and nodded as she listened. He was to wait here; the doctor would be down shortly; why didn't he sit down and relax until he came?

"How is my wife?"

"The doctor will be down in a few minutes."

"Is she all right? She isn't . . ."

"Oh, no." The nurse's eyes widened and she shook her head violently. "No."

She seemed to be telling the truth. She couldn't lie about something like this. Rogerson went back into the waiting room. The television was off now.

Dr. Earl was in street clothes when he came, tall, a youthful face, gray hair; he seemed a stranger to Rogerson. The doctor leaned against the wall as he talked, his eyes moving about the room as if he were taking a disinterested inventory of this squalid setting.

"She was in mild shock when she came in. She miscarried, but I suppose you know that. The hysterectomy was more or less routine."

"Hysterectomy?" Earl, apparently thinking Rogerson did

not understand the nature of the operation, explained it all, standing straight as he did so, choosing his words carefully. Rogerson followed the lecture for several minutes and then asked if he could see Marge.

"She's still under, of course."

Rogerson had started off but then turned to thank the doctor but Earl too was leaving; Rogerson looked back at the place where he had learned the news, felt a shudder pass over his body and went on to see his wife.

When he entered the room a woman looked at him from hollowed eyes, fixing him in a stare, and Rogerson stopped, about to explain, but then he saw Marge in the other bed. He went to her. She was unconscious, a troubled look on her white face, her hair damp and flat against her head. He lay his hand on her forehead; it felt cool. At the desk a nurse from the operating room had told him that Marge, just before the anesthetic took full effect, had begun to demand a priest. She was very insistent. The nurse thought Rogerson might want to know. Her duty done, she had gone away and Rogerson came down the hall to the room where they told him Marge would be and now, standing beside her, frightened by her ravaged countenance but accepting the nurse's assurance and Earl's that she was all right, he felt a tension leave him of which he had been only imperfectly aware before. It's all over. It's all over. That thought kept going past his mind and he stooped to kiss Marge's forehead. The fixed stare of the other occupant followed him from the room.

In the days that followed, Rogerson moved in a private cocoon while on the campus the chaos quickened. Wooley called a faculty meeting, wanting some sort of cohesion before the arrival of the legislative committee, but the auditorium contained less than a dozen people when Rogerson got there. Dismissing them after a twenty-minute wait, Wooley signaled to Rogerson.

"Why does everyone hate me all of a sudden, Matthew? Can you tell me that? My God, here we are on the verge of getting this place on a solid foundation and it falls apart. The letters I've received!"

Rogerson was unable to be moved by Wooley's predicament: he felt neither the triumphant elation he had anticipated nor the pity Wooley now invited.

"For all I know, that committee won't even show up. O'Connell phoned yesterday and ripped me up one side and down the other." Wooley sighed in a prolonged piping way, his lips fluttering in the exhaust.

Rogerson said something monosyllabic and he and Wooley emerged from the auditorium. "And resignations, Matthew. Half the faculty wants to leave."

"I heard Schmidt might go to Munich."

"I wish he would. He won't let me alone. He's been camped in Grace's office for days hugging a copy of his contract. He thinks I want to fire him and nothing I say convinces him otherwise."

That night at the hospital the nurse at the floor desk told him Marge was fine. She consulted a chart and added enigmatically, "Physically. I'm sure your doctor will want her to stay a few more days. It takes a woman time to adjust to this, you know."

Hoag had been to see Marge. Rogerson called him, asking if he would, and then ran into him in the hallway. The priest's progress was slow, he beamed into sickrooms, being relevant, but when he saw Rogerson his step got springier still and he advanced on him with outthrust hand. "I hoped I might run into you here, Professor Rogerson."

"I must return those books I borrowed."

"Keep them as long as you like."

"I've finished with them. You saw Mrs. Rogerson?"

The priest said he had, his eyes veiling slightly. "When are you going to give a lecture at the Newman Club? We'd love to have you."

"How is the series going?"

"Wonderful. Wonderful. I'm having an atheist present his views next Sunday night."

"Sounds exciting."

"Quite a serious fellow."

"I can imagine."

"Chances are he's a more truly religious person than you or I. I've come to think that a serious atheist must be very close to God."

"An odd kind of proximity, isn't it?"

"His ways are not our ways."

"I can see that."

"Mrs. Rogerson is coming along nicely, I'd say."

"Thanks for stopping by."

The priest dismissed it with a wave of his hand and continued on his way. "Don't forget that lecture now. I want all viewpoints represented in the series."

I have none, Rogerson wanted to call after him, but then decided that truth ought not disturb the tranquil course of Father Hoag's *aggiornamento*.

The campus situation worsened. No one was speaking to anyone else by the day the legislative committee arrived. Wooley had abandoned his original plan to have the committee meet the faculty in plenary session. Two committee members called on Rogerson at his office. One, a diminutive balding man of sixty, who ran a hardware store until a legislative session transformed him into a senator, looked uneasy and suspicious; the other, Senator O'Connell, was six feet tall, weighed two hundred and fifty pounds, had a round red face, crewcut hair and merry skeptical eyes.

"What's happened here, Professor?" O'Connell asked. He took the chair and left his colleague standing by the door. "I can't get anything but complaints and bitching. Even Wooley has a chip on his shoulder. He acts as if this inquiry was *our* idea."

"I guess everyone is overprepared. Nervous. Wooley has been very concerned about the condition of the school."

"You sound as if you're not." O'Connell smiled but his cold eyes did not twinkle.

"No. I'm not."

"Why aren't you?"

"The caliber of our students is not high. Neither is that of faculty. We make a good match. The better student leaves for more appropriate surroundings as often as not. Those who remain have their hands full with the little we can offer."

"You're against improving the place?"

"Can every school be the best school? The good ones just happened, I think. No one planned them. This place just happened too. It has a job to do, a modest job, certainly, but a job." Rogerson lit a cigarette, wishing he could get interested in the subject, but the truth was it bored him. "Onward is a respectable direction isn't it, Senator? Almost as respectable as upward?"

"You're counseling mediocrity?"

"The word meant serenity once."

O'Connell consulted a clutch of notes in his fat hand. "I see you've published a number of articles recently. And you and Professor Schmidt have applied for a grant you may very well get."

"Guilty," Rogerson said.

O'Connell and his colleague exchanged a glance and

the younger man arose from his chair. "Thank you, Professor Rogerson. I think you've been a little whimsical with us, but we're grateful for your time."

Rogerson closed the door after them and returned to his desk. Had he out of boredom scored one for the Old Bastards at last? He could believe that for the first time in years there was hope that the school might be protected from improvement. Good or bad? Rogerson was disinclined to decide. Dowlet and his breed would be better off elsewhere; so would Wooley for that matter. They took things too seriously, the school, themselves. And the disease was contagious. The self and its surroundings have limitations that cannot be wished away. To learn that is to become an Old Bastard. And there are worse fates, Rogerson mused. There are worse fates.

One afternoon a few days after Marge had come home from the hospital Laplace phoned Rogerson, asking him to come to his office. He insisted when Rogerson made excuses. The outer office was empty when Rogerson arrived but before he could comment on it Herb, agitated, said, "For Christ's sake, Matt, do you know what she's done?"

"Norah?"

"Norah. She called the police last night and asked them to come out. She gave them some crazy story about killing her mother." Herb threw back his head, looked at the ceiling, dropped his chin and looked at Rogerson. "And I jumped at the chance to get her back. The girl's flipped."

"Who told you about it?"

"Some goddam detective came here to quiz me about her. A lot of stupid questions and I demanded to know what was going on. At that, I had to twist his arm to get the story."

"Did he believe her?"

"You're kidding."

"Of course."

"Matt, what should I do? Someone has to go over there. *I* can't go. Wooley is having a post-mortem on the legislative committee's visit."

"How did that turn out, Herb?"

Laplace puffed out his lower lip and plunged a thumb toward the floor. Rogerson accepted the verdict with a neutral expression. "You might ask Emily Pruitt to talk to Norah."

"Who?"

"In the library. Emily Pruitt. She's an old friend of the family."

"How old?" Rogerson guessed and Herb shook his head. "Matt, could you go?"

He could go. Suggesting Emily was to postpone his own acceptance. Yet, if the forged letter from Emily lay behind Norah's action, she might have been calmed by a visit from the older woman.

Norah let him in and went before into the dim living room and sat in the rocker. "Did Laplace send you?" The voice didn't go with the tortured expression she had worn at the door.

"You shouldn't have gone to the police, Norah."

"They don't believe me."

"No."

"Matt, I did it. I'm guilty. I should be punished."

"You're punishing yourself."

"That's not enough. You know it isn't. Don't they have to investigate, Matt? Is it just a matter of taking my word?"

"What would they investigate?"

She didn't know. She had told them exactly how it happened, realizing as she spoke that they didn't believe her. They gave her that look; she could feel them exchanging glances whenever she turned away. "It isn't right, Matt." She kept saying that. He offered to call a doctor.

"Do you think I'm crazy?" Her anger calmed her.

"You should rest, Norah. There's nothing you can do about it now."

She couldn't accept that. He could feel it in the way she rocked. His eyes were accustomed to the room now; he saw her set jaw, the hands rubbing the arms of the rocker as she moved back and forth in it. She might have been her mother. She was calm when he left her.

Norah was on his mind for the rest of the day. When the police phoned he thought it was about Norah, but they wanted to talk about Harry. He had been taken in for forging checks and had demanded they call Professor Rogerson. Rogerson told them he couldn't come right now; he would be down first thing in the morning. Poor Harry.

Another victim of Jolly Rogerson. Like Rogerson himself.
Like Marge. Like everybody. He and Marge still steered
their conversations away from the one topic that required
no words to be between them. When he asked how she
felt she said she was all right and that was as far as
it went. But he spoke to her a great deal now of what
went on at the college, anecdotes from class, what had been
said in the lounge. That night he did not tell her about
Norah, however, and when Marge went upstairs to supervise
when the children got ready for bed, Rogerson sat in his
study thinking about Norah.

Crime and punishment. Order. Intelligibility. Norah
wanted so simple a thing, what we must learn we cannot
have: our life a sequence of events moving with meaning
to an appointed end, making sense. The guilty punished,
the good rewarded and for all the grays between an appropriate recompense. As if life were a drama and we
spectators of it, our deeds dropping to tragic doom or
lifting in a light rise to comic crowns. Rogerson lit a cigarette. Marge had come downstairs to sit on the couch in
the living room and look without interest at the murmuring
television. What if life is neither tragedy nor comedy, is no
drama at all, at least to the actors in it, is nothing we
are meant to understand? We are not viewers. He wrote
that on a slip of paper, then crumpled it. From the living
room the television mumbled unintelligibly. Rogerson pulled
the Mexican silver urn across the desk and eased from his
cigarette its tip of ash.

"I'm going up, Matt," Marge called. "There's nothing on
tonight."

"How do you feel?"

"Oh, all right. You know." She came into the study.

"You look much better."

She smiled wanly. "Working late?"

"Maybe I'll go up now too."

Their eyes met. "If you'd like."

"I'll be up in a minute."

"Matt . . ." Her voice was high, trembling with meaning, as if she had prepared something to say, but she stopped.

"Go ahead, Marge. I'll be right along."

She left and he looked around his study. Its clutter annoyed him. Suddenly he wanted it bare. He would clean up in here tomorrow. He thought of all that junk in the attic, the accumulation of years, saved as if it were a record of his life. It had to go. From the wall his Rembrandt woman smiled, permissive, agreeable, omniscient. Her days were numbered too. He picked up the urn of ashes, a funereal expression on his face; the metal like its contents was less than genuine, greening under the design. He tipped the urn over the wastebasket, watching the gray dust drift down and sift among the papers; a slight cloud hung in the air for a moment and then it too went. He put the empty urn on the desk and turned out the light. Marge had left a lamp burning in the living room and he switched it off. No plan, no plot that we need know. Each deed done with a minimum of maladroitness. Rogerson felt an impulse to write that down but repressed it. Then he went slowly up the stairs, to sow his seed in the wombless body of his waiting wife.